Conflict of Interest

A CASEY CORT NOVEL

AIME AUSTIN

Conflict of Interest
Sylvie Fox *writing as* Aime Austin

This edition published by
Penner Publishing
14900 Magnolia Boulevard #57914
Los Angeles, California 91413
www.pennerpublishing.com

ISBN 13: 978-1-944179-40-3

Cover Designer: Cover it! Designs

Conflict of Interest/Aime Austin. — 1st ed.

"Law is a revenue stream. Dead boys and girls are a cost of doing business."

—ANONYMOUS

"We have families too."

—Reverend Emery Wilkinson

1

Troy Duncan

December 28, 2005

“Why don’t you knock off early?” Spencer Milburn said to the kitchen crew. Milburn was the owner, proprietor, head chef, bar back and more of Spencer’s. All that and my boss too.

The fine citizens of Cleveland must have been getting their roasted pork belly, massaged micro green salad, and truffle fries with aioli elsewhere.

“You don’t think it will pick up later?” I asked, mainly for the benefit of the skeleton crew working under me. Spencer may have been head chef in name, but I was actually doing the job. He’d scribble down menu suggestions then waltz out to greet customers and hang out at the bar. If you asked me, those chef whites—which were actually black—because black was more hip—were no more than a costume for him.

I had to actually do the hard work running the back: work out recipes, place meat and produce orders, then train everyone in the kitchen down the line. Those people looked up to me and I didn't want them to think that I was just leaving them on a sinking ship. Because believe it or not, Spencer's was going down. I'd been in the restaurant business long enough to see the signs. Half-empty dining room. Monday night fish specials. Customers coming in with coupons.

I wasn't going to be the one to tell him that upscale bistro and coupon clipping senior citizens didn't mix. Milburn didn't take suggestions well.

"The holidays are hard on every restaurant. But Saturday night should be hopping. I'll see you then," Milburn said before heading back out to the bar. He was drinking too much also. I might cook for a living, but I didn't eat every damn thing that came out of the kitchen. He needed to lay off the booze, but we definitely didn't have the kind of relationship that would allow me to talk to him about that.

When the kitchen door swung closed, I unwound the apron strings from my waist. Leaving early obviously wasn't optional. I nodded to my guys. They turned off stoves, and wrapped food for the fridge or freezer. While they cleaned up, and left out the back door one by one, I started doing the kitchen calculations in my head.

Shrimp from tonight's taco special could become shrimp grits on Saturday. If I paired it with Hoppin' John or black-eyed pea salad, I could have a southern New Years Eve theme. I poked around the cold storage. Collard greens and ham hocks would pair well. There wasn't a soul who didn't like the idea of eating their way to wealth and prosperity.

White folks would think they were getting something exotic. Black folks would feel at home. Seemed like the perfect compromise for this area smack dab in the middle of Cleveland's so-called revitalization. Light some bridges, build a light rail and bam, you had gentrification.

When everyone had left the kitchen, and my knives were drying, I sat down in the tiny office and wrote out my suggestions for Milburn. He might bitch and moan about how he was the creative mind behind Spencer's, but dollars to doughnuts he'd have my specials on his New Year's Eve menu. Didn't make much difference either way, champagne and liquor would drive the profit on Friday. The next few weeks or months would be the true test. Pulling the last of the tape from the dispenser, I stuck my suggestions on the computer monitor where Milburn couldn't miss them.

After I changed, I bundled my stiff double-breasted jacket into my duffle bag. The uniform service wasn't operating during the week between Christmas and New Years. Spencer's couldn't require the staff to wash their stuff, but I most certainly wasn't going to walk around smelling like funk. Two days off was enough time for me to wash and iron.

Spencer walked back and forth through the kitchen and out the back door a couple of times. There was nothing for him to do in that alley because he didn't "do" trash. He was keeping an eye on me and my hours, plain and simple.

I got the message.

My knives were dry. The kitchen was clean. Time to punch out.

Chives. Damn. We were out. Back into the office I went. I added chives to the produce list. They made a much better garnish than parsley. When Spencer came back in this time, we didn't speak. I mimed punching out. I wouldn't cost him one penny more tonight.

I slipped each knife into its own pocket and carefully rolled the leather making sure there was no contact between the delicate blades. Ceramic knives could chip in a heartbeat.

I smoothed my fingers over the hand tooled knife roll. It had been a Christmas present from Lynell and the kids. Best one I'd ever received. Buckled each side carefully before I zipped up my jacket.

I switched my clogs for kicks and made sure my duffle and knife roll were fastened.

Checked the clock again. Only nine.

I liked going home early well enough. Especially during school vacation. If I left now, I could maybe watch a movie with the kids. Possibly even put them to bed early enough for me to get some time with Lynell. But I also got paid by the hour. If I left three hours early, that was sixty less dollars I'd have in my pocket at the end of the week.

I needed to leave because I was tired of Spencer watching me, and I couldn't think of anything else that needed doing. The twinge low in my belly wasn't hunger. It was regret and fear. I'd only been at Spencer's for a few months. The pay and opportunity to move up was too enticing not to take. I'd been at the downtown hotel for five years, but great hours and benefits hadn't made up for the lack of advancement or minuscule increases that hadn't kept up with inflation, nor growing kids.

Lynell hadn't been a fan of the move to Spencer's. It was looking like she may have been right about Milburn. The one time she'd met my boss, Lynell had said he didn't have a serious business-minded bone in his body. He was playing at being a restaurant owner, she'd said.

Cooks jumped around all the time, I'd told her. Those white boys made money hand over fist because they realized their worth. I'd taken a page out of their playbook when I hopped from the secure jobs I'd had to start work at this bistro, excuse me, gastropub in the Flats.

But every time I left this place, I doubted my choice. It looked like every other place on the water was jumping most nights. And when I stepped outside between the warehouses, it wasn't much different. I pulled the hood of my jacket over my head. It wasn't that cold, but I didn't like wind from the water turning my ears to ice blocks.

I swiveled my head around taking in the Wednesday night crowd. You could have heard a pin drop in the front of Spencer's, but the spaghetti place, the comedy club, and all the bars were lit up as bright as the bridges.

Shook my head and closed my eyes for a long minute. Didn't matter. This wasn't a problem that could be solved in a day or week. I'd ride it out a bit more and see what happened. A bunch of restaurants were going up on the near Westside that were looking for help. If push came to shove, I could apply at one of the chains in the Gateway district. I could make a giant batch of nachos as good as the next guy.

I hefted the duffle across my body and tucked the knives under my arm so I could shove my bare hands in my pockets. Hadn't been this cold when I'd left home.

When I looked over my shoulder, the door was open again. I went back and kicked the door closed with my foot. Don't know why Spencer propped it open. We had a bell for deliveries or locked-out employees. I guess if you had a lot of cash, little worries like theft and heat loss didn't concern you much.

The comment from Lynell about Spencer playing at being a grown-up popped into my head again. Tomorrow, or next week, or next month was when I would think about how I'd gotten myself into this situation and how I would get out.

I heard some talking in the alley near the dumpster. The one thing I'd learned growing up in Cleveland was that some shit wasn't my business. You poked your head into the wrong shit and you could end up shot. As a brother in Cleveland, I felt lucky to have escaped that fate, so turned the other way around the building. I pulled my hands from my pockets, though. First to tuck the knife roll a little more securely. Didn't want anyone trying to take it off me. Second, with my hands free, I could defend myself if it came down to it.

I blew a little bit on my exposed hands. Hopefully, I wouldn't be cold too long. The Rapid stop was close. I could warm up between there and East One Sixteenth Street.

Despite the cold, I put one foot in front of the other slower than I should have. The guys in the alley weren't moving, which said drug deal to me. As long as you didn't get in their way, dealers usually left you alone. Drug fiends were another problem, but if someone was getting their hit, they wouldn't need to rob me. And in a minute, they'd probably be too damned high to care.

What I worried about more than drug dealers was coming up short after Christmas. I'd gone hog-wild on the gifts planning to make it back during the holidays.

I didn't want my daughter to be the only one without an American Girl doll and all the stuff that came with it. Maybe that Xbox for Ellison been stupid for two reasons. The boy hadn't come up for air in three days. Kid's fingers were going to fall off. He was doing okay in third grade, though. Hopefully, Halo 2 didn't make him check out from school. Not that it was that great a school. But Lynell and I owned the house they were in. Didn't think a lick about it when we were looking for something we could afford. A few blocks away and we'd be in the Shaker School…

"Stop!" a voice yelled into the cold.

The shout jarred me from my thoughts, but I kept walking because no one 'round here was talking to me. Dealer had probably stiffed the fiend or vice versa. I'd let them hash it out well out of target range.

"I said stop!" The voice came at me like the crack of a whip.

I didn't bother to look around. Some kind of shit was going down, and I needed to get as far away from it as possible. I reached into my pocket to make sure I had my pass ready. Push came to shove, I'd ditch the duffle and book it from the East Bank to Settler's Landing.

It was a sad fact that black on black crime was what I had to fear. My father had always said we were killing our own so fast, didn't have to wait for the "the man" to do it for us. I picked up my pace, suddenly much warmer than

I'd been a minute ago. Nothing like fearing for your safety to heat you up.

I was too old for this shit, though. I didn't work in the 'hood for this exact reason. Lived as far out on the edge as I could afford, but still I was acting like a scared pussy.

What little hair I had stood against the back of my neck as stomping feet got closer and closer. I stopped because there wasn't anywhere to run. I was nearly at the station. A few drunk white people were slouching off the benches pasty under bright white light. Surely no one would try anything in near broad daylight.

Should I turn and face my attacker, or should I make a run for it? Maybe it wasn't anything. Probably nothing more than a boogeyman. I'd let the whole culture of fear and crime get into my head. Shame burned my throat. How was it I was afraid of someone who probably looked like me?

I turned.

Damned bright light blinded me. My left hand went up to shield my eyes from the light. "What's up?" I yelled toward the beam. I tried to pull off casual, though I was anything but. Sweat pricked my skin. My heart was racing. Dying had not been on my list of things to do today.

"Drop your gun," a voice yelled.

Gun? They must be police. I only relaxed slightly. They must have confused me with someone else.

I fit the profile.

I always fit the profile, until they figured out they weren't looking for me.

I fiddled in my pocket. I'd just get my wallet, show my old work ID from the hotel, then be on my way. That had always worked in the past. The light went from bright to blinding. I lifted my hand to shield my eyes again. I was moving too slow. I'd just explain.

"I don't—"

The pop-pop of a firecracker came first. The searing pain came next.

Oh, shit.

I was going to die.

I hadn't hugged Ellison in months. Zora still sat on my lap. But Ellison was too old. Jagged sharp pain radiated from my heart to my arms. My head hit something hard.

Mama, Daddy, Campbell, and Lynell were my last thoughts.

2

Marc Baldwin

December 28, 2005

"Police!" I yelled. "Drop your gun."

I thought my heart would leap from my chest. Adrenaline was shaking my hands. I pulled my own weapon. If I didn't get my hands under control, and I had to fire, it would go wide. It was him or me. I had to make it home tonight. My kids couldn't go fatherless.

Fuck.

What was I doing? My head wasn't on straight. I needed to focus, not get shot, not get killed.

Was this slinger carrying a shotgun? Who had a rifle in the city? Damned drug dealers were better armed than the police these days. Instead of putting down the shotgun, the guy reached into his pocket for a second gun.

In a single practiced move, I pulled the cold grip of my Glock from its holster. Crossed my flashlight hand over my gun hand and aimed.

Center mass.

Center mass.

Not head. Not knee. This wasn't TV. It was him or me. I wanted to get home to see my kids in Westlake. I wanted to ring in the New Year with my wife.

Guy wasn't moving. It was like he was looking at me and thinking. Thinking about stopping his advance on the police or thinking about shooting me, I couldn't tell. Didn't matter. I wasn't taking any chances either way. My cold fingers shook a minute, then I got my grip. I squeezed once on the trigger. The guy went down in less than a second.

My heart rate zoomed up with fear, down with relief, then up again. I breathed in and out a couple of times willing myself not to have a heart attack.

There was noise behind me, in front of me, around me. Were a crew of gang members or drug dealers closing in?

I spun around again and again trying to locate the enemy, but the only thing I saw were small clumps of drunk people. In a minute, the five people turned to ten. Ten to twenty.

Call this in. That's what I needed. Where was my partner?

"Webb!" I shouted.

Darlene was nowhere to be found. Damned rookie. They'd paired me with a woman and one who didn't have much experience at that. At least I'd saved her ass from getting shot. I'd worry about her later.

A man approached the perp.

"Step back!" I ordered the civilian.

"But he needs help or he'll die," the guy said kneeling down near the drug dealer.

"This is a crime scene investigation," I said waving my gun in his general direction. "Back off."

The guy scrabbled away.

It took me a minute to steady my hand and press the buttons on the mike at my shoulder. "Shots fired!" I shouted into the receiver. "Male, black down. Twenty-five. Has a rifle."

"Backup will be there shortly," a calm voice replied. "Do you need medical assistance?"

"No. I'm fine," I said. Where in the hell was Darlene? My weapon was in my left hand. How did it get there? Shit. I didn't need to shoot someone in that crowd by mistake. I holstered the Glock.

The sound of a car motor made me turn.

Darlene.

Finally.

My partner pulled up to me in the Interceptor. Throwing open the driver's side door wide, she stepped out cautiously.

"Get some tape," I barked. "We need to cordon off this area for investigation."

Webb went back and opened the passenger door wide. They were bulletproof and she was doing the right thing, providing coverage should we need it. The trunk opened and slammed. A large roll of yellow and black tape in her hands, she approached cautiously.

"What happened?"

"The guy had a gun. It was a lot more than drug dealing going on here. Sometimes dispatch doesn't get it right." I looked at the crowd coming closer again. Screaming sirens filled the air as more patrol cars pulled up. An officer got out, assessed the situation, and reconfigured the cars. Each of the four faced the perp. Our passenger and driver doors were already open. The other cars followed suit, then we had complete coverage. Civilians could no longer see what was going on. All the better. They always got the wrong idea about police situations. And now with the Internet...

"Sergeant Baldwin. Give me a rundown," a CPD officer demanded. I turned around to find a tall bullheaded man staring at me. I'd seen his face around but didn't know his name. The double bars at his shoulder let me know he was a captain.

"Should we call an ambulance?" Webb piped in. She'd left the car, where she'd retreated to safety, and walked to where the man lay on the pavement.

Captain Todd, I'd finally read and digested the name, waved away Darlene's question.

"The rundown?" I asked confused as to why I had to do this now. This kind of thing was handled at headquarters where there were cameras to tape my statement and lots of forms for me to fill out and sign.

The captain retrieved a small card from his jacket. It looked like the plastic Miranda card we all had, but it was more like a business card. He glanced at it, then slipped it back into his pocket.

"Was shooting necessary to defend your life? Was using your weapon a good idea in light of the perceived threat? Was what you did reasonable?" Todd asked all three questions in rapid succession.

I looked at him, my head tilted sideways. I felt like he was sending me a message. But my receiver was broken. Looking away from the captain's intense stare, I focused on the darkened factory buildings a short distance away. Then it hit me.

Garner training.

We'd done a three-day training probably a decade and a half ago on how to meet some court's test of whether an officer was guilty of excessive force. Those had been the three most boring days, twenty-four most mind-numbing hours of my life. I wished I'd paid attention. Quiet far too long, I gathered what was left of my thoughts, then spoke. The next few words could be the difference between getting back to work or endless desk duty.

"Approximately twenty forty five, Officer Webb and I received a call out from dispatch. They said there was drug dealing in the area between Spencer's restaurant and this office building." I gestured behind me to the looming dark structure. Anyone who'd been working during the holidays was probably long gone by now.

"At twenty fifty, we drove from our patrol area to West Tenth Street. Webb stayed with the vehicle while I initiated investigation on foot.

"Several men congregated outside near the Dumpster. I observed them engaged in suspicious activity. The assailant broke from the crowd and came forward menacingly. He had a weapon under arm—what appeared to be a short-barreled rifle.

"I identified myself, requested that he stop. When he finally complied, he turned toward me and reached into his pocket. Fearing for my life and those of the civilians around me, I discharged my weapon."

An ambulance screamed down the street, halting my report. Two men jumped from the vehicle. Their pounding feet echoed on the pavement. In seconds, they had a stretcher jacked up and rolling toward the perp. I looked at his face for the first time. The black hood he'd been wearing had fallen from his head when he hit the pavement. The perp's eyes were closed.

They all looked innocent when they were dead.

It was almost enough to make a cop second guess himself. Almost. But once you see a fellow officer on the ground, guts and brains splayed out for anyone to see, you never make that assumption of innocence. Not in the field anyway. Defense lawyers and the ACLU could argue innocence all day long. But that's not the way it was in the trenches.

"It's not fatal," an EMT said, his fingers on the neck of the perp.

The other lowered the stretcher.

In a single practiced motion, they loaded the guy on the rolling bed. In less than a minute, he was in the belly of the ambulance.

He wasn't dead.

Exuberance was followed by dread. What if...what if he wasn't a gangbanger? Something about his pants was off. They weren't nearly falling off his ass. I ran to the back of the ambulance to confirm what was in my head.

"Check his airway!" one EMT was directing another who was actually working on the body.

"Clear!" came back from the other as he positioned the head backwards.

"Oxygen."

The second guy lifted something from the wall of the van. He stretched a blue rubber band around the perp's head, covering his nose and mouth with a plastic mask. The EMT turned back to the wall and turned the valve on a green and silver tank.

"Breathing?" I asked, short of breath myself.

A stethoscope appeared.

"Yes," one of the men said, sparing me a glance.

"Get that jacket off. Collar around him," the first EMT commanded in some kind of short hand.

From somewhere in the van, the second EMT produced a blue and yellow foam thing that he carefully wrapped around the perp's neck. The first EMT popped a metal rod from the bed. It stood up like one of those poles they put on shopping carts in stores deep in the hood. Bags of fluid appeared and were slipped on to a hook on the rod. The second EMT inserted a couple of needles into the guy, adjusted the flow of fluid.

For the first time one of the EMTs looked at me. "Where was he shot?"

I had no idea. We shot to kill. This one wasn't dead. I couldn't get past that fact. Was trying to work out in my head how this was gonna blow back on me.

I finally shook my head in answer, but the EMTs weren't paying me any attention, they'd gone back to work keeping the perp alive.

"He's in shock or something. Cut off that jacket." Small feathers floated around the body. The sound of fabric ripping filled the van. Then blood was everywhere.

"Compression bandages. We've gotta go now. One guy hopped out and slammed the back doors. In a second, he was in the driver's seat. Siren wails accompanied the lights that had never stopped pulsing. The ambulance backed out and just like that, it disappeared around the corner.

I wandered back to the car. Time to go downtown. Officer involved shooting was nothing if not a mother fucking butt load of paperwork.

"Baldwin! Over here!"

I followed the voice. It was cold out here, but I was warm, almost hot. Maybe it was the dozens of CPD that had shown up on the scene. It was a sea of crime tape and navy blue jackets.

Someone in police blues, a robbery/homicide detective, or internal affairs was leaning over the spot where the body had been. He lifted a tube shaped leather bag from the ground. Under the watchful eyes of everyone, he unbuckled first one strap, then the second. The leather unrolled on the pavement. A dozen or so knives gleamed in the flashing lights on the scene.

"Knives?"

Leaving the leather roll where it was, the detective unzipped the black duffel. He pulled out a black jacket, shoes with staples all around them, sweatpants, and some dirty gym socks.

"You saw a gun?" the investigator said lifting his eyes to me. I read judgment and doubt in their depths.

My lower eyelids twitched painfully. They did that when I was tired or stressed or cold. Right now, I was all three.

"He approached me with his hands in his pocket."

"The jacket's in the ambulance," the investigator said thoughtfully. He directed two officers to get over to MetroHealth. They would impound his belongings. Search for a weapon. A small gun would make all this much easier for everyone.

"I'll drive you back to the station," Todd said on the move. Haltingly, I followed.

"I can..." I looked back at our patrol car helplessly.

"You can't. When you get there, don't say a word. Ask for your union rep. Wait until they get to the station before you make a statement. Got it."

Dutifully I promised myself to do what perps could never do, exercise my right to remain silent.

3

Troy

December 28, 2005

Bright lights as sharp as those at the Jake during a nighttime baseball game, pierced my eyelids. I lifted my right lid for the fraction of a second it took for me to realize I'd be blind if I didn't shut it quick.

A quick inventory of my body revealed there was something stuck in my throat. Whatever it was wouldn't dislodge when I tried to swallow. I opened the other eye hoping to find someone to explain this all to me. No luck. More lights.

"Where…" I pushed out. I tried to remember how the day had started. I'd showered. The kids had been playing or fighting or both. I'd left for work at the restaurant…

"Don't try to talk. You're in the hospital. You've been shot," came a reply.

Shot? With a gun? Who would shoot me?

"Am—" I tried again.

"Sir, please don't talk." A shadow loomed over me. I cracked my eyes again to see where the West Indian accent had come from. "I'm Nurse Joseph. The bullet has done substantial damage to your internal organs. As soon as an OR frees up, we're going to take you into surgery."

Surgery? Someone was going to cut me open. To take out a bullet? To take out more? I didn't want to come home half a man. I closed my eyes. If I needed emergency surgery, it might be the only thing between me and home or me and death. Maybe a date with a scalpel wouldn't be so bad.

Nurse Joseph was the last person who spoke to me directly. Every few minutes I opened my eyes as another person poked and prodded at me.

I was cold.

I think I was naked under a thin blanket. It was winter, why was there no heat? Or shock, maybe that was it. I'd heard shock made a person cold. Who knew if that kind of thing was true if it came from a medical TV show? The patients on TV shows always died, or had a miraculous recovery. Would the actor doctor be crying or high-fiving? Pain ebbed as my head floated away on a cloud. A swish of cold air stopped my mind from spinning. Reality came back with a snap. A poker of sharp pain burned my insides.

"You can't be in here," Nurse Joseph barked at someone.

"This is an official police investigation," a deep male voice replied.

"The patient is being prepped to undergo surgery," she said in a voice that probably stopped most people.

But not these men. "We need to ask him a few questions." Entitlement dripped from his voice.

Police.

"You can talk to him tomorrow," Joseph said her voice firm.

"Is he awake?" The cop asked. He wasn't backing down either. If they were in any place other than a hospital, I suspected Nurse Joseph would be more accommodating.

"Do you not see the breathing tube down his throat? He can't talk. In a few minutes, he'll be unconscious. You will have to do this later." Joseph enunciated the last few words as if the cop were a first grader.

"My boss isn't going to like this," the cop replied. He was backing down though. *Go Nurse Joseph!* I hoped she was at my side the entire hospital stay. I was going to need a fierce protector in this cold, cruel world.

"You tell your boss that as soon as he goes to medical school, and completes his residency in emergency medicine, he can make decisions about patient care. Until then, it's my call," another voice said, obviously a doctor. Had the man been there all along?

"We're going to need to move him into custody once the surgery is over." The cop was like a pit bull. Why didn't he go back to wherever he'd come from and leave me to live or die? Sharp pains pierced me as the doctor bumped the stretcher. I craved the surgery's promise of sweet oblivion.

"You know what? That's the next shift. Go wait in the cafeteria or something. You can ply your trade on the guys who come in at midnight," the doc said. Had the doctor just given me up? Where was Nurse Joseph? My head swam and things went from clear to hazy in a moment. Why was I in the hospital?

Gunshot.

Custody.

My mind cleared for the first time in what felt like hours.

None of this was making any sense. It must be a case of mistaken identity. I'd never crossed the line or gotten into trouble.

Custody meant jail or prison or both. I tried to think around the pounding in my head. Tried to figure out what had led me here. How many times had my dad railed against the school to prison pipeline? Every day he'd read one story or another from the paper about a kid from Hough or East Cleveland who jumped from one crap institution to another.

But I'd colored within the lines. I hadn't stepped one toe out of the box—except with Campbell. Getting married too young had been stupid, but wasn't illegal.

So I'd stayed out. Stayed out of trouble. Stayed out of gangs. Stayed out of the worse parts of Cleveland. So how had it happened? How had I ended up in the one place my father had worked so hard to have me avoid?

I shivered, not with cold this time, but with fear. All the stories my dad had told me from life down south in Alabama crowded out hope. They had been the stuff of nightmares, and now I was living it.

It wasn't sharecropping, part time schooling. But jail would be segregation of a different sort. Despite being confined, my head moved back and forth in protest. I couldn't let this happen. I couldn't be one of the black folks someone was making money off of. Teachers union, police union, prison guard union. With every throb of pain, I was letting my father down.

"He prepped?" The doctor asked.

"Yes," Nurse Joseph said.

My bed jerked. I opened my eyes enough to see that we were moving toward an elevator. The gasp of pain that came from my lips was involuntary.

Everything hurt.

Whatever they'd given me earlier was long gone. I'd never been in this much pain in my life. I was starting to see why some people begged for the mercy of death. I might be doing the same if the promise of anesthesia wasn't right around the corner.

"Sorry. You'll feel better soon," Nurse Joseph soothed. A roughened hand smoothed along my head.

I was wheeled to a room even colder than the hall I'd been in.

"We're going to give you something to relax," someone said.

I was awake again. This time in a different room. The curtains weren't blue like before but pinkish purple. Zora would know the name of that color. Machines hissed and beeped all around me. The tube was no longer in my throat. I lifted my hand to try to adjust the blanket, but something jerked my wrist back to the bed. I shook my hand experimentally.

Handcuffed?

I was shackled to the bed. Was I in jail? Did jails have hospitals? They had to, didn't they?

"Troy Duncan?" a voice asked.

It took all the strength I could muster to nod my head. Damn, that hurt a lot. Fortunately, or not, the rest of my body from the chest down was numb.

"You're under arrest for felonious assault. You have the right to remain silent," the officer started in the all too familiar litany. I'd seen cops reading rights to hundreds of television criminals in my life. Never in a million years did I think it would be my reality.

"Do you understand the rights I've just read to you?"

No, I didn't understand a thing that was going on.

Gunshot.

Surgery.

Arrest.

None of it computed. I nodded anyway, the way guys always did on TV. I was innocent. It could all be sorted out later. When I was healed. When I was home.

"Lynell," I croaked out. The cop being here was one thing, but maybe someone had called my fiancée.

No one answered my plea. Someone in scrubs lifted my eyelids, lifted the blanket, prodded at me. In a flash, the space below my ribs went from numb to burning pain. I must have flinched, because the woman stopped moving her latex clad hands for a second and looked me in the eye.

"Sorry."

She moved liquid-filled bags from one hook to another.

"What's happening now?" I croaked out the question.

"We're required to move you to a secure floor."

"Secure?" For my safety? Who was a threat to me?

"We'll move you to the jail infirmary as soon as you're stable," a cop said. He was slouching by a bank of monitors.

I got it. They thought *I* was the threat.

Me.

The guy lying in bed with the gunshot wound. Clamming up, I exercised my right to remain silent because I didn't think my comment on the irony of the situation would be well received.

4

Marc

December 28, 2005

"You're going to need to get your stories straight," Captain Todd said. We were sitting across from each other in one of the interrogation rooms. I'd dumped guys here after arrest, but I'd never stayed. All that detective stuff was above my pay grade.

"Me and who?" I asked. I'd been alone when the guy had threatened me.

"Webb. Darlene Webb. That's her name right. About five years on the force?" Todd said flipping through a file folder. What did he have in there anyway? I hadn't been asked to write a single report yet.

"Darlene's my partner. That's right," I answered warily.

"You didn't hear this from me, but you should talk to her before the CPPA lawyer comes."

"But there's no story to get straight." I looked right and left, wondering if I were being taped. If what I said in this minute could derail my career. I shook my head. Nah, Todd wouldn't do the dirt on me like that. I continued, "The guy was carrying. He didn't stop after I warned him. Then he reached into his pocket. Fearing for my life, I unholstered my weapon and took aim," I said, the words already becoming familiar in my mouth.

"That's a great speech, Baldwin. But you're going to need to address the fact that the guy had no weapon."

For a long moment, the hum of the overhead fluorescent lights buzzed louder and louder until it was all I could hear. My head swam with dizziness, the way I felt after a couple of drinks at The Zone Car. But I wasn't drunk or high or anything like that. I was starting to get flat out scared. Todd was looking at me like every word from my mouth had the power to end my career. The hum of the lights was like an annoying summer fly. I shook my head again, willing away the irrational fear clawing at my insides.

"What do you mean?" I asked. Surely, Todd would explain it now. That the gun had been found in the dumpster. That the perp had thrown it to a gang member they were still pursuing.

"He's a cook at Spencer's. New place in the flats," Todd explained.

"What? Cooks don't carry? I've seen one or two gangbangers with jobs." I said jabbing at the fake wood table.

"He was *carrying* his knives, a dirty uniform, and a bus pass," Todd answered his eyes boring into mine.

"Shit," I whispered. He was right. I needed to talk to Webb. I could count on the union to back me, no matter what. The politicians were another story. I'd been in Cleveland long enough to know that elected officials would circle the wagons to save themselves first. That might include saving me, it might not. Rookie Webb might be the key to my getting cleared.

"I'm going to walk out of this room. You'll have fifteen minutes with Darlene Webb. I suggest you use it wisely."

A couple of minutes later, my partner came into the room. The admiration which usually filled her eyes when she glanced at me had changed to wariness.

"What happened to you?" I asked. "You shouldn't have let me go out there on my own. I could have been killed without backup. That's lesson one. I thought I'd drilled that into you on your first day with me."

"I'm sorry," she said. Darlene's hands were shaking. Tissue shreds floated from her palms to tabletop.

"Don't be sorry. Be smart. Next time—"

"I think you should find a new partner," she interjected.

Her words came at me, harsh. She looked at me like I was glowing radioactive waste.

"Fine." It would be good to be rid of her. Maybe my next partner would be someone with more than affirmative action under her belt. Someone who would know the meaning of backup.

I glanced at my watch. Ten minutes stood between now and midnight. "The rep will be here. We need to have a single story to tell him."

"I'm going to tell the truth," she said. Naïve is what that was. But she didn't want to hear that from me, her soon-to-be former partner.

So much for talking and compromise. Funny, that's what women said they wanted. But at the end of the day, I'd handle her like I'd handle any other woman. I'd tell her how it was going to be.

"Twenty forty-five we received a call from dispatch. Suspected drug activity at Eleven Twenty-three West Tenth Street. We drove from our patrol position on the west bank of the flats. We entered Tenth Street from the west side. Strategically, we chose to leave the car on the street rather than pull into the alley. No reason to be backed into a corner.

"While you radioed for backup, ran plates, something, I approached the suspects. There were approximately five black and Hispanic males surrounding a dumpster. They appeared to be engaged in illegal activity.

"One male broke from the pack. He jogged toward me in a menacing manner. He had what appeared to be a rifle under his right arm. I identified myself. Shouted for him to stop. He continued to advance. I shouted again. When he finally stopped, he reached into the pocket of his coat. Fearing for my life, I took out my weapon and fired.

"Got that?"

Darlene didn't say anything, but she nodded her head.

"I don't mean to throw you under the bus here, but you realize you're gonna have to answer why you were hiding in the car, right? They may put you in admin for a bit, but I'll go to bat for you. Try to get you back out on patrol. You have potential, but will need some more field training, even if that's not with me."

Her wary look was back, but she nodded nonetheless.

"You think you can remember all this when Todd comes back to question you?"

"Of course," she said, her voice wobbly. "I'll tell them exactly what happened."

A knock sounded at the door. Then it opened. Five men entered the small space.

"Here's what's going to happen," Todd started. "It's late. No one's at their best without sleep, so we're gonna keep this simple. I'll take a statement from Patrol Officer Webb first with the union rep. Then we'll take a statement from Sergeant Baldwin. After that, we'll all go home and reconvene in the morning after everyone's had sleep, shower, and a coffee.

I nodded. It was okay with me. We had our story. The guy wasn't dead. After a few days, the fuss would die down, and we'd all get back to work.

Todd had been as good as his word. Half hour later we were done.

"We'll call you," Todd said holding my gaze like a vise.

5

Augustus Duncan

December 29, 2005

There were two crappy things about being old. First, I never slept anymore. It was as if my body had decided with the little time it had left, being awake was best. Second, being old made you frightened of everything. Driving made my hands shake. A knot of teenagers seemed like a menace. In my more thoughtful moments, I think all of it was fear of my own mortality.

So the insistent banging on my door was more than a little scary. I didn't exactly fear jackbooted thugs would show up at my door any minute. But growing up in segregated Alabama had made me more than a little bit scared of late night visits. Can't remember a neighbor Birmingham whose house was visited past eight thirty that had a good outcome.

I pressed pause on the video I was watching, eased myself from the chair, ignoring the pain in my hip, and walked to the door. The peephole revealed my boy's—ah I never knew what to call her—Lynell.

"It's late, girl," I said in greeting after I opened the door letting in cold night air. "Myrtle is laying down upstairs. What's going on?"

The woman pushed past me, with my grand babies in tow. They didn't do more than lift their hands in tired greeting. Something told me they'd rather be home in their warm beds.

"Troy didn't come home," she whispered after she'd pushed the kids into my living room.

I stood in my vestibule looking down at this woman my son chose and wondered why in the hell she was so insecure. He'd picked her and still it wasn't enough.

"Maybe he went out for a drink after work. The man's well past eighteen and certainly past twenty-one. Does he need to call you before he meets friends?"

"He usually comes home straight after work."

"Lynell, you know I do not get involved in anyone's personal mess. I'm sorry that you're put out..." I really wanted to say insecure, jealous, and just a tiny bit crazy, but after eight years of holding my tongue, I wasn't going to tip my hand now. "But I don't know what we can do to help."

"I called his job, and they say he left at nine."

"You called his job? He's only been working there for a couple months." This girl had no sense, calling Troy's job like some afternoon talk show guest. It was like she wanted to get him fired. That way he could be up under her feet all damn day. Goodness knew she never left the house.

It was an amazing feat that she'd made it the few miles to ours. Her worry must have won out.

"Should we call the hospitals? You think he got into an accident?" the girl asked her voice bordering on hysteria.

"You have the car Lynell. He can only go as far as an RTA bus pass can get him, which isn't very far. If there'd been an accident, I'm sure it would have popped up on the news here. I glanced back to the living room, where the kids had changed the channel from my movie and were watching some age inappropriate late night television.

"Have you heard from Campbell?"

Took her five whole minutes to get to Campbell. That had to be a record.

"It's late. I'll make up the guest room for the kids. You can sleep on the couch. Why don't we all get a good night's sleep. It'll be fine in the morning."

"Do you think—"

"I *think* it's time to get to bed. I hope you left a note for Troy."

Lynell's eyes widened, and I knew she hadn't thought of that. Instead of running here like a bat out of hell, the girl should have gone to bed and stayed put. No doubt, Troy would have been home in the morning, and I would be none the wiser about their domestic dispute of the moment.

Now he'd get home, wonder where his girlfriend and kids were. He'd either go and sleep off some liquor or he'd be here banging on my door at three in the morning. I didn't want what precious sleep I did get to be uninterrupted.

I looked at the couch's proximity to the door. That would be Lynell's problem. I got the grandkids situated in Troy and Malik's old room then took myself down the hall.

"What was all the fuss about downstairs?" Myrtle asked me when I finally lowered myself into the bed.

"Did we wake you?" I asked. I'd felt my wife shifting on the double bed.

"Naw. I was up way too late reading," she said her voice thick with sleep.

"I don't know how you stand those true crime books."

"It's kind of fascinating how humans do the craziest things. The one I'm reading now, the guy stole three different girls off the street. He kept them in the backyard under a tarp for years. And his wife helped him."

"He was married?" I had to chuckle to myself. My wife didn't put up with anything she considered unseemly. I couldn't imagine me trying to keep a couple of women in the backyard. She'd have turned me over to the police in a heartbeat.

"So his wife helped deliver his babies," she continued.

"From the girls he kidnapped?"

"Yeah, he had like six kids. Two from each girl."

"Nutso. Must have been some white guy."

"Of course. Can't imagine no black man getting away with anything like that. People 'round here call the police when a dog barks too damn long."

"That's for sure." I paused, trying to find a way to frame the crazy downstairs, then just spit it out. "Lynell is downstairs on the couch."

"Oh, God. What's her story now?"

"Troy didn't come home early enough for her."

"He works at a restaurant. The hotel did have more regular hours. But she has to understand that even when a restaurant closes at ten, you can't just walk out the door."

"Maybe if she cooked, she'd know that," I said playing on Myrtle's one issue with the girl. She didn't go for the easy bait.

"Yeah, well. She's the one he picked."

"I miss Campbell."

"Me too, Gus. Me too." Myrtle scooted under the covers then pulled the comforter over her shoulder. "Let's go to sleep," she said with her back to me. "Those kids are gonna be up early and hungry. I'm going to have to get a jumpstart on the grits."

Even with my late night fussing with Lynell and them, I still woke up at four, like I did every day. Took myself a quick shower, got dressed and tiptoed the best I could with my bad hip, down the stairs. I needn't have worried. Lynell, snoring on the couch, hadn't heard a damned thing.

I turned up the heat a little, then put on my jacket and cap. Took a while to warm up the truck, but once I got it running, I cruised on over to Troy's house. Their neighborhood was quiet. But everything slowed down in the week between Christmas and New Years. Parked in his driveway and stared at the house. Looked quiet. I knocked on the door then rang the doorbell.

Hmpf.

I went back to the truck and got my extra set of Troy's house keys out of the center console.

Let myself into the house. Except for a bunch of mess in the living room with the Christmas tree up, and paper wrappers everywhere, not to mention a whole nest of wires attached to the TV, nothing looked out of place. There wasn't anyone in the bedrooms. I locked up and got back in the truck.

Maybe Lynell was right. Maybe Troy was at Campbell's house. That would be something. I looked at my watch. It was close to five. I couldn't call Campbell's house. And I needed to be getting home anyway. Who knew what Myrtle would need me to get out of the freezer? Those kids ate through the stuff we served like they were starved half to death.

"Got the grits on," my wife said when I let myself into the kitchen. "Wow, it must be something out there. You brought the cold in with you."

I kissed my wife on her graying head. She'd been saying the same exact thing for thirty something years. "Do you need anything from the shed?"

"Oysters."

Dutifully, I went back outside and got the frozen oysters.

This was the best part of the grandkids coming over. Myrtle went all out. I dropped the bag of oysters in the sink and sat down to look at today's paper.

"I don't know why you still get this rag," I said unfolding the cold newspaper. "There's never a lick of good news in here."

"How else am I going to keep up on what goes on around here? If I don't keep my eye on things, the city will have sold the land under my feet for a new stadium."

"You live in Cleveland Heights," I pointed out. This suburb was far outside the jurisdiction of the city.

"You know what I mean. Next thing you know they'll need this land out here for a soccer stadium or hockey or some sport Cleveland hasn't built something new for yet."

"Ah. Damn. There was a shooting in the Flats last night. Drug dealer got shot by the police." I read for a bit. "Cops are saying the guy pulled a gun on them. The paper says the bystanders said he was an unarmed black man."

Myrtle dried her hands on a towel and leaned over the table next to me. "Let me see that."

I pointed to the short page-three story.

"Gus! Did you see the end of this? Some woman says the guy was holding knives."

"Probably what the cops thought was a gun."

Myrtle shook the paper. "Not brandishing a knife. Knives. Do you think that's Troy?"

My wife started spinning around like a top. I worried that at her age that she'd fall down and break a hip if she wasn't careful.

"Stop," I said grasping at one of her outstretched arms. "This city has hundreds of thousands of people. What are the chances it's Troy? Let's be realistic. He's probably staying with a friend or something after tying one on. This guy is someone else's kid."

"I'm calling the hospital," Myrtle said flipping through a phone book she kept in one of the cabinets. I didn't stop her. What wise man got between a mother and her worries? I pulled the receiver from the wall phone so we could get this over with and on to breakfast. I did love her deep fried oysters.

"What's the number?" I asked.

I dialed the digits she read from the phone book and handed her the phone. We didn't have a touch-tone phone in the kitchen. Had never bothered replacing the golden yellow hardwired phone that had come with the house. So Myrtle was on hold for a bit while waiting for a live person to come on the line.

"I'm calling to find out if you admitted a patient last night," Myrtle asked. I could hear the tears in her voice. She'd worked herself up into a tizzy. Only when they promised her there was no Troy Duncan at MetroHealth would she put down the phone and get back to breakfast. Speaking of, I walked over to the stove and turned down the fire under the grits. Spitting and bubbling of the thick white liquid told me they were getting a bit thick.

"Troy Duncan. May eight. Nineteen seventy-one. Okay, I'll hold."

She motioned for me to put a lid on the grits. I found one in the cabinet and popped it on the heavy pot.

"What! He was admitted when? What's his diagnosis? I'm his mother. Myrtle Duncan. We'll be right over." To me she said, "He's at Metro—"

"I heard you." I already had my jacket and cap back on and was halfway out the door.

"What do we tell Lynell?" Myrtle asked.

"Let her sleep. We'll get the lay of the land and come back. It may be nothing more than a slip and fall. I don't want to get her and the kids wound up over nothing."

I flipped the fire off under the pot and ushered us out the back door.

If Cleveland was a ghost town during the day, it was positively deserted this early in the morning. A normally forty-five minute drive to the near west side only took us twenty minutes.

"Gus, can you please not kill us on the way. I don't want our whole family to be in the hospital."

I eased off the gas pedal a tiny bit, even if it was only to pull into the huge hospital parking garage. My family didn't much go to the hospital. We'd been at Cleveland Clinic for the birth of the two boys, but I couldn't remember much after that. Maybe when one of the boys broke his arm was the last.

Nothing had changed about hospitals, though. We walked through the doors into a vast open area with scrubbed floors and a distinctly antiseptic smell. Unlike any hospital I'd ever been in, there were no people. Given the bad news that fronted the newspaper every morning, I wondered where everybody was.

The big sign on the main desk said the hospital wasn't open until eight thirty. It wasn't even seven yet. Following directions, we took ourselves to the Emergency department on the ground floor. This was where everyone was. We wove our way through the throng of people toward someone who would likely have an answer.

A woman who looked like she was well toward the end of her shift was rolling around behind the reception desk.

"My son, Troy Duncan, was admitted last night. What can you tell me?" I asked without the usual introduction. I couldn't manage polite or respectful this early.

"Is he okay? Can we see him?" Myrtle added. I could already hear the quaver in her voice. Those boys had long displaced me as the center of her universe. I ached for her now. She'd always feared for their safety. Life had been hell for her brothers in Alabama. Once they were teens, she often woke up in a cold sweat scared they'd been carted off by the Klan.

"One moment while I check the computer," the receptionist said before keying in a few letters.

"What's his date of birth?"

"May eighth, nineteen seventy-one," my wife answered in an instant.

"Hmmm. He's on the twelfth floor."

"How do we get there? What room?" Myrtle's eye wandered over to the elevator bay. My vision was still good enough to see that there was nothing in the directory indicating a twelfth floor. Eleven was oncology. Nine was stroke. Eight was psychiatry. There was no ten either. Trauma was seven. If he wasn't on seven, maybe it wasn't too bad. Maybe twelve was overflow patients and not grown children on the verge of death. I leaned forward on the desk in anticipation of the answer.

The receptionist tapped at the keyboard, her eyes no longer on me or Myrtle. She shifted uncomfortably in her chair. Was that floor where they had the morgue? I'd always assumed that the dead were stored in the basement. I eyed the directory again. Morgue was missing from that list in addition to floors ten and twelve.

"Why don't you wait over there," she said gesturing to a grouping of blue and green upholstered chairs. "I'll have someone come down and speak to you about your son."

"Can you tell us anything about his condition? Or what happened?"

The receptionist hesitated a long moment looking like she was wavering between sympathy for an obviously overwrought mother and whatever was on the screen in front of her. Decision made, the woman spoke. "I'll leave that to…to the professionals. Please have a seat. I'll page the nurses' station on twelve right now."

The emergency room had no shortage of activity. Ambulances came and went. Children in the throes of pain cried in their mother's arms. Neither Myrtle nor I spoke. I didn't want to infect her with my fear and worry; she already had enough of her own. I glanced over at the woman who'd been at my side for more than forty years. She was staring straight ahead, probably holding back tears.

My watch indicated we'd been waiting twenty-five minutes. I was about to step up to the receptionist again and insist on seeing Troy, when an announcement came from a clipboard-carrying woman in dark blue scrubs.

"Troy Duncan. Anyone here waiting for news on," she glanced down at the clipboard again. "Troy Duncan."

"We're his parents," I said, standing so my voice could be heard over the growing crowd.

"Follow me," the woman said disappearing through a set of double doors at the end of a narrow hallway. I helped Myrtle up, and we followed the woman as best we could. "Wait here," she said before leaving us in a small room that looked like it should have the sign, "Bad News Delivered Here," on the door instead of Patient Conference Room.

"Should we call Lynell?" Myrtle pointed to a phone on tiny table jammed in a corner. "We didn't leave a note. I don't want her freaking out that *we* disappeared."

"In a minute," I said, because the sound of footsteps outside our little room was getting louder by the second.

The knob turned. I waited to see what kind of doctor would be facing us. Instead I was shocked to find myself nose to holster with two police officers.

"Cleveland Police," one announced as if their supercilious demeanor and shiny black guns didn't scream cop.

They stood on opposite sides of the room, hands on hips displaying their firepower.

I waited.

Weaker men would have tripped all over themselves with questions or explanations.

"How do you know Troy Duncan?" the older one in a gray suit asked.

"He's our son." My answer was clipped.

I was in a name, rank, and serial number kind of mood.

The other guy, younger, in a better fitting navy, plaid sport coat, spun around a chair and sat backwards across the seat. He scrutinized each of us. I have no idea what he was looking for, but I don't think he'd found it.

"How long has your son been slinging?"

"Excuse me?"

"Drugs. Dealing. How long has he been in the game?"

"Our son has never done anything illegal," Myrtle said. She looked like she'd been slapped. "You must have him mistaken for someone else."

"The felonious assault charge is not a mistake. He's been charged with assaulting a police officer. An attempted murder charge is not out of the question. Duncan's being held on the secure floor of the hospital. When he's stable, he'll be transported to the hospital wing of the Cuyahoga County jail."

My brain was having a hell of a time computing what I'd just heard.

Arrest.

Charges.

Jail.

Troy?

"Can we see him?" Myrtle asked, a pleading note in her voice.

"There are no visitors on the secure floor."

There was a lot we needed to do. None of it could be done here. I rose then offered my wife a hand on her elbow.

"Where are you going? We're not done with our questions," the gray cop said. His hands had moved from his waist to his gun. Quickly, I calculated. I'd lay odds that no cop would shoot me in a hospital conference room.

"Excuse me," I said as boldly as I could.

Good manners got in the way of intimidation and they let us go without incident. I strode with purpose, my hand firmly on Myrtle as we exited through the ambulance port.

We had to circle the complex to get to our truck parked on the other side. Once seated in the car, Myrtle spoke.

"Shouldn't we have stayed and tried to see him? He has to be scared being all alone. We still don't know what's wrong with him."

"As soon as we get home, I'll call to speak with whoever his doctor is. But first thing I think we'll need to do today is get Troy a lawyer."

6

Marc

December 29, 2005

"Marc!"

"What?" I said rolling over. I really needed a good night's sleep before facing another round of police rigmarole. It would be days of paperwork before I was able to get back out on my beat.

When I didn't move fast enough, Jan jabbed a well-placed elbow in my ribs.

"Channel five."

Sleep fog left my brain in an instant.

TV.

I hoped to God the story wasn't on TV. I'd never seen anyone in the department come out of that kind of coverage unscathed. I found the remote and tuned into WCLE. I didn't have to wait more than a few seconds to hear my name.

"Cleveland police officer, Sergeant Marc Baldwin has been placed on administrative leave following the shooting of an unarmed black man on the west bank of the flats last night.

"The victim, identified as Troy Duncan is a cook at Spencer's. Bystanders say, the officer failed to identify himself and shot the man. Let's go to Rick McDaniel for a live update. Rick?"

"Thank you. I'm here in the entrance to the alley behind Spencer's on West Tenth Street. As you can see, the scene is still cordoned off as police investigators comb the area for evidence. We had the opportunity to speak with an eyewitness.

The station cut to a pre-recorded interview. The interviewee's name scrolled at the bottom of the screen between the channel number and the station's logo. He was some shaggy, long-haired guy I wouldn't have looked at twice.

"We'd been watching comedy at the club next door. While we were walking to the Waterfront line, we heard a car roll up. The black guy was leaving work out the restaurant's back door, and the police drove like five feet away from him. The cop never said he was a police officer, and the black guy didn't notice him. He was hunched down in his jacket.

"It was like thirty degrees that night. Next thing we knew, the police officer was shooting. Then the guy fell on the ground bleeding. When the cops opened his bags, there were only dirty clothes and knives in them."

It cut away from the guy in the flats, back to the two talking heads behind the desk at the studio.

"We've reached out to Cleveland police, but they haven't returned our calls. We'll update our viewers with breaking news as it happens. Weather, after the break."

A car commercial blared from the screen. I grabbed the remote to mute the noise. The kids slept across the hall, and I wasn't ready to face them yet.

"At least they didn't use your name," Jan said, sitting on the side of the bed. The smell of bacon and coffee filled my nose.

"I could have sworn they'd used my name."

"You're tired Marc. They said an officer has been put on leave. I can't imagine having to explain any of this to the nuns at school."

Jan worried a whole lot what people thought about our family. I'm pretty sure I heard my name, but maybe that was my imagination. Maybe I *was* tired. I turned toward the bedroom door.

"You made breakfast." I know my tone was less than friendly, but for a woman who insisted on having a gourmet, chef's kitchen in every place we'd ever lived, she didn't turn on the stove too much.

"The kids are on vacation. They should get something more than cereal and skim milk." Then she turned that snark right back on me. "You don't care about breakfast. I can't remember the last time you ate a meal here. What about what was just on TV? Did you shoot somebody?"

"I told you last night." She'd been awake when I'd finally gotten home.

Worried, but awake.

Cops' wives learned to deal with the stress of being married to men in the line of duty in one of a couple of ways. Jan's brand of crazy involved her staying awake until I got to bed. No matter what time I arrived. Caffeine fueled her through a lot of mornings.

"You said your firearm discharged. Then you rolled over and went to sleep." Her bangles jingled as she pointed at the TV. "They're saying a cop shot some unarmed black guy. That's a whole different kettle of fish."

"Hon, it's no big deal. Just some drug dealing gang banger. I'll get the paperwork out of the way today during my shift, and it will be all squared away."

Jan stood by the bed, arms crossed. She puffed air through her lips a few times. Realizing she wasn't going to let me go back to sleep, I gave into one big yawn. Then, I got myself out of the warm and comfortable bed and into the shower.

I usually loved working the second shift. Gave me time to get some stuff done during the day. And if Jan was off work, gave me time to slip her a little action.

With the kids home, neither was going to happen. After the late night I'd had, my plan was to sleep in as long as possible. I was going to need my wits about me to deal with the potential shit show coming my way. I toweled myself off and decided coffee would have to stand in for sleep today.

At the dining room table, the kids were tearing through bacon and toaster waffles like they'd never seen a square meal before.

"You want some breakfast?" Jan turned to me from her perch on the buffet. The TV in the living room was muted, but I could see that she had it tuned to one of the local stations. I raised my eyebrows.

"Can you turn to something else?"

Jan flicked to some Technicolor sitcom on one of the family friendly networks. Michael and Donna were way too old for that crap, but I didn't say anything. I was pretty sure that the news wasn't going to come back to the shooting again, but I didn't want to risk it.

The smell of bacon and syrup got to me right quick. It was too cold to hop on over to Denny's or the Day Café. It probably wasn't a good idea to meet with my guys anyway. I'm sure Todd or someone like him would get on me for fraternizing at a time like this. Toaster waffles it was.

"Can you add a couple of over easy eggs to mine," I said.

Jan, who's favorite phrase was probably, "this is not a restaurant," held her tongue for once and retreated into the kitchen.

The waffle wasn't half bad. It even kind of looked like the picture on the box in the freezer. I was dipping the last bite into the egg yolk when the doorbell chimed some classical music tune.

Not for the first time did I curse that thing. It always made me jumpy. Set my teeth on edge. I nudged Michael with my foot. He broke his stare at the screen across the room and ambled toward the door. He was only twelve and already full of attitude. Teen years didn't look to be shaping up so great if his current surliness was any clue. I saw a lot of overtime in my future.

Captain Beau Todd strode into my house like he owned the place. In deference to my wife, he took off his hat and shoved it under his arm. There was more brass on the guy's chest than in a marching band. Someone in full dress uniform was the absolute last person I expected to walk through my door.

I stood, suddenly conscious of the wrinkled jeans and Browns sweatshirt I was wearing—the "B" peeling from the chest. Slippers slapped on the floor as I walked the two feet to the entranceway.

"Captain Todd." I shook his hand formally. "This is unexpected. These are my Kids Donna and Michael. My wife Jan."

Todd dutifully shook my wife's hand and nodded toward my kids. I gave Jan the side eye and she corralled the kids upstairs. The Christmas Xbox that I'd hooked up in Michael's room was probably the incentive fiercely whispered under my wife's breath. We'd made a two-hour daily limit rule that was about to be violated in the worst way.

"Do you want to..." I pointed to the living room furniture a mere two feet away. I'd bought this open plan house brand new, but it didn't really have anywhere formal to have a dinner, much less discussion with someone five pay grades up the ladder.

"The dining room table will be fine," Todd said. He unzipped his jacket and hung it on the back of a chair. I hurriedly removed the plates, syrup bottle, and orange juice from the table and plopped it all on the kitchen counter.

"Sorry about that. Breakfast," I shrugged in a way that said family time, surely you understand.

"You were a difficult man to find this morning," Todd said setting his cap on the table.

Busted.

I'd been so damn surprised to see someone from the top brass in my house that I hadn't given a thought to that house being far outside of Cleveland's city borders. He pulled out a folder I hadn't seen tucked under his arm.

"A quick database search let me know this Edgewater Drive address is very popular," he said tapping on a sheet he'd pulled from a folder. Looked like some personnel shit I'd filled out a ways back. "I counted no less than twenty officers sharing the same apartment number. Who will I meet if I stop by there when we're all done here?"

I stared at the busy grain swirled on top of the solid oak table. Fuck. I didn't need this. A couple dozen of us were kicking fifty a month to someone's kid. He made sure we all got any mail that came to us in a timely manner, and he got to live rent free.

"Sir. I'm sure that's not the reason you're here," I said redirecting the conversation. No way was I going down for something as petty as an address violation. Half the force would be dismissed if that rule were enforced. Then who would be left to protect Cleveland's civilians?

"Troy Duncan is the reason I'm here," Captain Todd said without a hint of cordiality in his voice.

"Who's that?" I asked though I damn well knew.

Todd had the good grace to ignore my question. "Troy Duncan is in the secure wing of MetroHealth. He's being charged with felonious assault and assault on an officer. Our preliminary investigation shows that he was unarmed at the time of the shooting."

"What about the knives? I saw that on TV this morning."

"Knives in leather pockets, rolled up, and twice buckled does not count for a weapon."

"What are the charges for?"

"A way for us to go out fighting. He didn't stop when you called out to him. He did stick his hand in his pocket in the face of an officer. None of that is kosher. We're behind you all the way on this. But you need to know what you're up against."

"Up against?" I was genuinely asking a question this time, not playing dumb. "The way I see it, the shooting was justified. I was planning to log some overtime during the holidays. Pay for the Christmas gifts, you know what I'm saying?" I leaned my head toward the tree that was still up in the small room. Unwrapped toys littered the little skirt the tree wore.

Captain Todd did not look persuaded. "We tried to keep this quiet. If it had happened in Hough or somewhere on the Eastside, you'd be in the clear. You know the city hired that outside PR firm to hype its image." I nodded. There had been a couple of memos and an hour-long presentation on the city's branding or some shit. The river wasn't on fire anymore. It was at the center of so-called revitalization.

Todd continued, "Part of that image includes the Flats. Eyewitnesses plus hipster central equals TV coverage. It's been a slow news week. You're not page one in the *Plain Dealer* today. But you will be tomorrow."

"What do I need to do? I assumed that stuff about leave was just reporters talking out of their ass." I said in resignation. Geography was messing with my job. If this had happened on East Seventy-sixth, no one would have batted an eye.

"Nope. It's all true. I'd have told you first if I could have found you faster."

Chastised, I sat back, ready to take my medicine.

"I'm here to officially put you on administrative leave. That means you get to stay home, be with your family during the holidays." When I lifted my hand in protest, he continued, "We don't need any more officers riding desks. Todd opened the folder and spread the contents on the table. "Here are all the forms that you'll need to complete for an officer involved shooting. Let my office know when they're done, and we'll send someone out to pick them up.

"When can I get back to work?" I asked. Overtime was one issue. But hours cooped up here were another. I loved my family, but they were sometimes better from far away. Jan ruled the roost. I'd learned to stay out of her way.

"Consider this a much needed vacation. I'm sure your family will be happy to have you home during the holidays. When we're done formalizing our investigation and clearing the decks, you can come back. We'll assign you a different patrol area," he said matter-of-factly. Todd carefully fitted his round hat to his square head. I nodded. The Flats assignment had been a plum that would no longer be mine. Up until last night, corralling drunks had been the hardest part of my shift. If I had to go back to the east side, my work life would get a whole lot harder. I could only hope I wasn't patrolling near any CMHA buildings. Public housing wasn't what it used to be.

"Oh, and while you're at it. You may want to look for a place in Cleveland for you and your kids."

Todd tapped the folder against his palm, then stood. He put on his jacket and let himself out without so much as a backward glance.

"Jan!" I yelled up the stairs. I was in a pickle. I hoped she had some ideas on how to get us out.

7

Augustus

December 29, 2005

A skeleton crew was manning the offices of Vernon Dinwiddie at nine in the morning. His office, like the streets of the city beyond the dirty windows, was nearly deserted. The woman who'd greeted us had acted like she'd drawn the short straw having to work during the holidays.

"You sure he's coming?" Myrtle asked after we'd given our names to the secretary manning the persistently ringing phones. My wife folded and unfolded her arms, her scarf, her gloves, and her hands before I laid my hand on her arm, stilling her movements.

"I called his emergency line," I said. "The woman I talked to promised he'd be here."

My wife shredded tissues while I paged through issues of Ebony, Jet, and Black Enterprise. I guess there wasn't much diversity among this lawyer's clients. His full page listing in the yellow pages had said he practiced criminal law, discrimination cases, and something else I didn't understand. Black folks in Cleveland was probably in enough trouble to support a whole slew of lawyers.

At ten-fifteen, a woman led us into Dinwiddie's office. The lawyer was as small as an elf, and dressed like one too. His cowboy boots pointed up at the toes and a shiny rock on a string was knotted around his throat.

"Good morning. So sorry to see you on this solemn occasion. Please tell me all that you know," he intoned, his voice as sober as a priest giving last rites.

I sketched out the details as best I could given what little the cops had told us. I slipped the lawyer the article I'd torn from the morning's paper. He scanned it and looked up at me.

"That's all we know. We're here because they've charged him with a felony. I don't think he did anything wrong. My boy isn't like that. But I've lived long enough to know that innocence doesn't matter."

Dinwiddie ignored my cynicism and pulled a folder from the far side of the blotter. He flipped it open.

"While you were waiting, I placed a number of calls to various sources I've gathered over the years. The police didn't tell you the whole story."

I tried mightily hard to tamp down my rage as the lawyer laid out what had happened after Troy had left work.

My boy had been shot in cold blood. Left to die on the freezing cold pavement of the alley.

I wanted nothing more than to tear out of there and drive to the house of the cop with the quick trigger hand. If I could get away with it, I'd shoot one of his kids and leave them to die on the side of the road. Maybe the man would show some remorse then. If he didn't I'd shoot him dead.

"Gus?" Myrtle's hand landed on one of my balled up fists. "Do you know where he was shot? Will he be okay? When can we see him?" She asked the questions I couldn't get out.

"I wasn't able to get all that info, and I didn't want to keep you waiting while I made more calls, but I will try to get you in to see him as soon as possible, but until I get more info, I'm not ready to try to spring him yet. Let's just say that your son is safer in the hospital than anywhere else right now, okay? We don't want him in county jail where officers would have unfettered access to someone they'd be quick to label a cop killer."

"What do we do?" Myrtle asked. It was in neither of our natures to sit quietly. That had worked in Alabama to keep us alive, but up north things were far different—in some respects, at least.

"I know this is a lot to take in, but I want to discuss with you a three-pronged approach."

"We're listening," my wife said.

"First, I'll be glad to defend him on the felony charges. I hope to get those dismissed. They're no more than a smoke screen trying to throw off attention from what likely happened. But if we don't get a preliminary hearing, or the county goes straight to indictment, then we'll have to play that hand as it's dealt."

"What are two and three?" I heard Myrtle ask. I was still seeing red and unable to speak a coherent sentence.

Dinwiddie sat up a little straighter. Then he stood. It didn't make him appear any taller. I resisted the urge to make a joke about him standing up. He'd probably suffered short jokes most of his life. It was what had likely turned him into a lawyer. Couldn't fight in the streets, so he duked it out in the courthouse.

The small joke I made in my head eased the rage—if only a little.

"Second," he was saying. "Second, we need to call for an external investigation. Any internal look will favor CPD. It always does. Third, I'm going to recommend that you sue—"

"Bring a lawsuit?" Myrtle asked shaking her head. "Against who?"

My wife had always believed that too many people sued. She was probably the only black woman in America who supported so-called tort reform. It was one of a few things that would get us into an unending argument.

"This would be in federal court," Dinwiddie answered. "We'd sue the officer, his partner, and the City of Cleveland for the...wrongful...injury inflicted upon your son."

"How much is this going to cost?" I asked. If lawyers were anything, it was expensive. This conversation probably cost more than my monthly pension check.

Dinwiddie moved over to the hollow wood door and closed it. The sound of the ringing phones was diminished but didn't disappear altogether, confirming my belief that nothing good had been built after 1940.

"I didn't start this law firm or buy this building outright by taking pro bono cases. I want to say that up front. What has happened here, however, is a grave injustice for not only Troy but your family as well. I will not charge you for the criminal case, or my effort in getting state and federal investigations off the ground. I will, however, take your wrongful death case—"

Myrtle jerked forward in her chair.

"He's not dead. My Troy isn't dead, right?"

"I misspoke Mrs. Duncan. His lawsuit with the city for the shooting and pain and suffering, I'll take on contingency. This means there will no upfront money from you. If I don't get money from the city, then I won't get paid."

The lawyer walked back behind his desk, sat in the chair and rolled up to the papers he'd been looking at earlier.

"Here we go," he said handing me a thick stack of papers. This is the agreement I'll need you to sign."

Panic began to set in. It always did when I was faced with a sea of words on paper. Both Myrtle and I had escaped the south, but we hadn't escaped the substandard education system. School hadn't been more than a few months when I was a kid. By high school, after the Supreme Court ruling, I had been too far behind to catch up right. Then I'd joined the army. They hadn't cared much about education for black infantrymen.

"Let me look at that, Gus," Myrtle pulled the papers in front of her. She extracted granny glasses from her purse and slipped them on her ears.

"Mr. Dinwiddie," she started, her voice was all business. It was the voice she used when white people tried talking down to her. "I see here that there's only one agreement, concerning that lawsuit you mentioned. Where's the other, for the criminal defense?"

The lawyer gave her an appraising look and picked up the receiver on his phone. In the ten minutes that my wife had read the first agreement, the second one had come in by way of an assistant. She intercepted the handover and took that to read as well.

"It says here on page three that anyone from the law offices of Vernon Dinwiddie and company can appear in court on Troy's behalf. We came here today because of you, not any associates or just graduated lawyers. Let's change this so that you'll be the sole representative for Troy unless you're sick or dying, okay?"

Dinwiddie narrowed his eyes for a short moment then nodded. Another phone call and another document. Myrtle took her time reading again, then she signed both. "Gus, sign here," she pointed handing me a blue ballpoint pen. I added my name to hers.

The lawyer took them and laid them on his desk.

"Can you have copies made before we leave today? I make it a rule to have copies of anything I sign," Myrtle said. That was true. My wife was pretty diligent about things like that. No one ever came back to her and said she was responsible for something she wasn't.

I half stood from the chair. It was digging into my backside, throwing my hip more out of whack. And I wanted to get back to the hospital. Press our case about seeing our flesh and blood.

"Not quite yet," Dinwiddie said gesturing for me to sit back down. "I need to get some information on your son."

Myrtle answered all the usual questions about his full name, birthdate, and his job history.

"He have kids?"

"Two," I answered. "Ellison and Zora. He named them for famous black writers." I was proud as punch about that. He didn't bow to Lynell's desire to give them made-up names. If that woman had ever worked outside the house, she'd know that naming your kid Tynesha wasn't good parenting.

"Lastly, you mentioned Lynell earlier. How long have they been married?"

It was like Dinwiddie had opened our upstairs hall closet and all the family's dirty laundry had fallen out.

Myrtle and I looked at each other for a long moment. Chair wheels squeaked against a plastic floor pad as Dinwiddie leaned forward. I broke the silence.

"Troy and Lynell have lived together for about eight years, probably. But Troy is married to someone else."

"What's *her* name?"

"Campbell. Campbell Wells."

8

Troy

December 30, 2005

“Campbell?” I called out. My voice sounded different, hoarse. The person I heard couldn't possibly be my wife. The woman I'd married at nineteen lived on the other side Cleveland Heights. We'd said our goodbyes long ago. No way would she be here in a hospital.

I must be dreaming.

Everything after leaving work early was hazy, though. I wondered if I was in some kind of dream. Maybe some kind of nightmare.

"Yes, Troy it's me. I came to make sure you were okay."

Her voice was distinctive enough to have roused me from the drugged sleep I’d had here for the last who knows how many hours, or days, or weeks.

“Troy?”

My wife stood next to my bed. Everything was surreal, the pain, the hospital, the estranged wife. Would this be like *A Christmas Carol*? Would other ghosts from my past and future visit? The light jingling of chains made me believe it was possible.

"Troy! You need to wake up." A red tipped hand snapped its fingers by my ear. "Every minute you drift off in la-la land, you're wasting. Time is running out."

The tube had been long removed from me, but getting words out still hurt my throat and just about everywhere else. I pushed the little miracle plunger that gave me some pain relief and waited a long minute before replying.

“What are you doing here?”

“I’m still your next of kin.” Campbell looked me up and down. I wasn't sure I'd measured up, passed whatever test she was giving. I'd learned long ago not to ask.

“What happened to me? Why am I here?” Not a single soul had given me a straight answer. One thing I could trust from Campbell would be one hundred percent unvarnished truth.

Campbell paced back and forth in the tiny room. Eventually, she sat, her butt perched right on the edge of the small folding chair that had held a uniformed cop the last few times I’d surfaced.

“They’re saying you got into an altercation with the police, and got shot.”

“I was shot? Oh, my God. I lived?" Campbell gave me a look that said I was stating the obvious. I didn't miss that look. I crooked my head trying to assess my body. "I guess I must have lived. Altercation? That can’t be right. I’ve never been in a fight in my life.”

“Not if you don’t count fourth grade. You got into it with Arnoldo Fife.” People who had known me since I was three always had a way of reminding me of my checkered childhood.

"He did that stupid duck walk making fun of your butt. He deserved what he got." It had been a good move, taking on Arnoldo Fife. To this day, I stood behind that one. Not a single soul had made fun of Campbell after that. Not for the next eight years anyway.

"What? You both got suspended."

"Lynell's not here," I said, done with the walk down memory lane. Seeing Campbell was interesting, but where were my fiancé and kids?

"Maybe you should marry her."

Trust Campbell to go right for the jugular. She could push my buttons faster than anyone else. The end of my marriage was my kryptonite. Avoidance shifted my brain from one unpleasant legal matter to another.

"They're charging me with some kind of felonies," I said the memory of someone reading me my Miranda rights coming back full force.

Campbell sat back a little farther. She looked at the man-sized watch hanging from her wrist.

"I only get thirty minutes to visit. After that, no one can visit you for another whole week. Got that? So let me say what I came here to tell you."

"Okay," I slurred. The meds had run through my veins, and I wasn't feeling much pain, and the pain I did feel, I didn't give a shit about. The appeal of drugs was suddenly very understandable. The fuzzy brain I could do without. For now, high was winning out over sober.

"There are a couple of stories floating around out here. But basically, the police are saying you were in a knot of drug dealers and addicts in the alley behind Spencer's. They tried to break it up, and you came at them. They shot you in response—"

Indignation nearly launched me from the bed. I would have been across the room and out the door in a heartbeat if I hadn't been shackled to the bedrails and as high as a kite.

"That's not true, Campbell. You have to know that."

She nodded, but there was a little hesitation in the way she moved her head.

"Campbell!" I shouted as best I could. It came out as a hoarse wail.

"Sorry. I was never a fan of Lynell. She's straight from the hood. I thought it was a small possibility that she—"

"What? Turned me out? Took me over to the dark side? Just because I wasn't good enough for you and your family doesn't mean that I'm one step up from a common criminal. You know my parents didn't raise me like that."

My ex looked at her watch again. "Fifteen minutes, okay. Your story has been on the news at the top of the hour on every channel. Bystanders are saying that you weren't doing anything wrong, and the cop was trigger happy."

"That sounds a lot more like the truth."

"Anyway, your parents have hired a lawyer."

"When's he gonna get me out of here?"

"I don't know all that. I'm pretty sure the courts are probably closed for the holidays."

"Shit. How are the kids?"

"Look, Troy. I'm not getting involved in your life again. I'm doing this as a huge favor to your parents. They'll visit you next week once their registration has cleared."

"How did you—"

"Pulled a few strings, okay? Daddy made a couple of calls, and here I am."

"He's still running your life, huh?"

"Six minutes. I don't think we should spend it arguing. Can I look at your wound?"

Grudgingly, I nodded. If it really was another week until I could get a visit, I didn't want to waste my last few minutes of human contact. She lifted up the blanket, then the blue and green patterned gown. Her gasp was not a vote of confidence. As she laid them on my skin, I noticed that her long thin fingers hadn't changed. Gently, she pressed around the bandage, her hands moving in ever bigger circles. Her face was the same mask of concentration she'd worn when she was trying to work out what our tenth grade geometry teacher was going on about.

"Where does it hurt?" she probed.

"Everywhere." Once I said it, I realized it was true. My head had been pounding for days. I wasn't sure of the cause. Part of me thought it wasn't getting any sleep. This place was a hive of activity nearly around the clock. The other cause might have been what was hidden behind the bandage plastered back there. I tried not to think about that too much because it itched like hell.

"Move your legs, Troy."

I willed my brain to listen to her command, but something wasn't working right.

"Are they moving?" Why hadn't I realized that there was no pain in my legs? "Are they?" I asked again. My hand rattled the chain anchored to the hospital bed rails.

"No, Troy. No."

"Oh, my God. Do you think...? No one has said anything about... Can you ask a doctor what's going on?" I could hear the rising panic in my voice, but I didn't give a shit about sounding like a pussy. There wasn't anything Campbell didn't know about me.

My wife pressed a button next to the bed and scrambled out of the room.

A minute later, she brought back a doctor, at least that was what I took the embroidered lab coat to mean.

"Tell me what's going on? Why can't I move my legs?" I asked. I rattled the chain around my wrist. The steady beeping of some kind of monitor turned into a near high-pitched drone of sound.

"Sir. Sir. I'm going to need you to calm down."

I took a deep breath and waited. The beeping slowed.

Instead of speaking, he took some kind of probe from his breast pocket. He threw off the covers fully and poked at my feet.

"I'm pricking your foot. Do you feel anything?"

I moved my head from side to side, afraid to ask the question I didn't want an answer to.

He probed somewhere else on my foot. At least that what I assumed as arm clad in stiff white cotton moved around my body. "Here?"

For every "here" question, I shook my head again and again. When he poked me in the groin, the pain provided pure relief.

"There. I feel it there," I called out. "I can feel something. What does all this mean?"

"The bullet entered on the left side of your abdomen," the doctor said. "It traveled through your large intestine, landing at T-ten of your thoracic vertebrae. While we were able to repair the damage, and resect your bowel, we couldn't remove the bullet. its location is inoperable."

"In English, please," I insisted. "Am I going to be able to walk?"

"At this time, due to the bullet's location, you don't have any sensation from the waist down."

"Does that mean I'm paralyzed?"

"Yes, you will not be able to walk again. Given your situation, I'm not sure when you will be able to start rehabilitation treatment."

"My situation?" I asked. "I have insurance," I said. It was the one thing I'd insisted on before taking the job at Spencer's. There was no way I would leave the kids without coverage.

"Insurance is not the problem. We're going to discharge you to the jail's infirmary as soon as you're well enough."

"Infirmary? Will I need a wheelchair? Who's going to make sure I'm healing?"

"There's a doctor assigned the county jail. He will be responsible for your care going forward. But don't worry about that right now. You will be here probably another three or four days."

"Time's up," a sheriff's deputy announced as he pushed the door in nearly hitting the doctor in the back.

The doctor didn't budge.

"You," the sheriff jerked a thumb in Campbell's direction. "It's time for you to go. Your thirty minutes was up ten minutes ago."

Campbell took her time, winding her scarf, and pulling on her coat. The deputy snapped his fingers "If you don't haul ass, I'll deduct this from next week's visitation."

She'd never been one to be easily intimidated, but I could see her do a quick mental assessment and err on the side of caution.

"I'll call your parents," she said before gently pulling the door to behind her.

9

Augustus

December 30, 2005

"Where's Daddy?" little Zora whined over the kitchen table. We'd sat the kids down for lunch. Myrtle had hoped grilled cheese and tomato soup would be enough to quiet their fears. My wife was wrong about little, but she'd been wrong about that. They had been on a starvation diet. Grits and eggs, fried fish and hush puppies, and now the sandwich and soup hadn't caught their interest.

Even Ellison had been pushing his food around for the last day or so. Normally, we were trying to get this kid to stop stuffing himself. He slid the sandwich on its plate toward the middle of the table.

"You eat it, Granddad. Can I watch TV?"

Normally I would eat his leftover food. When the kids were here, I was lucky to get enough to get full. Ellison ate like the teenager he'd be in four years.

"You really need to get something in your belly." I pushed the plate back in his direction. The kid didn't have the words to express his anxiety. I didn't either. A voluntary hunger strike wasn't the answer, though. I was about to offer to run to the store and get him that handheld computer game he'd asked us to buy for Christmas, when relief came in the sound of the doorbell.

Lynell, moving faster than I'd ever seen her was pulling the door open before the last chime echoed through the house.

It had been ten long years since Campbell Wells had stood on my doorstep. Her pointy chin and wild hair were a welcome sight.

"Come in out of the cold," I said moving around Lynell and grabbing my daughter-in-law by the hand.

"Sorry it took me so long."

I took her coat, hung it on the coat rack. She crossed our living room and pulled out the piano bench. The piano was right next to the dining table where Myrtle and the kids sat.

Despite her eagerness of a moment ago, Lynell hadn't moved from her space by the door.

"Should your kids hear this?" Campbell asked. She looked Lynell directly in the eye. Something the kids' mom was unable to reciprocate.

"There's no sheltering kids these days. They have to grow up fast," Lynell said, her eyes on the floor.

I half agreed with Lynell, but if they'd been my kids, I'd have filtered what I would have told them. Zora already looked like she was carrying the weight of the world on her six-year-old shoulders. It was times like these that I wondered how our people had made it through slavery. Parents being separated from kids at the whim of a cruel master. Tried to shake my head clear of those kinds of thoughts. Going that way could land me in my bed for two days while I tried to figure out human behavior.

"I spent forty minutes with Troy this morning."

Lynell moved from the door to the couch. I think her legs could no longer hold her up.

"What did he say?"

I saw Campbell purse her lips, lick her teeth, and pause before she spoke.

"He asked about you and the kids," she said. In that moment I'd never been prouder of the girl. She'd matured a lot over the years. I glanced at Myrtle, and she nodded at me in understanding. Campbell had been kind when she didn't have to be.

"Oh, thank goodness he's awake. He can talk? What else did he say?"

"Not much. I answered a lot of questions, told him what I know. The cops haven't said much to him, and he's been out of it on some kind of narcotic. I mainly came here because I want to tell you two things in person. Neither is good news."

Ellison leaned all of his nine-year-old weight on the table, nearly tipping it. Zora hunkered down in the padded floral chair. Both kids looked like they were bracing for an explosion.

"Go on," I said from my seat on the couch.

"Because he's charged with a felony, he will not be discharged from the hospital in two or three days, which is how things are normally done. Troy will be transferred to the jail's medical unit until his case is...resolved."

I laid a heavy hand on Lynell's arm to silence her. I could tell she was about to launch into a litany of questions. The girl had a roundabout way of understanding things. But I didn't have the patience right now to watch her mind work through stuff on her way to understanding.

"You said there were two things, Campbell. What's the second?"

Suddenly Campbell rose. She walked around the small table and laid her hands on Myrtle's shoulders. The two had always been close. Myrtle had missed Campbell absence more than I had. After nearly twenty years of being in our house every day, she'd disappeared like a puff of smoke only to be replaced by a sulky, withdrawn Troy moving back home.

"The doctor thinks that the bullet may have severed his spinal cord."

"May?" Myrtle blurted.

"What does that mean, Granddad?" came from Ellison.

"Is Daddy paralyzed?" Zora asked.

Campbell looked at the girl for the first time. "How do you know that word?"

"Daddy said that's why people are in wheeling chairs. Their spine got broken, and they had to roll around instead of walk. Is that what's wrong with Daddy. Will he need a wheeling chair?"

"Zora? Is that your name?" Campbell asked. My grandbaby nodded. "You're right. Your daddy is paralyzed from the waist down. He'll probably be in a wheelchair when you see him next time. But he can't do that until he's all healed up. That's gonna take a while. Okay, sweetie?"

Zora's six-year-old head bobbed solemnly.

"Oh, my God, he's going to be half the man he used to be," Lynell cried out, throwing herself across the couch and onto my lap. "Je-ee-sus come save us. Our provider won't be able to work anymore. How will we make it?"

Campbell went into the kitchen and returned in a moment with a few tissues for Myrtle. Until than I hadn't noticed the tears streaming down my wife's cheek as her worst fears became reality.

My daughter-in-law kissed the top of my wife's head. She leaned her head down on Myrtle's shoulder. Tears merged on their cheeks. I'd missed Campbell so much sometimes, but this was not how I imagined her return. With news that my son's life had been severed in half like his spine. I could see it all now. We'd always divide his life into before the shooting and after. The sword of Damocles had fallen. The other shoe and the penny had dropped all at the same time.

"What do we need to do?" I asked. Hoping and wishing things hadn't happened wasn't going to change a thing. We needed to fix this, and quick from the sound of it.

"You're going to need to get him out of there. Whether it's bail or getting the charges dropped or whatever. He can't stay there. I think they'll kill him." Campbell had always been one to lean heavily toward pessimism. But her eyes were clear. She believed what she was saying wholeheartedly.

So did I.

Dazed, Zora looked around the room at everyone, her mother and grandmother were crying. Her brother looked like he wanted to punch someone. I watched her eyes zero in on the bringer of bad news.

"Who *are* you?" She pointed an accusing finger at Troy's wife. Out of courtesy to Lynell, we'd moved Troy and Campbell's wedding photos upstairs. Replaced them with yearly school pictures of Troy's and his brother Malik's kids.

"Campbell. Campbell Wells." She'd never taken the last name Duncan. I'd once loved her fierce desire not to replace one slave name with another. Now it just made me sad.

"How do you know my daddy?"

"They met in elementary school," I answered. I stood abruptly and walked toward the door. A sharp sweet smell tickled my nose as I lifted the red wool coat from its hook. The oh-so-familiar smell of patchouli hit my nose. But I couldn't let myself fall into the past. I needed to hustle this girl out the door now before all of Zora and Ellison's childhood was gone.

"Why did you go see him? Why couldn't my mommy see him?"

"They only allowed immediate next of kin," Campbell answered matter-of-factly. I could see how it would never occur to this childless woman to filter her thoughts. Especially after Lynell had sanctioned disclosure.

"What does next of kin mean?"

"Only family could see your dad. I'm the closest family he..."

Zora turned her head from Lynell to Myrtle to me, her face screwed up in misunderstanding.

"Campbell is Daddy's wife," Ellison said to his sister. My head snapped up. I'd had no idea he knew that. Nine wasn't what is used to be.

"How can she be daddy's wife? Momma's daddy's wife."

"Daddy had a wife before he met momma," Ellison said his voice full of the superiority he liked to wield over his sister." He pointed. "That's her. That's why momma says fiancé to everyone. Daddy can't be married to two people at once."

It was too much for the little girl. This was the final straw. My grandbaby finally broke down and cried. Unlike the rest of us, her tears weren't for her father's paralysis. They were for the loss of innocence.

10

Marc Baldwin

December 31, 2005

“Channel Five!” Jan yelled.

I was beginning to hate the television. The days where I could sit back and enjoy the Indians, Browns, and Cavs were long gone. These past two days the set was always on mute while the judge and jury of public opinion convicted me on screen.

Misspelled words scrolled across the bottom of the screen in a constant march. It was starting to give me a headache. I didn’t say a word, though.

Jan was afraid to turn it off. It was like she thought some kind of revelation was going to shine from the box. More like endless condemnation from what I could see.

I closed the refrigerator I'd been investigating. Like there was nothing to watch on TV, there was even less to eat in our kitchen. I came to stand beside my wife. She stood, arms crossed, remote clenched in her fist.

"What do you want me to see?" I glanced around, happy the kids were safely tucked away upstairs. Something told me it wasn't going to be a listing of First Night celebrations in the county.

"Benedict Arnold."

"Who?" I racked my mind. "Didn't Bobby play that character in some kind of Brady Bunch episode—"

"Shhh!" Jan silenced me then turned back to the screen. A commercial break ended and she punched up the volume.

The room the CPD used for press conferences filled the screen. The sound of cameras clicking and static filled the air. Captain Todd came on screen. More upper level brass filled in behind them.

I turned on my wife. "Why are we watching this? It's like a train wreck." Blood and guts had never been my thing. It's why I was still on patrol instead of doing something like homicide.

"So, what? You want to bury your head in the sand? The more knowledge you have, the better."

"What are they gonna say that I don't already know? I was there, Jan. I know what went down. Civilians don't call it the Blue Wall for nothing, you know? Todd and the others will protect me no matter what. It's what we do. It's what I'd do for them. It's what they'll do for me."

Jan sucked her teeth derisively then turned back to the screen. "Then what is Darlene Webb doing at that end of the sea of blue."

I stalked across the living room and stood less than a foot from the screen. What in the hell was going on? I was trying to work out in my head whether I was angry for being excluded or—

"Maybe they're going to toss Darlene to the dogs, hon. She's a rookie."

"Good morning," Todd said. The American, Ohio, and Cleveland flags stood tall behind him. His introduction was accompanied by more clicking. You had to wonder who all these people were and why there were so many cameras. We only had one newspaper and three real TV stations. This wasn't New York or Washington with endless news channels, or even Los Angeles with its celebrities.

A good five minutes passed while Todd announced every person on the city of Cleveland payroll who would speak. The list was long from the Mayor, county prosecutor, chief of police on down.

Backing away from the television, I sat down on the couch. Something that had seemed as simple as a discharge of my weapon was turning into the shooting of the century. Inwardly, I cursed the twenty-four hour news cycle. There was time to fill over the holiday season, and it looked like I was going to be it. This week's sideshow.

Merry Christmas and Happy New Year to me.

The press conference started without the usual preamble. That meant they were serious up there.

"On the night of December twenty-eighth, there was an officer involved shooting on the west bank of the Flats. Nine-one-one dispatch received a complaint of illegal activity in an alley behind a restaurant. Cleveland patrol officers were called to investigate drug activity. Troy Duncan, thirty-three from Cleveland, approached an officer in a threatening manner, and he was shot. Duncan is in the secure custody of the Cuyahoga County Sheriff's department.

"Unfortunately a lot of rumors are floating around, fueled by media coverage. Our officers have done nothing wrong. Far from it. I'm here to announce that we're seeking to indict Troy Duncan for his actions that night."

A reporter jumped up and waved her hands. Not waiting to be called on, she shouted "What are the charges?"

"The charges will be determined by the prosecutor in consultation with the grand jury."

"What about the bystander testimony? Will that be presented to the grand jury?"

"All the facts will be presented. The grand jury has sole discretion over any charges filed."

"Why are you skipping preliminary hearing?"

"As you know, the county has the discretion to determine how any case is handled. Given the potentially incendiary nature of cases like these, we prefer a grand jury over a hearing."

The number of reporters standing increased from one to a dozen. They all shouted questions, Todd flicked his hand toward one man. "Chris?"

"What is it that you're trying to hide? Grand juries are secret. Preliminary hearings are public."

"We are not hiding anything, Chris. Police procedure is not on trial here. That's what would happen if we don't keep the door closed on this. Let's not pretend that tension doesn't exist between police and the black community. I want to short circuit any unnecessary protest and keep this as clean as possible."

"Is that because your officer," she shook out a small piece of notebook paper, "Sergeant Marc Baldwin shot an unarmed black man in cold blood?"

The clicking started again as the room erupted in shouted questions and fierce note taking. The county prosecutor, Lori Pope replaced Todd at the podium.

"I ran for the office of county prosecutor because I wanted to bring transparency to our county's justice system. There will be no rush to indictment or rush to judgment in the Duncan case. We are holding this press conference to inform everyone what the state of this case is. Unfortunately, we're in the middle of the holiday season and for obvious reasons, we're operating at a reduced staff level. The news media, however, has run with a story, while only reporting on half the facts.

"This city is in a sensitive place. It's my job to let everyone know, black, white, and otherwise that we are doing all that we can to make sure justice is served for everyone involved."

"What about the bystanders?" a reporter asked. "Their story is in complete contradiction to what the two of you are asserting."

"First, we are not asserting anything. We have opened an investigation and will only make any determination after gathering the facts. If information turns up that suggests that Duncan did not commit a crime, the grand jury won't indict."

"Are you saying you have more information than you're revealing here?"

"Chris, we always have more information. Our policy is generally not to comment on ongoing investigations. We're making an exception here in the spirit of continued peace within our city and as I said before, transparency."

The police chief, Kelley McCormick, came to the podium. "Our office is conducting an investigation of its own. Our department thoroughly investigates all officer-involved shootings. There's a special unit whose only job are these kinds of internal investigations. We have interviewed dozens of eyewitness," he said. McCormick took a long pause then turned toward Darlene. She stood a little straighter and taller, nodding slightly at him. He turned back to the crowd. "And we're sure that we will have all the facts in place to complete our investigation. Internal Affairs will issue a report."

The questions and answers continued. The mayor, a county commissioner, and a retired judge all said their piece.

"What do you think?" Jan was chewing her lip.

"That was good news. Did you see them signal to Darlene? She's going to be the one who covers me. She was there, knows how it all went down. At first I thought it was shit, that she wasn't anywhere near me, backing me up. But now I think that's going to help. She can testify as to what we agreed happened, and I'll be in the clear. Duncan will go to jail where he belongs, and I'll be back on the beat come January."

I let out a breath, relaxing for the first time since the shooting. Darlene on the panel was a signal. Todd and the force were going to bat for me. It all clicked. This was what was best for me. I was foolish to have doubted the system, even for a minute.

11

Casey Cort

January 3, 2006

"Happy New Year. Ms. Cort," Judge Margaret Lynch intoned from the bench. "What matter are we here on today?" For a second I marveled over the friendly tone of the jurist.

Nothing in my last few years of practice had prepared me for this. Criminal judges couldn't seem to remember my name, or remember to assign my cases when it was their turn in the arraignment room.

Domestic relations judges in divorce court had favorites, and I'd never been one of them. I didn't even want to think about how badly the juvenile judges had treated my clients, much less me. That part of my career was best permanently blocked from my mind.

A few donations would have cured the issue of judicial recognition, but I had never been in a position to dine at Massimo and line the pockets of the career judges constantly running for office. Well, money could have helped and maybe a change from the dirty-blond "nowhere color" hair. I thought of Lulu sitting not too far away in the gallery. Her rhinestones cast light all around the courtroom. Maybe all I was missing was a little bling.

Damn.

Someone said good morning, and I was already on the fast slide to no self-esteem land. I needed to brush off the past. Wasn't the phrase of the moment: move on. Buying myself time, I pretended to shuffle my papers and get comfortable at the decades old wood table.

"Good Morning Judge Lynch. I'm here on the matter of In re Jacqueline Lopez. The child is here, your honor with her guardian *ad Litem*. They're in the hallway. I'm representing Jackie's guardians, Bonnie and Steve Mitchell." I pointed to the couple to my left. They'd done me proud. Steve was in a navy suit. Bonnie's face was framed with pearls. I could barely get my other clients to ditch their low-slung jeans. The Mitchell's appearance was a triumph, a mark of my practice's upward mobility.

"Looks like there's going to be a lot of celebrating going on after court," Lynch said looking out at the small knot of people. I followed the judge's gaze. Lulu Mueller gave a thumbs up from the gallery. My best friend's first case had been a little bit earlier in the day. Watching Lulu's adoption case proceed successfully this morning had given me hope. It hadn't been false.

"We're ready to proceed, your honor," I said.

"Dalton Lacey. Good firm. Nice of you to come on down and see us in the basement. And twice in one day at that."

"I'm actually in private practice, Law Offices of Casey Cort. Volunteering through Dalton's pro bono initiative," I explained. “Lulu and I were on law review together in school.” Over sharing a bit much. Sheesh. Thank goodness, the judge ignored me.

“What have we got here today?” The judge’s question was all business. “No money, no love,” and “no firm, no love” were the unwritten policies of the county’s courts.

“Steve and Bonnie Mitchell have been first unofficial and then legal guardians for Jacqueline for nearly six years. They took Jackie in when she was two. She doesn’t know any other parents,” I said starting with my opening gambit.

“Have her birth parents consented to the adoption?” The judge interrupted.

I was ready for this. It was an uncontested hearing. All the judge had to determine was that Jackie’s adoption by the Mitchells was in the child’s best interest. That was a standard I knew like the back of my hand. When all was said and done, the basic requirement in divorce, abuse, and adoption cases was the same: kids being safe and loved.

For the first time in my checkered career, I thought I was actually going to achieve it. I glanced down at my notes before continuing.

“Jackie’s mother is deceased, your honor. Her father has consented. I personally went to see him at Mansfield and had the form signed and notarized.”

“Looks like your papers are in order Ms. Cort. Good thing your friends at Dalton helped you out there.”

I took the dig in stride. I did that when it looked like the judge was going to rule my way. What was a little lost pride in the face of victory?

Ten short minutes later, the judge got to the meat of it.

"Pursuant to Ohio Revised Code section three one zero seven, I find that the adoption of Jacqueline Lopez, date of birth June nine, nineteen ninety-six by Bonnie and Steven Mitchell to be in the best interests of the minor child. I'm entering a final decree of adoption. It is so ordered," the judge decreed lifting the metaphorical sword of Damocles from hanging over the child's head.

"Does that mean I can be Jacqueline Mitchell?" the girl asked the judge. Jacqueline and her guardian had come in from the hall for the judge's questions and ruling.

"Absolutely," the judge said mimicking the girl's solemn expression. "Let me be the first the shake your hand as Jackie Mitchell."

The girl took the judge's hand with her own. Then Jackie added her other hand and promptly cried over their intertwined body parts.

"Sorry. I'm sorry. I'm just so happy."

"You should be. You'll have now what most other kids have. Two parents who live with you, love you, and will always be yours."

Bonnie took a huge heaving breath, her bosom rising and falling in the stiff fabric of her dress. I dared look my clients in the eye then, and promptly regretted it. Steve was outright crying, especially when Jackie bounded down the few steps from the podium and ran into his arms. I looked away when my eyes smarted.

Shoving papers into my bag, I gave the new little family some time to celebrate.

"When will get her new birth certificate? She really wants to change her name at Mt. Carmel."

I looked back at the bench, but the judge and bailiff had disappeared into chambers, the wood door shut tight.

Thankfully, I had enough experience in Cuyahoga County to answer this one easily.

"I'll get the judge to sign the decree today and walk it through to the clerk's office. I'll get you a certified copy as quickly as I can. The new birth certificate, though, will come from the Columbus. That may take a few weeks."

"Thank you. Thank you and all the people at Dalton Lacey. I'm so glad I signed up for the free assistance program. You've made all our dreams come true," Donna said. The hug that came after was warm and tight. I swallowed past the lump in my throat.

"You're welcome. Why don't you guys go out and celebrate. I'm going to pop in to talk to the judge," I said lifting my messenger bag and coat.

After the parents and guardian left, it was me and Lulu in the vast wood and stone courtroom. I always appreciated the work of the WPA at times like this.

"So what do you think?"

"I think," I started giddy with my small victory. "I think I'd love to do this full time. I've never left a courtroom with someone as happy as the Mitchells. I mean some of my clients who *didn't* go to jail were relieved, if not exactly happy. The divorce or juvenile custody ones are never happy coming or going. This, though, this felt great. I don't know why I always thought the law was all about the bad shit. If I can figure out a way to get paid for this, I'm really going to leave the criminal law behind me."

"I'm so fucking happy for you," Lulu crowed. "Criminal law wasn't you. The shit that went down never seemed to sit well with you."

"All criminal defendants deserve a vigorous defense. It's their constitutional right," I protested. Even if I didn't like criminal law much, it got my back up when people dismissed the importance of a vigorous defense. Getting railroaded would be the worst thing in the world for an innocent man.

"Yeah, yeah. I don't see no cameras up in here. I know you swore to uphold the Constitution and all that shit in Columbus, but no one's holding you to that. You shouldn't have any hesitation about making money with your degree and being happy."

"Catholic guilt makes that hard." When the doors to law firm practice had been shut tight—with me on the outside—I'd done what was available, and what, in my heart, I thought was right. I made my best efforts to help myself and those who needed the help the most. Or maybe that's what I told myself to make a set of bad options feel better.

"Since when do Catholics have to live in poverty? Hard to believe with that compound the pope lives in. I have all sorts of Jewish guilt, but you know what? I take a bit of my Dalton Lacey salary, donate it to the ACLU and get to live another guilt-free day."

"I don't need permission to be happy," I said hearing the defensiveness in my tone.

"Kind of sounds like you do. Come on. Let's walk our decrees through then maybe get a drink. There's this website I've heard about—eHarmony or something like that. It's supposed to be really good at matchmaking."

"Dating?"

"Third time's a charm, right."

"Can you believe how warm it's been today?" I said as I pulled on my coat in the ornate vestibule of the courthouse. Normally, there weren't many fifty-degree days in

January. But I'd take them. Leaving the courthouse with an arctic wind at my back was an experience I'd get to save for another day.

"Last week was warm too. Maybe global warming or some shit like that. You know we can't count on this to be anything more than a minute. I think it's God's way of keeping us in Cleveland."

"Yeah, well. A girl can hope. Where do you want to go?"

"Where else? West Sixth."

Suitably gloved, wrapped, and buttoned against the inevitable cold that would sweep in off the lake come nightfall, I pushed open the heavy door. A large knot of people milled about on the front steps and on Lakeside Avenue. I looked back at Lulu. My best friend glanced at her watch.

"It's a protest march."

"How do you—?"

"Dalton Lacey sent out a memo today. Reverend Emery Wilkinson is leading a protest of the way the city is handling the Troy Duncan shooting. It's supposed to be a candlelight vigil."

I'd only ever seen Reverend Wilkinson on television. He was Cleveland's answer to Jesse Jackson and Al Sharpton, all wrapped in one hell of an expensive overcoat. Whenever there was something amiss in the black community, you could be sure to see Wilkinson being interviewed on TV or leading a protest in the streets.

My victory of minutes ago fled my mind as I watched Wilkinson in his fur-lined coat, fiddle with a bullhorn in his leather-gloved hand. An aide standing next to him flipped a switch, and Wilkinson lifted the horn to his lips.

"Let's pray," he intoned. Hundreds of heads, most in hats, bowed. "Let us pray for Troy Duncan and his family.

A fine man…an honorable man was cut down in his prime for no reason other than the color of his skin."

The bowed heads came up erupting in a chorus of "amens" and "preach it." Then fists, a few at first, then more and more rose in anger over the picture of injustice Wilkinson painted.

"Let us pray for truth and justice to win out. Proverbs twelve seventeen says, 'When you tell the truth, justice is done, but lies lead to injustice.'"

A hiss of agreement rolled through the crowd as their agitation grew. I could hear a few "lying mother fuckers."

"Let us pray for redemption and forgiveness for Sergeant Marc Baldwin." A couple of boos stole through the unforgiving and restless crowd.

"The Gospel of Luke says…Luke says we must forgive men their trespasses if we want our heavenly father to forgive our own. So let us include Sergeant Baldwin in our prayers. If anyone needs God's love and forgiveness, it's him." There was a long moment of silence before he whispered "amen." into the horn.

When Wilkinson spoke this time, his voice was booming. The soothing preacher's voice was long gone.

"We're gathered here today to let the powers that be know that we can't be brushed aside, closed out, and treated as if our voices don't matter. Our men are in danger, not just from each other, but from the police as well."

The crowd responded with a litany of "amens" and "hallelujahs.'"

"An innocent black man in Cleveland, a man like Troy Duncan, should be able to walk the streets free of fear of injury or death at the end of a policeman's hand, Taser, nightstick or gun."

"Preach it," someone shouted.

"We're here tonight to let Police Chief Kelley McCormick, Cuyahoga County prosecutor Lorraine Pope, and Mayor Foster Gates know a single thing. There will be no peace until there is justice for Troy Duncan. No justice, no peace."

As if by magic, everyone had lit candles in hand. I hadn't realized while listening to Wilkinson talk that dusk had fallen.

In moments, the courthouse we were standing on the steps of and the city hall not a quarter mile to the east, would bleed hundreds of workers. This was the first full day back to work after the holidays. With the street blocked off, the evening commute for most of those folks would be hellish.

Seconds later, those selfsame workers stood on the steps, unsure of how to navigate their way through the growing crowd of protestors. I spied Wilkinson sharing a word with someone. None of this was by accident. I had to admit, he'd done a masterful job.

Not a few seconds later, news cameras arrived, followed by police in riot gear.

"We should go," Lulu said pulling at the sleeve of my coat.

"Wait a second," I said mesmerized. It was like television news had come to life right before my eyes.

As if on cue, the protestors started chanting, "No Justice. No Peace. No Justice. No Peace."

Slowly, as though marching down a wedding aisle, the protestors moved. I watched the police. Usually aggressive in situations like this, they stood still behind huge plastic shields and helmets. I had no idea if this protest was permitted, but a huge show of firepower by white police against unarmed black and brown protestors would surely spark something. This didn't seem like a good time to watch my first in-person protest and risk something like that. Innocent people got caught in the crossfire all the time. Troy Duncan being one of them if Wilkinson's version of events was to be believed.

"I'm ready," I said as Lulu grabbed my hand. She jog-walked us west, while the protestors fanned out to the east. "Why so fast? You really think a simple protest like that could spark off a riot?"

We stopped in the first bar with an "open" sign. It wasn't anything special, nothing like the wine bar down the street that held young lawyer functions once a month, but the beer was cheap, and the happy hour snacks looked good.

"My parents were in the south during the Freedom Summer. They watched peaceful agitation turn ugly too many times to count. It may be forty years later, but some things don't change."

What did I know? I'd take her word for it. My parents hadn't even been involved in any kind of protest movement. They had been too busy learning English and working two jobs each.

After we hung our coats on a hook by the wall, we settled into one of the many empty wood seats.

Slow night.

The wall-to-wall screens grabbed my attention. They were usually filled with whatever game was on. In Cleveland, a city that had held on to all of its sports teams with an iron grip that meant that there weren't many nights without a game. I looked at the wall and saw the Cavaliers were scheduled to play the Milwaukee Bucks. Tip off was at seven.

Lulu ordered beers and nachos for us while my eyes were glued to the television. The protest we'd walked away from was front and center on the four screens behind the bar. Each screen caught the action from a different angle. The protestors had made their way from the courthouse to city hall. There Wilkinson stood before a podium. To his left was Vernon Dinwiddie. Every high profile case with a black plaintiff or defendant brought the small man out of the woodwork. This was no different. I wondered how he did it. Did he chase ambulances or did the families come to him? Either way, I wanted to hear what the men at the podium were about to say.

"Turn that up," I asked the bartender.

He pushed a button on a remote and the closed captioning disappeared while anchor voices blared from invisible speakers.

The Chyron caption under Dinwiddie's name said he was a lawyer for Troy Duncan and family. No surprise there. That man was attracted to controversy like a moth to flame.

A large poster loomed behind the lawyer. I assumed the picture of the attractive black man in the chef's whites was none other than Troy Duncan, who as far as I could figure had committed the crime of being black—an easy one to commit in Cleveland.

Dinwiddie was railing about justice when the mayor stepped out into the fray. The mayor, not being your average run of the mill worker could have, no doubt, escaped through the basement parking lot, or a back door. Between Mayor Gates, Wilkinson, and Dinwiddie, there was no shortage of ego and testosterone on the city hall steps. This was about to get interesting.

The bartender muted the sets again when new patrons filled the bar.

Ungluing my eyes from the screen, I took a larger than necessary sip of the beer that a waitress had plopped between Lulu and I.

"Do you know anything about all that?" I asked. Being at a big firm, meant Lulu sometimes had the inside scoop on city politics. Her firm had represented the city in various capacities over the years when the matter was outside the scope of expertise for the City Attorney's office.

"No more than you're seeing there on screen. What happens here in Cleveland is a travesty of justice. There isn't a year that goes by without one of these incidents. You know why that protest was super organized and on point?"

I shook my head.

"It's because they do it once or twice a year. It's like a surprise reprisal of a yearly play. Police brutalize a black person, Dinwiddie and Wilkinson are on the scene. The city promises justice, the police threaten justice, and the family gets a little money and no justice. But nothing changes."

"Maybe I should call you Ms. Pessimistic Downer instead of Lulu," I said. If this was a yearly reprisal, it was one I'd be happy never to see again.

"It's true, Casey. You know it yourself."

I didn't ask the question in my head: when was the last shooting? If I said it out loud, I'm sure Lulu would come at me with all kinds of shit about how I should know those things about my city. She was probably right that I should, but I was as guilty as the next white person about turning a blind eye to police violence.

Who wanted to think about the dark side of the police? I wanted to be able to rely on peace officers, guilt free. Ugh. I'd give anything to discard the knapsack of white privilege I was lugging around.

I bit into one nacho, then a second. The gooey, melty cheese, and meat would be hell on my newly trim waistline, but it was much easier than talking about what was going on outside the front door.

"So you were saying you had some ideas for my dating life?" I asked in a not so subtle attempt to change the subject.

Lulu was quiet a long moment, as she scrutinized my face. Mentally she acquiesced to the change.

"Right, so, there's this dating site that everyone at my firm's been talking about. I hear it's even better than JDate."

"What's the difference between this thing and the usual online hookup service?"

"When you sign up, you have to answer a super long list of questions. They match you with potential dates, but you should have more in common with them than usual guy off the street."

"Have *you* tried it?"

Lulu stuffed a bunch of chips in her mouth, and shook her head at the same time. That girl could eat half a platter of junk food and not put on half a pound.

"Then why do you think *I* should do it?"

"You want to get married and settle down, right?"

"Sure," I said hating myself for being so traditional in a world that had changed. "What about you?"

"I need a minute to work on my career. Nothing says no to partnership like marriage and family."

"But I with no such lofty aspirations can date?"

"For fucks sake, don't act so thin skinned. You were engaged to Tom right out of the gate in law school. You were talking marriage with Miles. Am I wrong thinking a family is important to you?"

"More important than my so-called career, apparently."

"Skip it, then. We can go on being single besties forever. That's quite fine by me."

We'd come to the crazy cat lady spinster part of the evening a bit earlier than usual. I wasn't drunk enough for that fantasy. I took a big gulp of beer.

"I can't remember the last time you had a date," I said looking pointedly at my friend. My last two relationships had been crappy. But I'd shared every embarrassing detail with Lulu. She was really good at deflecting, rarely sharing at all. I gave her a look that said I wasn't going to be persuaded. After a long considered silence, she glanced at me from under her lashes.

"I've maybe seen a partner at the firm," she said under her breath, like white shoe spies were lurking around between cracked vinyl booths.

"Married?" I whispered. I'd never even suspected she'd been out with anyone. My radar was all askew.

"What kind of skeeve do you think I am? No, not married. But not quite kosher either."

"Have I met him?" I asked. I was really wondering if she meant not kosher in terms of his religion or not kosher because was an old ass man who should be dating someone in his own age and income bracket. But I stuck to the simple.

Lulu paused for an unnaturally long time. The blue screens stole my attention. The cameras cut from pictures of Troy being upstanding and honorable, to a picture of a cop in dress uniform standing in front of a flag, to angry protestors shouting at the mayor.

When Lulu spoke, I tore my gaze away from the screen.

“You know what? Maybe later on this. I've already said too much. You're in the office all the damn time, so I don't want to tip my hand. Okay? Maybe when this adoption pro bono program is over in a few months."

I brought my eyes back to LuLu and lifted my mug. "To boys.”

“To boys.” She hit my mug with her own.

12

Marc

January 10, 2006

I slammed the thick stack of papers on the table. The CPPA rep, and his nameplate jumped. He nearly fell out of his seat. I didn't try to hide my small smile of satisfaction.

Francis Parker, Attorney-at-Law. Fucking pansy ass loser. I lay my hand on my hip, but it was empty. No Sam Browne, no holster, nothing. There was no damned gun, because of course the brass had confiscated my weapon. It was probably for the best. The urge to pull my piece and wave it in his face was nearly irresistible. If I'd learned one thing in twenty plus years of policing, it was that a gun was a hell of a persuasive tool.

"What the fuck are you doing for me? Why in the hell did the county sheriff knock on my damn door at six in the morning with a stack of papers? 'You've been served,' he said. Like I'm some fucking common child support dodging, bench warrant having criminal. Served me in my home. My wife and kids were there. They saw this."

"Marc!" Parker raised his voice, slightly. "No one else can accept court papers on your behalf. That's why it's called personal service."

Sarcastic son of a bitch. When people needed an urban foot soldier out in the trenches, I was an expert. But the minute I walked in an office, suddenly everyone knew better than me.

"So what does this say?" I slid the papers across the desk. I'd tried sitting at my dining room table to work my way through the thick stack. But there was a bunch of gobbledygook legal speak in there.

"Get some coffee." Parker motioned to the open door.

"I'll stay put," I said parking my butt in a chair. I wasn't going to be dismissed so easily. If I walked out that door, he'd take ten phone calls then see me off with promises of later. This was my life, and I wanted to know what I was up against—*now*.

"Fine," he said. He pulled open a drawer and slipped out a pair of reading glasses.

He took his sweet time flipping through the pages, nodding, using a highlighter in a couple of places. Itching to do something, I stood and started pacing the small office. He'd graduated from Miami University and Cleveland Marshall. I had no idea if those schools were great. Certainly weren't Harvard. Cleveland wasn't the kind of place Harvard graduates flocked to, though. From watching the news, sounded like they all went to New York City and worked for big banks or San Francisco and worked for dotcoms.

Cleveland wasn't that kind of player in the labor market. I hoped my kids grew up and left. I'd miss them, but even I knew there were greater opportunities elsewhere. Ten years ago, I'd have said that I'd love it if they were on the job. Now that everyone was anti police, they needed to seek their fortune elsewhere.

"You're going to need to find yourself a lawyer." Parker concluded, dropping the papers and his glasses.

"Since when? Doesn't the union represent all officers in cases like this?"

"This usually true. But we have two issues going on here. First, this is a civil suit."

"And..."

"Troy Duncan's family is suing you for money...a lot of it."

"But it's *his* fault. He stuck his hand in his pocket after I'd told him to stop. Why aren't you suing him for fucking with my career?"

"Whoa, man. Slow down. I'm on your side, okay?"

"This guy...Vernon Dinwiddie...is asking for millions of dollars." I may not have understood every single thing in those papers. The bottom line demand of ten million dollars came through loud and clear though.

"Look. The guy's lawyer did this for two reasons. First, he's coming out strong. It's just a great first shot across the bow. He's saying that your perp is not only innocent, but he was hurt, really bad. Dinwiddie's alleging permanent paralysis."

"Does he have a case?" I asked sitting down and leaning closer to Parker. His hesitation in answering made me think the kid might be able to make something of all this.

"That depends on a lot of stuff," he equivocated.

"Like what? What could this guy say that would make a jury give him a bunch of money?" When he didn't answer, I stood and leaned my weight on my hands. I looked him right in the eye. "Is there a reason that lawyers can't ever give a straight answer?"

"Marc. I don't think we should get into this now. As a matter of fact, I'm pretty sure we *can't* get into this now. I was going to call you today. If you hadn't come down, I'd have called you anyway. Because…because the CPPA can't represent you in this matter *or* any possible criminal proceeding."

"You said that already, but you took these papers anyway. What's the story? Why can't you represent me?"

"The CPPA is representing Darlene Webb."

"What does that have to do with me finding a lawyer? I pay union dues just like Darlene. I've probably paid a lot more dues over the years than she has. She's been on the force, what, ten minutes? Seems like in any decision to pick between two people, if nothing but the fact that I have greater seniority, I should have come out on top."

"Last year, the Ohio Supreme court ruled that we cannot represent two people with markedly different interests. For years we'd been skirting around those rules, with Chinese walls and all that. But the court made itself clear last session. It's in section twenty six of the new collective bargaining agreement the union signed with the city at the end of the year."

I remembered seeing something about this in one of the endless bulletins the union posted on their board in the squad room. Honestly, other than getting us okay wages and better overtime I didn't think much about the Cleveland Police Union. They'd done their job and we'd done ours. Now it was looking like I was going to have to do their job too. Dollars to donuts, Francis Parker wasn't going out in a patrol car and driving through Hough on a Friday night.

"What do I have to do?" I asked resigned not to battle it out with this suit.

"You should rest assured that we'll pay for your representation. You will not be out of pocket."

I tried not to let my laugh escape. Of course these fuckers were paying. I hadn't been turning over nearly a thousand dollars a year to line the pockets of these desk jockeys for no damned reason.

"Fine. What do I do now?" I asked again. He'd been squirrely with the answers.

"You take this complaint and this file with you to the city law director. Their office will give you a list of attorneys to visit. Let us know who you choose, and we'll make proper arrangements."

"Complaint?" I said.

"The civil lawsuit. The possible internal disciplinary hearing, we'll handle. That's a private arbitration. But if there are any possible criminal actions against you, then your new attorney will handle that as well."

I snatched the list out of his hand. "This looks like fun."

"Off the record." I nodded, and he continued. "Off the record, you're going to be better off. We're overworked here. We don't handle cases in common pleas all that often. But these guys on the list have experience. If I were you, I'd pick a woman or a black. They'll make for much better optics. Plus, you have a no-lose case. The Supreme Court, the one in D.C., has made it nearly impossible to put an officer down for a shooting. Okay? This will be cake."

Five hours later, I wanted to curse Francis Parker. I was sitting in my car on Superior. I'd badged a meter maid who tried to make me move. Let her report me. A possible abuse of authority write-up to get out of a parking ticket was looking like the least of my problems.

Not one of the so-called common pleas lawyers from the law directors list could take the case. Not one.

Darlene Webb was either the smartest or the dumbest chick on earth. While I'd been cooling my jets waiting for Todd to get back to me on my reinstatement, she'd been pleading her case to every Tom, Dick, and Harriet in the Cleveland bar.

I'd been ushered out of more offices, and turned away more times than a doorbell ringing Mormon. The dash-board clock said that it was three o'clock. But I didn't want to go home empty handed. According to the lawyers, I had less than thirty days to find an attorney who could handle my case and file an answer on my behalf. It might be an easy win, but I'd need a fucking lawyer; otherwise, it would turn into a sure loser. The idea of explaining this latest failure to Jan across the dinner table wasn't appealing. I flipped open my phone.

Ten minutes later, I was back on Lakeside in the City Law Director's office. This time I didn't take anything fobbed off on me by some secretary. I demanded to see the law director himself. He was going to have to explain to me who in the hell was going to represent me.

"The list you gave me this morning is a bust. Darlene Webb has conflicted me out of half of the Cleveland bar," I said without preamble.

The lawyer, looking mighty comfortable behind a desk the size of my dining room table, peered through his glasses at me. He didn't speak. I shifted in my seat.

"I've got nothing against black people," I said. "I just want you to know that. As long as everyone follows the law, and obeys the cops, they got no problem with me."

The minute the words left my mouth, I regretted them. The light-skinned black man sitting across from me, took a moment to smooth his hand across his balding head. "Don't move," he said holding up a single finger. "I'm going to make a call."

He turned his back to me and flipped through a Rolodex I'd seen in the middle of his credenza. Plucking out a card, he turned back and lifted the phone.

"Mr. Brody," he boomed in a much friendlier voice than I'd gotten. He explained my particular dilemma. The law director scratched his jaw as he listened. Minutes later, he pulled a pencil from a metal cup on his desk. He scratched something on a sheet of paper. After he hung up, he handed the sheet to me.

It was personalized, from the desk of, and all that. My eyes followed the scrawl down the page. It had a name and an address.

"Who is this Casey Cort?"

"I don't personally know her. But this is a recommendation from the Brody family. I don't have to tell you who they are, right?"

"No sir," I said. "Liam Brody used to be the county prosecutor." Every indictment I'd ever seen carried that guy's name from the time I'd started as a cop until he'd gotten a better job as Attorney General.

"I spoke to his brother, Patrick Brody. He's the presiding judge in the county. This is a personal recommendation from him. If I were you, I'd walk on over to the Illuminating Building right now."

"Okay," I said standing and zipping my coat for the millionth time that day.

"My advice: you need to get out ahead of this thing. I'd start today."

I shook the man's hand and thanked him. I didn't tell him that I hadn't exactly been sitting around twiddling my thumbs. I didn't say that Darlene was turning out to be anything but loyal. She'd busted through the blue wall and was stomping all over what cops everywhere stood for. I didn't mention that I'd been a team player from day one. Never had I run to a dozen lawyers trying to throw my partner under the bus.

"It's every man for himself out here, huh?" I tossed over my shoulder before I pulled at the brass knob.

"The city has the back of every sworn officer in the city," he said.

It was the most diplomatic bullshit I'd ever heard. But I took his advice anyway. I left my car in its illegal spot and walked the two blocks to Public Square.

13

Casey

January 10, 2006

Letty came into my office and slammed the door behind her. That was weird by any standard. I braced myself for what was next.

"You have a walk-in," she said.

I held in my sigh of relief. At least I didn't have to do an emergency jail visit, soothing a defendant new to the system and totally freaked out. Those had a way of ruining what I'd planned on being a quiet night.

The clock on the wall read four o'clock. I rubbed the back of my neck. Replacing the cases I didn't want with cases I did want wasn't as easy as waving a wand or calling a Brody. Presiding Judge Patrick Brody had done just that for me a couple of years ago. I didn't expect a repeat performance.

One call from him and I'd been able to slip out of Juvenile Court hell in a couple weeks. He'd anointed me important, told them I was too busy, and the judges and magistrates there had let me go faster than a Marlin from a sport fisherman's line.

Extrication from criminal defense work was proving to be a little more difficult. I'd pestered enough judges during their swing through the arraignment room, that I was getting regular assignments. Ten assignments per month netted me seventy-five hundred, enough to pay the bills. The domestic cases were gravy. Filling up that money hole left by turning down criminal assignment with adoptions was looking like it was going to be a long-term plan. Really long term.

"Casey?"

I looked back at Letty. "I'm tired," was my shorthand response. I was learning that you didn't burden staff with your money worries. Loyalty wasn't forged in shared adversity. Not when your assistant had to worry about her paycheck.

"I think you should see this guy," she said pressing her own case.

"Why?" I rolled my head. Neck cracking sounds rang in my ears.

She thrust a piece of paper toward me. "From the desk of City Law Director, Thomas Gordon..." Then my name was scrawled below. I looked up.

"He's saying that this recommendation came personally from Tommie Gordon not fifteen minutes ago."

That woke me up from my afternoon sugar slump. I scooted forward in my chair, rereading the note. Letty wasn't mistaken. My name was on the notepad of the City Law director.

"What's the story?" I asked buffered by a little bit of a second wind.

"He wouldn't say. He only wanted to talk to you. Not me."

I opened my drawer, popped an instant dissolve pain-killer from my supply, and chased it with the cold tea from either today or yesterday. That, I couldn't quite remember.

"Give me three minutes. Then send him in."

I folded the open files on my desk and slotted them in my ongoing file drawer. Detritus ended up in the bin under my desk. When my door finally opened, all that remained on my blotter was a single legal pad and a sharp pencil. I stood.

"This is Attorney Cort, please have a seat," Letty said pulling out a chair across the desk. I shook the man's hand, and we both sat. My assistant pulled the door closed behind her, much more quietly this time.

"How can I help you?"

"I'm Marc Baldwin," he said and paused like he was Mel Gibson. My hours didn't leave much time for entertainment, though I was pretty sure he wasn't a major or minor celebrity. He didn't have the body of a local professional athlete either.

"Should I know who you are?" I asked before I could think better of it. "I saw you were recommended by Tommie Gordon, but he didn't call before you came."

"Actually, the recommendation is from Judge Patrick Brody."

The pencil that had been firm in my hand moments ago plopped on the cardboard backed calendar I used as a blotter.

Two thoughts flashed in my mind simultaneously. This was going to be a big money case for one. What would I owe for this recommendation was the other. Because the Brodys were the very definition of "strings attached."

"What do you have there?" I asked. He had a thick-looking folder under his arm. Most clients would have slid it across the desk by now pushing their personal kryptonite off onto me, happy to be relieved of their burden. Baldwin was the exact opposite—clutching at it like a life raft.

"You've heard of the Troy Duncan case?"

It hit me like a ton of bricks. "Reverend Wilkinson prayed for you last week," I blurted out.

"I might need that," he said his mouth in a wry twist. He handed over the file this time.

A complaint lay on top. Vernon Dinwiddie had outdone himself, I thought as I flipped through all one hundred twenty pages. I flipped back to the top page. In the United States District Court for the District of Ohio, Eastern Division, it said. Of course, I should have known that. Any lawyer worth his salt would file the action under section 1983 of the U.S. Code among a laundry list of other state and federal statutes. I tried not to let my last federal court disaster get me down.

"You've read this?" I asked, stalling for time while I gathered my thoughts. It wasn't every day that a gem of a case plopped in your lap. But the last time it had happened had turned out to be kind of a disaster.

"I glanced through it."

I bet he did. He had all the bluster of someone easily overcome by dozens of pages of legal documents. But half my job was boosting confidence and stroking ego. The other half? Engaging in a bit of bluster myself.

"What's in the folder?" I waved my hands in a give-it-to-me gesture.

He handed the other bit over. Inside there was a quick memo to file of the kinds of criminal charges police officers faced when they used excessive force. The attorney who'd put this together, someone from the police union, had practically laid out a strategy on this one. Of course, he was probably an expert. Like Lulu said, this wasn't CPD's first time at the rodeo.

I sat back and considered my potential client. He looked innocent enough, white, stout, with a short brush cut of light brown hair. He was wearing a button down and jeans, neither of which looked like they'd seen much use. A common pleas jury would love him. They'd be falling all over themselves to deny the victim's family money or acquit him. Federal court, though, was another matter entirely.

"Why isn't the police union representing you?"

"They say it's a conflict of interest. They're behind my partner, Darlene Webb."

Now that was curious. The papers were full of police officers sticking to the same story no matter how the facts played out. Defections didn't usually happen.

"Does Darlene have a different story from you?"

"I wouldn't think so. We talked about it with Captain Todd right after the incident where I discharged my weapon, and I'm pretty sure we were on the same page."

"And now? Do you think she has second thoughts about her statement?"

"Why are you asking all of this?"

"Because if you were," I held up the first and second finger of my right hand, "like this, then the union could represent the both of you no problem. A conflict of interest arises...happens...when the two defendants have a different story." I split my finger apart like a peace sign. "Or when one defendant has agreed to testify for the government..."

Marc Baldwin shifted back and forth in his seat.

"Look, it's late. Why don't we do this? You tell me everything that happened that night. I'll go home, have a look at all these papers and we'll meet again tomorrow."

"Will you take the case?"

I wanted to say, let me see, I'll think on it, and let's talk tomorrow. The new me wanted to be an early bird, wanted to get the worm. Ignoring the tiny flutter of unease in my stomach, I nodded vigorously.

"Yes, of course I'll take it."

"Have you handled anything like this before."

"Do you remember the federal judge who...left Cleveland, allegedly having taking her kid from foster care?" I stumbled all over the truth with that question.

"Grant something?"

"Sheila Harrison Grant. That was me."

His blink was slow. I have no idea what he was making of that in his head.

"Why'd she run? Did she think she'd lose?"

"Look, I can't talk about other cases with you. I'll say this. I would have probably won her case, but the judge dismissed it because the defendant was no longer in the jurisdiction. That's all I'll say. Just as I'll keep everything you tell me confidential, I have to do the same for other clients. Got it."

He nodded. "So you know Judge Brody?"

"I know all the Brodys," I said plainly. "They're big time, but on the state level. Not one of them has a toe in with the federal government. We'll have to fight and win your case on its own merits. We'll talk about this more tomorrow, though."

"What time?"

"Let's say one in the afternoon. Why don't we both go home? We can review the facts tomorrow when we've had a good night's sleep."

"Do I need to bring anything?"

"I'll need to review all of this first. If I need anything else, I'll have Letty—she's the one who showed you in—call you to confirm in the morning."

"Okay."

"I know this seems pretty bad. The whole city is tuned into the Troy Duncan case right now. You need to keep your head down, though, and after today, you do not talk to anyone about this, not without me present, do you understand?"

"I do."

"Give your contact information to Letty on the way out. I'll see you tomorrow."

Baldwin stood and opened the door. The clicking of keyboards and the hum of the photocopy machine filled the small space I shared with other attorneys.

"Oh, are reporters hounding you at home?" He seemed to be the only person in all of this I hadn't seen on television.

"Uh…no."

"How—"

"My address is a pretty big secret." His answer was cryptic.

"Try to keep it that way."

14

Troy

January 12, 2006

"When will I be able to see my family?" The nurse who'd swept by my bed was the first person I could remember seeing in the last two days who wasn't an inmate.

"I'm a nurse," she said brusquely. "Not in charge of visitation. You'll have to talk to a deputy about that."

"My wife said that I get a half hour a week," I said not letting her tone dissuade me. "I really want to talk to my family."

I knew it had been well more than seven days since Campbell had seen me, how many, I wasn't sure. It had felt like half the hospital staff were blowing through noisemakers while I'd been coming to terms with the news about my paralysis. I was still holding out hope that I'd walk again. My mom and dad and the lawyer had to be working to get me out of here so I could see some kind of specialist who could tell me the whole truth, tell me what my chances were of carrying my soon-to-be wife over the threshold. I looked toward the nurse again trying to catch her attention.

She finally paused organizing gauze or whatever it was she was doing that kept her from looking me in the eye. Exasperation huffed from her lips.

"Unfortunately for you, you're in lockup." Every word was sounded out syllable by syllable as if I were a foreigner. "You don't *get* anything that the sheriff's deputies don't *let* you have. Get *that*?"

"What about my constitutional rights?" My father may have schooled me how black people's rights got trampled over, but I wasn't dead, so I still had some.

"You gave up your rights the moment you committed a crime," was the nurse's sharp response.

"I didn't—"

"La, la, la, la, la. Don't think I haven't heard it all before," she said. I was grateful that she didn't jam her thumbs in her ears and wave her fingers at me. "The bathroom is over there. I'll be back to check on you in the afternoon."

The bedpan that had been tucked along the rail was gone. That bit of memory stood from the haze of the last few days.

"Wait. Bathroom? I'm...my legs. They've stopped working," I bit out in mortification. Paralysis was one thing. The whole job of going to the bathroom, something I'd been doing on my own for thirty plus years, was another.

"What do you expect me to do about that?"

"The doctor at the hospital talked about a bowel program," I said my voice nearly a whisper. I wish I'd started with that instead of visitation or constitutional rights.

Emptying my bowel was more important than fifteen minutes of visitation.

"What? We are not equipped for this," the nurse sucked her teeth in obvious displeasure. "Please don't tell me you have a catheter as well?"

"Um, no. I can handle that part. Where's the funnel?"

Once the doctor had removed the catheter, a nurse had showed me how to hold myself over a funnel. Fortunately, I could feel when I had to pee. The other, though, was going to take more work to get under my control.

"Ah jaysus. I'll see if we have any in supply. Haven't had a paraplegic in here in a long time. Jesus on the cross, I can't believe someone didn't warn me. The doctor's gonna love this."

"When can I see him?" I asked. Maybe I could plead my case to the doctor. Maybe he'd figure out a way to get me what I needed which was up and out of here. I'd hated the cold, bright light-filled hospital. I'd go back there in a heartbeat, though. The jail infirmary was a strictly third world affair.

"Dr. Carlsen?" she squinted at me.

"I guess," I said lifting my shoulders. That one movement was a triumph. Someone should have warned me not to take standing, walking, and sitting for granted for all those years.

"Hmphf. I have no idea. State gives us two weeks before we have to do a medical evaluation. So I'm guessing before the end of the month."

"What about a wheelchair or rehabilitation? The doctors at MetroHealth said I'd need to learn how to do everything…for myself…again."

They really couldn't expect me to lie in bed all day every day for two whole weeks. That seemed like a lot of cruel and unusual punishment.

"Look, Mr. Duncan. You're facing some pretty severe felony charges. They're saying on television that you nearly tried to kill an officer in the line of duty. I'm from a long family of cops and don't take too kindly to your kind trying to kill our kind, okay?"

Nurse Ratched stalked over to the next inmate who needed care. I hoped he got better than I had.

My head swiveled around on the bed. I was going to die in here unless I figured something out. I couldn't imagine there was a chance that my mom or dad were getting in here to see me or coordinate the kind of medical care I probably needed.

Certainly, I didn't want my kids here, no matter what. Campbell had said something about Dad hiring a lawyer. He's who I needed to see. Closing my eyes, I tried to remember all I could from Campbell's visit last week. Did she ever say who the lawyer was?

It was so hard to remember anything after that guy had told me that my legs would never work again. That there was a bullet lodged so deep in my spine, no doctor could or would operate.

I pressed the emergency button. Nurse Ratched came back, full of eye rolling teeth sucking indignity.

"What do you need?"

"I need a lawyer visit," I said back to that constitutional rights thing again. Surely, I was entitled to medical care and lawyer visits. If I couldn't get one, then I really needed the other.

"You don't get to arrange them. The lawyer gets to arrange them. I'm sure your big time lawyer will get you out of here on some kind of technicality. Cause that's what they do. Defend the guilty. That Dinwiddie's going to go to hell. And you'll be right behind him in line to greet the devil. Don't page me again unless you're dying, and even then, don't bother."

Dismissed, I closed my eyes and thought about strategy. Dinwiddie. That was something I hadn't known ten minutes ago. The teeth sucking had been worth it. I was sure I'd heard the name before on TV when someone else had been railroaded in Cleveland.

No way in hell did I want to die in this place. Which meant I needed to see a doctor and get into a rehab facility or I needed the Dinwiddie guy to get me the hell out of here.

A bell clanged for a full thirty seconds. I hadn't heard anything like it since I'd graduated from Cleveland Heights High School. A deputy with a metal counter clicked by me. That deputy was followed by another who stood by my bed a long moment while the first radioed his numbers.

"Hey, what time is shift change?" I asked trying to make my voice as frail and friendly as possible.

"Five minutes. Why? You planning on breaking out?" The deputy chuckled at his own stupid joke.

"No reason. The nurse said she was going to bring me something. I guess I'll ask the next one."

"Yeah. You do that." The deputy took his counter and walked away.

Thirty minutes later, an older black woman bustled in, her uniform starched within an inch of its life. She unhooked the chart from the end of the bed. I crossed my fingers, under the covers, and prayed she'd be nicer to me than the last.

"Oh, you're going to be a mess," was her greeting. It wasn't exactly friendly, but it wasn't hostile either. "When was your last bowel movement?"

I swallowed my mortification. "At MetroHealth they gave me a suppository." Exactly how many days ago, I wasn't sure. The normal feeling of pressure and bloating that came with constipation was missing along with a lot of other sensation.

"Are you going to have get a suppository every day?" She asked while paging more slowly through my records.

"I think so. But could I ask you to tell me how I can use the phone?"

"There's one in the hall."

"I can't walk."

"Chile, that's a long walk then." The nurse laughed and walked away with my chart in hand.

Five minutes later, she was back with a funnel, a suppository, and a cell phone.

I reached for the phone first.

"Mama," I said when the line was answered. "I need you to get my lawyer here. It's urgent. I can't say too much more, I have to go. Love to you and daddy and the kids."

The nurse pressed a button ending the call, then slipped the small gadget into her uniform pocket.

"You don't tell a soul I did that," she admonished.

"My lips are sealed."

She lifted the blankets from the bottom up. She wrapped one of my hands around my penis, the other around the funnel. I let go of any control I'd had on my bladder. I shook into the funnel. She removed it and the plastic collection bag, and deposited them onto a rolling tray.

"I'm going to turn you over and insert this suppository. I'll pass out meds for everyone else, then I'll be back with a bed pan."

She rolled me on to my side. Latex gloves were snapped into place. The sound of plastic separating from foil filled the small space we shared. Seconds later, she snapped off the gloves.

"Don't move," she said. The nurse patted me on my right shoulder.

Like there was any chance of that. All that was left of body strength was in my forearms and hands. I wouldn't be moving on my own for a long time.

15

Augustus

January 18, 2006

Myrtle, Lynell, and I cooled our heels in the deserted lobby of the Cuyahoga County Jail while we waited. Last week, all three of us had come down to the jail to register in person. Now we were all on Troy's visitation list. Only one of us could see him probably, but we'd all come in the hope the rules could be bent. It had been nearly three weeks since anyone but Campbell had seen him. I hoped someone in this institution had an ounce of compassion for grieving, frightened parents.

Cold air and snowflakes swirled through the cavernous space when the outside door opened. Vernon Dinwiddie, leather briefcase in hand, came through the gap in the door.

I nodded in greeting at the lawyer. He was my ace in the hole. Given the way the sheriff's deputy had put us through our paces a week ago, I didn't think our right to visit was guaranteed. But with Dinwiddie there, not only could he demand his own visit, he could help one or hopefully two of us see my son.

After that ten-second phone call from Troy last Wednesday, I hadn't been able to sleep more than a few fitful hours in any given night. According to Myrtle, Troy hadn't sounded that pitiful since he fell out of a tree in Campbell's backyard and broke his arm when he was six years old.

"Have you seen him?" Dinwiddie asked while he clapped his leather-encased hands together for warmth. The slapping of the palms of the leather gloves echoed earning us a cross stare from the deputy manning the desk.

"We registered last Wednesday, which was the day we could visit inmates with the last name A through something. But they don't allow same day registration and visitation."

"What about Monday?"

"Martin Luther King Day. Visitation was suspended for the holiday."

Dinwiddie's harrumph held all the frustration I'd felt. The registration requirements and rules were arcane. A maze of hoops to jump through for thirty damn minutes every seven days. Reminded me of my parents going down to register to vote in Tuscaloosa where filling out forms was an existential exercise—because no one had ever planned on allowing them to vote.

We stood off to one side as Dinwiddie swaggered up to the reception desk. I liked that swagger. Told me he was a man used to getting his own way.

"Someone's gotta see him today," Lynell said full of mock indignation. "Zora needs to know her daddy's okay.

The girl ain't never woke up without her daddy there. She's waking up screaming at night that he's dead."

"I'm sure he's fine," Myrtle said firmly patting the girl's arm. God knew Lynell could go from zero to hysterical in a hot minute. Not for the first time did I wonder how Troy had gone from Campbell to this one. Their personalities were only one thing about them that was as different as night and day.

"You've got to prepare the kids, though," I said. "Once the lawyer gets him out of this mess, he may not come right home. The doctors at MetroHealth were talking about substantial rehabilitation."

"I can do that myself you know. I'm a certified home health aide. I'm at my house all day. Can't they just give me the instructions?"

"He's not one of the kids you babysit, Lynell," I said. How she could think running a daycare and caring for Troy were even in the same universe, I had no idea. I looked her in the eye to make sure she was listening. "He's a grown man who can't walk. Why don't we worry about getting a ramp at your house and whatever else we need before talking about when he's going to get home."

Lynell looked like she was going to argue when we all turned at the sound of shouting.

Dinwiddie was on tiptoe, his body half way across the desk as he argued with the deputy on duty. Better him than me. I wouldn't have been able to hold my temper. Then two Duncans would be in county lockup. For a short second I considered that. I'd probably get to see my son if I was on the inside.

"Can I ask you a question?"

I hated when Lynell did that. I just wanted her to ask the damn question already, not preface it with a whole lot of stuff. I turned away from the Dinwiddie drama and nodded toward Lynell.

"I...um...didn't make the January mortgage payment," she stuttered out. I refrained from pointing out it wasn't a question.

"Why not?" I squeezed between tight lips. This woman wasn't my child, so I worked hard not to scold her. But who in the world missed a house payment? That was first, car second, then food for your family. Maybe the last two could be switched depending on how you got to work. On a day like today when the arctic winds blew across Lake Erie from Canada though, a warm house wasn't optional.

"Troy would have got paid that Friday when he worked the New Year's shift. But..." She left the rest unspoken.

There were three more deputies at the desk now, but Dinwiddie was still going strong. A show of force and firepower didn't stop him. He'd tossed his briefcase on the ledge and the words "have your badges" and "constitutional rights" could be heard above the silent glares of the men in uniform.

"Don't you have anything in savings?" I asked turning back to Lynell. We'd lent—given—them the down payment for the house on East 118th. I didn't remember the mortgage being more than five or six hundred a month. It was something one of them could easily handle, made easier by having two regular incomes, most of hers under the table.

Lynell fiddled with the gold rings on nearly all her fingers. She had a little home shopping habit, but not to the tune of busting their budget, at least I hadn't thought so.

"We got the kids those games for Christmas," she said, her chin tucked in her neck in embarrassment. And she should be mortified. Who spent their mortgage money at Toys R Us?

"And?" I prided myself in not prying in my kid's affairs, but when someone asked for money, I figured I was entitled to as much information as a bank loan officer.

"Well, Troy had gotten that big raise. My family shares everything, you know, so I got my sister's car out of impound, and paid a little toward my momma's debt too, so they could enjoy the holidays."

From what Troy had said, "sharing" in the Powers family only went one way. When Lynell and Troy had gone broke after Zora was born, I'd told Troy he needed to support his little family and ignore the rest of them. The Powerses would use him up and spit him out. Turned out I was as right as rain because the minute my boy was out of the picture, Lynell had gone and given away his money.

"Gus, after we're done here, why don't we stop on down at Spencer's and get Troy's last check and whatever else he's owed," Myrtle said coming up with a solution like she always did. "Lynell, you're to send the payment right away, plus whatever they tacked on for being eighteen days late. If you get too behind, the bank will take the house in a minute."

Placated, Lynell went and found space on a nearby bench. She was like a scolded kid, running away from a further lecture. I was still thinking of giving her a lesson in money management when Dinwiddie jogged over to Myrtle and me.

"He's not here," the lawyer said.

"What do you mean he's not here? Did they let him out? Is there a place we have to go collect him?" I was already mentally moving the car in my head, then trying to figure out if we could keep him at home on the couch for a couple of days while we figured out the next steps.

The lawyer shook his head vehemently. “There was an emergency. He was transported back to MetroHealth. I’ll meet you there.”

I thought my heart was going to leap from my chest. Adrenaline surged through my body before my brain could make the shift in thought. My pulse pounded like I was running in place.

The hospital.

God damn it.

Damn. Damn. Damn.

My lips were moving in prayer on their own. Couldn’t stop that reflexive plea to a God who had forsaken me more times than I could count. Maybe today he’d spare my son since he hadn’t that night in the Flats.

I knew they should never have moved him to the jail. It was probably to save money. Always was. County wanted to house their inmates on the cheap. Hospital beds were never cheap.

“Gus?”

I must have been standing there a very long time. Dread had kept me rooted to the shiny linoleum. I’d leave as soon as I could think of one good thing that ever came out of a hospital. I glanced at Lynell who was standing by the front door crying.

Babies.

I remembered babies were the one good thing you could get from a hospital.

“Gus!” Myrtle shouted unaware of my internal bargaining and prayer.

“I’ll get the car. You girls wait out front.”

They looked like snow covered popsicles when I finally pulled up to West Third Street. "Sorry." It was all I could muster. I had no explanation for driving at the speed of molasses. None.

The rest of the trip to MetroHealth took maybe fifteen minutes. Not enough time to warm up, that was for sure. I dropped them by the front door and looked for a parking spot. The woman manning the front desk had an eye out for me and beckoned me over as soon as the revolving door closed behind me. Maybe Dinwiddie had used his considerable influence to smooth our way here.

"Mr. Duncan?"

"That's me."

"This man will escort you to the twelfth floor now."

I looked around the lobby and a thin white man walked up to me. Here we go again. He didn't introduce himself, and I didn't offer my hand. Our son being a prisoner in the hospital didn't make for a lot of smiles and handshakes. Nonetheless, I followed him like a duckling imprinted on its mother.

The man was quiet and somber looking in his gray suit. At the elevator bays, he finally nodded his greeting then slipped his card into a hidden slot above the call button. The door whooshed open instantly. After we got in, it was only seconds before we reached the top floor. Maybe the express elevator ride was the reason my stomach was doing flip-flops in my abdomen.

Myrtle and Lynell turned when we came into the small waiting area.

"Anything?" I asked sitting in the empty chair between them.

"That guy in the suit and Dinwiddie went back somewhere as soon as we got here," Myrtle said.

I looked left and right. The silent man had disappeared like smoke.

"Did the guy say anything to you?" Myrtle asked. She'd pressed her side against mine. I gave her the only support I could conjure up, throwing an arm around her shoulders.

I shook my head. He hadn't seemed like the kind of guy who wanted to answer a bunch of questions I didn't want to ask in the first damned place. I took a deep breath of antiseptic-tinged air.

I remembered sitting in Cleveland Clinic waiting rooms, first when Malik was born, then when Troy came along. Looking at the tiny people swaddled in blankets, fear for their future was the farthest thing from my mind. The possibilities then had seemed boundless. Everything from professional athlete to concert pianist had bounced through my mind. City planner and chef were okay though.

The lawyer and the gray man came back down the hall, stopping in front of the chairs where we sat.

"Mr. and Mrs. Duncan? Ms.... Powers?" I nodded. From the corner of my eye, I saw the women nod in acknowledgement as well. "On the behalf of MetroHealth I want to say that we're sorry for your loss. We did everything we could, but the gastrointestinal perforation had become septic."

"What are you saying?" Myrtle said jumping to her feet, throwing my arm off nearly wrenching my shoulder from the socket. "What are you saying? What are you saying? Are you saying my little boy is dead?"

"He didn't make it. We're sorry."

Sorry. He sure as hell didn't look sorry.

"How long has he been laying here dying?" I asked.

"He was pronounced at twelve oh six p.m."

"You stood next to me in the elevator as quiet as you please. You didn't think to say anything then. Didn't even introduce yourself. Are you a doctor here?"

"I'm the medical director at the jail. I act as a liaison between the jail and the hospital," he said.

I'm not sure how much of that I took in. After the medical director stepped back, I couldn't hear anything but crying. The man's mouth was moving. Dinwiddie was pulling a mobile phone from his pocket and speaking. I pulled Myrtle close, letting her tears soak my shirt.

Nothing was what was inside me. Not a single thing. Not anger, not pain, not loss.

Nothing.

The man in the suit disappeared. Dinwiddie dropped the phone in his bag.

"I just got word that the grand jury issued a no bill. They refused to indict Troy," he said. "A judge would have probably released him tomorrow."

"One day too late," I whispered.

"You can come back and see him now." The man in the suit had suddenly reappeared like an apparition. Maybe he *was* a ghost. Maybe I was imagining all this. Maybe I'd wake up and this would all have been a nightmare. The worst I ever had, but I'd wake up and I'd be the father of two sons again.

Myrtle clutched my hand so tight I knew it wasn't a dream. For a long moment, I thought she'd break my fingers. For another moment, I realized that would be okay. It was the least I deserved for my failure as a father. I'd messed up on the one job I'd taken for granted that I could do. What kind of parent was I if I'd failed to protect my son? I was alive and he was dead, and somewhere along the way, I'd fucked this up. I closed my eyes against the recriminations.

Death couldn't be walked backward.

The four of us trudged single file through some doors. A sheriff's deputy stood when we got to room 1239. He couldn't meet my eyes either. For a lot of self-righteous white folk, they sure as hell looked guilty.

"I'll call you in a few days," Dinwiddie said. We'll talk about amending your complaint."

"Amending?" Lynell asked through her tears. "What are you talking about?"

"Wrongful death."

16

Marc

January 18, 2006

"Marc!" Jan's voice was shrill.

"I'm already downstairs," I answered.

I'd been sitting on the couch, a kid on either side. Now that they were back in class after the holiday break, there was no gaming after school. Rather than unhook the console from Michael's bedroom TV, I'd insisted he and Donna do their homework in the living room where Jan and I could see them.

The bold orange words "Special Report" scrolled across the bottom of the screen.

When I turned up the sound, the kids looked up. I didn't send them upstairs because the truth about what was going on was getting harder to hide. I wasn't sure they'd bought the vacation excuse after the second week I was home. Who knew what they were hearing at St. Raphael. No matter how hard I'd tried to bury my head in the sand, I had the sinking feeling that my life was about to change and not for the better.

The phone bleated in the kitchen at the exact same moment the reporter started talking. Michael dumped the books from his lap and ran to get it while Donna sat transfixed—her eyes glued to the screen.

"Dad, it's Captain Todd." Michael held up the phone like a beacon.

"Tell him to hold on," I said turning up the sound as another few bars lit up on the bottom of the screen.

"This is a Channel Five special report. Troy Duncan, the unarmed black man who was shot in late December has died at MetroHealth hospital from complications relating to the bullet wound he suffered. In a related story, prosecutor Lori Pope announced this morning that the Cuyahoga County grand jury declined to indict Troy Duncan on felony charges. Let's go to Rick McDaniel at the hospital. What can you tell us, Rick?"

The screen changed from the desk anchors, split, then switched to McDaniel.

"Troy Duncan was pronounced dead at twelve oh six this afternoon. The specific cause of death is unknown but it appears to be due to complications from his gunshot wound. We were able to talk to Vernon Dinwiddie a few minutes ago. He represented Troy Duncan, and now represents his surviving family."

Tape rolled and the short, black attorney appeared on screen. He looked slick as oil in a pinstriped suit and navy wool overcoat.

"Rick," Dinwiddie started, "this here was a tragedy that didn't have to happen. Not less than twenty-four hours before Troy Duncan was transferred from MetroHealth to the jail infirmary, the grand jury failed to indict him on any charges. But that information hadn't filtered into the system. Instead of going home or to rehabilitation where he could receive quality care, he became a victim of a broken system."

McDaniel, probably seasoned by such rhetoric didn't flinch. But Donna did. I dropped an arm across her tiny shoulders.

"Shot at the hands of a white police officer. Housed in a jail infirmary that had no provision for caring for him. Instead of getting the medication he needed, he was denied care until he became critical, until it was too late," Dinwiddie said.

Channel Five cut the tape and Rick McDaniel was on screen again.

"We reached out to Cleveland Police and the Cuyahoga County Sheriff, and they had this to say." The reporter took a small notebook from a pocket somewhere and started to read.

"Cleveland police chief Kelley McCormick says an investigation into the shooting is ongoing. The deputy county sheriff says the death was unfortunate. The county will launch an investigation into procedures concerning the care of seriously ill prisoners. We here at Channel Five will continue to follow and report on this most important story."

"Thanks, Rick. This concludes our special report. We'll be back if any further news breaks in this most tragic story. We now return to our regularly scheduled program."

Donna took the remote from my hand. She was still gripping a pencil in her other fist. The sparkly pink hair stood stiff on the end of the pencil. Erasers used to be on the end when I was a kid. A lot had changed in the last thirty years.

My daughter turned the volume up to ear bleed range before she figured out where the button was that killed the sound.

"Daddy, did you really shoot someone dead? You always said killing people was wrong."

I had said exactly that when she was five or six or so and had seen something on TV that she shouldn't. Neither justifiable homicide nor excusable police action had entered into that conversation.

"The guy was a criminal honey. Sometimes that happens when people are doing bad things. It's not how we'd like things to end up, but it was him or me."

"But the lady on the news said there was no…in…whatever, that he would have been released from jail." That was Michael. He stood looking at loose ends.

"Just because someone isn't charged with a crime, doesn't mean they aren't guilty. I'm one hundred percent sure that guy Duncan was out to do harm to me or my partner."

Michael still held the cordless in his hand.

"Son. What happened to Captain Todd?"

Michael jammed the plastic to his ear. "Oh. I think he must have hung up." He gave me the phone. The dial tone confirmed what he said.

"What happens now?" Jan said. I hadn't seen her come down the stairs. As unsure of herself as a teenage girl at her first co-ed dance, my wife stood twirling her hair looking between the kids and me.

"What happens now is you start dinner, the kids finish their homework. Today's a normal day just like any other," I said.

Like a slow motion movie segment, the wife and kids moved to what they were supposed to be doing. Despite the frigid air, and falling snow, I stepped outside the front door. Away from the oppressive judgment of everyone, it was a little easier to breathe.

The phone in my hand jangled. I looked at the foreign object, not remembering bringing it outside with me.

"Baldwin," I barked into the receiver.

"Captain Todd. You saw the news." It wasn't a question.

"Yes, sir. It's unfortunate."

"The death isn't really the problem, Baldwin. It's the prosecutor's refusal to indict."

"Why?"

"This town is black and white. Always has been. Reverend Wilkinson and Mayor Gates will be looking for a scapegoat." That the scapegoat would be me didn't have to be said. This had really gone sideways, but I still wanted to set it all to rights.

"What happens next?" I was ready to put this all behind me. Get back on the job. Even if that meant desk duty, I'd take it. Paid administrative leave wasn't all it was cracked up to be.

"We'll continue our investigation. You'll stay on leave. And you need to hope and pray the prosecutor doesn't indict you."

"Wait. What?" I was sure I must have heard incorrectly. I was the cop. I hadn't done anything wrong.

"Indict me? For what?" I could hear my voice rising. Sideways didn't cover cops going to jail. I'd die quicker than Duncan in lockup.

"Murder. Manslaughter. Assault with a deadly weapon." Todd listed the three felonies in rapid succession.

"Do you think that could happen? I shot the man in the line of duty. I was doing my job." Jail wasn't for the likes of me, someone who'd always been on the right side of the law.

"The badge can protect you from a lot, but maybe not from this. Times have changed. The blue wall has chinks."

"Shit," I said my hands were tingling against the plastic, numbness right around the corner. My breath fogged the air. If I went to jail, frostbite would be the least of my problems. I wouldn't survive it. Unlike the people I arrested, I didn't have a whole group of family and friends in lockup to protect me.

"Sounds like maybe you need to be with your kids," Todd said relieving me of any further conversation.

"Thanks for calling."

I jammed the phone in my back pocket. I didn't need my kids. I needed my lawyer.

17

Augustus

January 24, 2006

For all the warm days we'd had this month, the day of my son's funeral had to be the coldest in January history. The temperature outside was about the same as on my insides. I was learning firsthand how cold and cruel the world was.

"Jesus welcomes you," the sign over the church's door had read. I wanted nothing more than to rip down that sign and throw it into the Cuyahoga River. All this crap about Jesus saves, Jesus loves, and Jesus is all around. Where in the hell was Jesus when Officer Baldwin had pulled his gun? Where was Jesus when my son was shot in the gut? Where was Jesus when nurses ignored him for days on end in the jail infirmary?

"Where was Jesus?" I asked under my breath as we made the long agonizing walk between the pews to our reserved seating in the front of the grand church.

"I was wondering the same thing," Malik said.

My legs nearly crumpled under me at the sound of Malik's words. At the sound of a voice so much like, but so much different than my other son.

"I've got you, Dad," he said gripping my arm tight.

"I'm fine," I said after I regained my footing. Once in our pew, I turned to look toward the doors at the back of the nave. It was easier than looking toward the coffin. I could see the tiny stitches they'd used to sew Troy's mouth shut. His hair was too shiny to be real. But I had to look away from those imperfections. That body in there wasn't my son anymore.

I stood with my back to the front of the church as the pews filled with mourners, onlookers, media, and of course, politicians. Anger pulsed so hard through my brain that I thought my eyes would bulge out of my head.

Dinwiddie and the funeral director had whispered back and forth for long minutes about a public versus private funeral. I'd cut them off saying a funeral should always be public. Who knew what people a life had touched, and those people should be able to say goodbye. I'd been thinking more about the people who'd worked with him in the kitchens all those years, some illegal, who I'd never known enough about to add to some invite list, but who I thought might mourn for him all the same.

But maybe I should have had some kind of keep-the-hell-out-of-here list.

I nodded at people who mouthed their condolences, then turned back when the minister tapped once on the microphone and said "Let us pray."

I bowed my head, not because I had anything to say to God, but because I couldn't look at that coffin. Myrtle squeezed my hand. I turned to my wife, and she gave a weak smile. I squeezed back. The woman had always been the love of my life. We'd laughed together, eaten thousands of meals together. We'd raised two boys together. I never thought we'd bury one together.

Never.

A new voice compelled me to look up, up and over the coffin. Revered Wilkinson had stepped up to the podium. I'd never seen the man off the television screen. He looked broadcast ready, with slicked hair and flawless skin. Kind of like Troy. It was a macabre thought that I pushed away.

"This man," he boomed. "This young man was taken too early. Troy Duncan leaves behind a wife of twelve years, and two young children. They're sitting before all of us grieving a father and husband who will be forever lost to them.

"Despite the evidence of a loving wife, parents, and children, the first words from the Chief of Police when a no bill was filed for Troy Duncan were, 'Be kind. Marc Baldwin has family.' I'm here to tell all of them out there that we have families too.

"Since the times of slavery, our families never meant much to those with the power to sever them. In a heartbeat, a slave master would part husbands and wives, mothers and sons, fathers and daughters. Our families have never mattered to them.

"But they matter to us. Little black boys and girls should be able to grow up assured their parents are safe. In today's Cleveland, maybe that's not something we can give them.

"Let's vow today not to abandon the Duncans. Lets vow to do what we can to keep our families safe. Let's vow to hold our elected officials accountable for keeping our families safe, and absent that, bringing our families justice.

"Mayor Gates, Police Chief McCormick, we have families too."

I wanted to stand up and holler my approval. At the same time I wanted to kick him in the teeth for using my son's funeral as a political grandstand.

A second later, I sorely missed Reverend Wilkinson when my other son Malik took the podium.

"Good morning. Thank you for coming out to remember my brother Troy. I never thought…I never thought I'd speak at my brother's funeral. He was two years younger than me. I figured we'd grow old together. Now I'm an only child."

Malik swallowed past his Adam's apple two or three times. His voice, even stronger than before, came through the podium.

"I don't want to talk about his death today. I want to talk about his life.

"There are so many stories that I could share about growing up. We had sixteen years together in that house in Cleveland Heights.

"But while I was thinking about exactly what I'd say today, I decided to choose just one story that really exemplifies who my brother was.

"When I was twenty-five, I was working mightily hard to impress the woman who would become my wife. Jennifer loved good food, good wine, and good company. I could only provide the last one of those." There were a few laughs in the crowd. "But I had a plan. My brother had just graduated from culinary school. He'd done a summer sommelier course in Florence, Italy. I figured he could make dinner, bring wine, and I'd pass it off as my own.

"He said, 'you can give a man a fish, or teach a man to fish.' That was his polite way of saying he wouldn't let me pass off his knowledge as my own. Every night for a week, he taught me how to make a classic French meal for Jennifer. After we were done cooking and eating, he drove me all over town looking at wines.

"Come Friday, he sat on his hands in my kitchen and watched me make Niçoise salad, Cassoulet-Au-Canard, and éclairs for dessert. I was mad for a hot minute, especially when I was trying to squeeze custard into delicate pastry, pot a choux, he called it. But I learned two things. One, he was a great teacher and mentor, and how to cook...prepare, he'd want me to say prepare, a meal I've made at least once a year for Jennifer."

My other daughter-in-law was pretty stoic, but I saw tears leaking from her eyes when I glanced her way.

"Troy wasn't perfect," Malik continued. "He wasn't a martyr. He was my brother, my parents' baby, and a really great daddy, and I'll miss him."

Everything after that was a blur. More speeches, more sermonizing. I almost broke down when I had to shoulder the body of my son in its shiny wood coffin. I nearly threw myself into the hole the backhoe had carved into the frozen soil. But I held on for Myrtle, for Campbell, for Lynell, for Zora and Ellison. While they cried, wept, and sobbed for Troy, I vowed revenge or at least justice.

18

Casey

January 27, 2006

Maybe I needed to find a place to hide out.

Permanently.

Like Pittsburgh or Detroit.

Controversy had a way of finding me. If it wasn't the Strohmeyers and Brodys, then it was Sheila Harrison Grant. I'd never had any desire to be in the public eye. Lulu had been right about one thing, I'd always assumed I'd get married, have kids, maybe work part-time when all was said and done. None of this is what I'd planned for.

This was my phone ringing off the hook. Reporters hounding me in and outside of the building. Every last one of them had the same damned question: How would my client hold up to criminal charges?

The thing was, I had no clue.

When I was a kid learning to swim I remember what it was like when I'd mastered freestyle across the small kid pool. I was so proud of myself, I thought I could tackle the world, or at least the big adult pool.

The next weekend my dad had taken me and some friends to a fourth of July celebration at Edgewater park. I'd crowed all week about my new swimming prowess. Not ten seconds after Dad had rolled out our picnic blanket, I'd pulled off my T-shirt and shorts and was running into the lake.

I swam out blindly amazed that I was above water. Then I stopped, looked around, and panicked. I was in the middle of Lake Erie. Seaweed and currents and unknown flotsam pulled me back and forth. For the life of me, I didn't feel like a swimmer, but a drowner.

It was exactly the same now. In the last few months, I had been really getting my footing outside of Juvenile Court. I had learned to negotiate plea deals like a champ. I was learning how to weave my way through divorce and shared parenting and making sure my clients were at least satisfied, if not happy—because divorcing clients were never happy.

With one second of ego and bravado, the moment I'd accepted Baldwin's case, I was flailing like that summer in Lake Erie. Which was why I was cooling my heels in Cleveland Heights. Despite the subzero temperatures, I was standing outside Miles Siegel's building working up the courage to press the doorbell.

"Casey?" I heard a familiar voice shout. I looked up to see Miles shivering on his front porch in a maroon T-shirt and jeans. I pushed the bell then, his buzzer system, like mine didn't work until someone called up.

His front door was open when I got to the third floor.

My ex-boyfriend was as still as handsome as ever. One look into his deep brown eyes and my stomach got all twisty. I thrust my hand forward to defend myself from the onslaught of emotion. Miles ignored the gesture, instead pulling me into a bear hug.

"Casey. So good to see you, I've missed you," he said patting my back.

This touching people you'd once had sex with thing was way more uncomfortable in person than it looked on television. It hadn't gotten any better with practice.

"Missed you too," I said. But in my case, it was true. Acutely true. I'd been thinking about sharing the rest of my life with this man, when he'd unceremoniously and sanctimoniously dumped me. By his calculation, he was on the right side of the law, and I was on the wrong side. He hadn't had room for any wrong in his life.

We'd left it there with all that "we'll be friends" crap. I'd never planned to see him again, but the Marc Baldwin case had made me desperate. Federal court with all its procedures and rules scared the shit out of me. Especially after I'd lost my first and only case in the northern district—trying to get a client's forfeited drug money back. That judge had shut me down after a single hearing where I'd flailed about without so much as a clue. I had no desire to repeat that performance. My fear of public shame outweighed my fear of personal humiliation.

I stepped into my ex-boyfriend's apartment. The refinished wood floors and blemish free molding gleamed at me mockingly. I'd forgotten how picture perfect everything in Miles' life was. It was like walking onto a sit-com set. Basketball in one corner, bike pegged to the wall. Perfect paint and expensive furniture. All he was missing was a theme song.

"Place looks nice," I said for something to say. Or rather to keep me from saying something stupid or needy. I had it in me to do both.

"Did you ever paint yours?"

I'd talked about painting. I'd talked about a lot of things, but for so many of the months I'd lived there, I'd figured I'd make more money, or get married, or be something less than a permanent fixture on North Moreland Boulevard.

"Nope. Same textured walls lined with college girl posters." Damn. I'd tried not to sound needy and instead had come out pathetic.

Miles backtracked to a distressed leather sofa I knew to be really comfortable. I lifted my messenger pack and hung my own coat on a free coat rack hook. The man had an antique coat rack for fucks sake. How had I ever thought we would be compatible?

"How's your mom?" I asked hopping from one land mine to the next. Miles thought her perfection personified. When he'd compared me to her, I'd come up lacking. Quite.

"Mom and pops are good. They're doing a swing through southeast Asia."

Of course they were. His parents were the kind of people who planned a vacation around the world like it was a trip around the corner.

"What countries?" I was loathe to work out what that would mean and embarrass myself. My international geography wasn't what it should have been.

"Vietnam, Malaysia, Thailand, and Cambodia. I think they didn't have time for Laos. Probably because mom wanted to spend time in Singapore. It's one of her favorite places."

I kind of had to wonder if it really would have worked out between us. In a moment of blazing clarity, I realized that I kept seeking out rich guys. Men who were way out of my league. It was like I was living the life of one of those pathetic heroines I read about when I was a kid. They were always standing around waiting for some king, or knight, or prince to swoop in and save the day. The girl would get to live happily ever after in the castle, a step up from whatever shack she'd been born in, and have a great guy to boot.

Life maybe didn't work that way. Rather than delve into some kind of deep self-examination, I pulled papers and folders from my bag and stacked them on Miles' reclaimed wood coffee table where even the nicks and scratches were in all the right places.

"I...um...called you because I needed your help."

"You working in federal court these days?"

"Been doing some smaller civil cases," I bluffed. The one time Miles had run into me at court had been the only case I'd had there. "But this is a big one, and I need some help sorting a few things out."

"If it's not in your wheelhouse why'd you take it?"

"Patrick Brody—"

Miles reared back like I'd punched him. "You still talking to that corrupt family? If you don't stay away from them, you'll wind up in jail one day."

"I know, Miles." I acted suitably chastised. I didn't need him telling me that the Brodys could be toxic. I'd long been on the receiving end of their enmity.

"Do you? I think there's more to it than meets the eye," he said cryptically.

"You know something I should?"

He shook his head. "Office stuff I can't disclose."

Now that was the first full of shit statement to come out of his mouth that morning. There was no kind of Brody investigation going on within five hundred miles of this exact spot.

Not one.

The Brody family quashed the mere hint of an investigation like a southerner crushed a June bug.

"The referral was actually from the Cleveland law director, Tommie Gordon" I clarified unnecessarily. I had no idea why I was still justifying myself to him.

"Sounds like you're moving up in the world," he said, both large hands braced on the back of the couch.

"Yeah, well, I don't plan to be in common pleas forever."

"What do you need help with?" he asked coming around to my side.

"You've heard of Marc Baldwin?" I asked waiting for the explosive reaction anyone would have hearing I was working on the city's most infamous case. A slow blink was all I got from Miles.

"Who hasn't? Even my mother managed to e-mail from Asia to ask about Marc Baldwin."

"Wow, she found a computer there?"

"Asia isn't sub-Saharan Africa," he said with a bit of condescension I chose to ignore. "What about Marc Baldwin?"

"I'm his lawyer."

"You're shitting me," he spat out. Finally a reaction from Mr. Wordly-know-it-all.

"Unfortunately not."

"Is that what all this is?" he said hefting the thick stacks of papers I'd dropped on the table.

"Yes. I just got Dinwiddie's second amended complaint. The other two hundred pages are the original and first amendment."

"The court gave leave for a second amendment?" He asked. It was usually hard to get a court to allow a plaintiff to change the complaint more than once.

"Wrongful death," I answered. The fact that the plaintiff had died due to injuries caused by the gunshot wound had been more than enough excuse to allow Dinwiddie his way. Even I hadn't been fool enough to oppose his motion.

"Oh, right. That." He was silent for a long moment. I almost asked what he was thinking, but I'd lost the right to ask questions like that. "What do you need from me?" he asked. I guessed the niceties were over.

"Let's make a deal," I said in place of an answer.

"Okay, Monty Hall." Miles' half grin made me lose my place in the conversation for a moment.

"I'm serious," I said breathing through my accelerated heartbeat. "Everything we talk about concerning this case has to be off the record."

Miles' smile morphed from cute to condescending. "Sure, Casey. I mean I'm in the U.S. Attorney's office, and you're mostly in common pleas, but whatever you need."

We were a few blocks from each other, not across a great lake. But the divide between us might as well have been that wide the way he made it out. But this wasn't some city mouse, country mouse laughing matter.

"I'm serious Miles. I need to be able to talk to you freely without you running to your boss trying to trump up a charge against my client. You have to promise me this won't be your career maker."

"What like Eamon Brody? 'Cause for all your help, I lost my first jury trial. Then you picked the law-breaking philanderer over me."

"Okay, sorry. Truce." I held my hands up in surrender. I officially gave up. I was done fighting the same fight. Broken up, we didn't have to do this anymore. The conflict went out the door the same time the sex did.

"Fine. What do you need from me?"

"I need your advice on how to best tackle the answer here." I was proud of my response. It wasn't a fraction of what I needed, though.

"Now comes the defendant, he denies all the allegations. Then move on to discovery."

"That's your advice? Deny everything? You could have told me that on the phone," I huffed, embarrassed that I'd driven over here over something that could be this simple.

"Or you can admit your client shot an unarmed black man without provocation or justification and hope the city pays out the maximum," he said delivering the second punch of the one-two combination.

"You think he did it that way, without remorse?" Even I wasn't sure what had happened that night. I wasn't sure we'd ever know.

"I've been a black man longer than I was a cop or have been a prosecutor."

"You think this is about race?"

"You think it's not?"

"He was investigating drug activity in the Flats. A guy came out of an alley. He had a right to be cautious. I'd be cautious if a guy came out of an ally on a dark and cold night."

"But you don't carry a gun, or a badge, or a responsibility to the public to not abuse either."

I'm sure my mouth was gaping like a fish. "I had no idea you felt this way," was the feeblest, worst line ever. But it was all I could manage to squeak out.

"This is why things didn't work between us, Casey," he pronounced. "Your moral compass is all over the place."

"My moral compass. How can you talk about how bad cops are on the one hand? You *were* one for five years. And now you're a prosecutor, right? How many times did you jump on me, first for not turning in the Brodys, then for defending Jarrod Carter? You practically dared me to tell you he was the guy behind the Container Girls case.

"Was he?"

"You know I can't answer that. He's in jail for possession and intent to distribute methamphetamine. So even if he was the guy behind it, he can't be anymore."

"The statute of limitations hasn't tolled on those crimes."

"I'm sure you won't let me forget it. Speaking of forgetting. This was a mistake. I'm sorry to have bothered you for help with your lofty federal court knowledge. I'm sure I can cobble together something from my fourth tier law school education and my experience in common pleas."

I slipped from the couch to my knees. Close to the coffee table, I started pulling all three hundred pages of federal pleadings together. Miles' hand stilled mine.

"I'm really sorry about that. I'm being a total shit. Sometimes my life is completely schizophrenic. I'm working with the very same people who shoot and lock up people who look like me, sometimes with no basis whatsoever."

I dropped the papers back on the table.

"So why do you do it? Why aren't you on the other side of the aisle? We could use your first tier Ivy League ass on the defense side."

"You're Sisyphus rolling that boulder uphill every day. He never gets to stop doing that for eternity. I want to be Zeus. On this side, I can decide what counts for law, order, and justice. I want to wield prosecutorial discretion fairly."

"Then why were you so disappointed in me. You have to know it's my job to vigorously defend my clients no matter what someone might think they've done."

Miles pulled me to him in a hug. "I know, love. I'm sorry." His voice was a whisper. For a time, I resisted. But I wasn't made of steel, so I melted. Right into the arms I'd missed so much over the last months. For a long moment, we sat like that, his chin on my head, my ear laying against his chest. His hand started doing lazy circles on my arm. The heart under my cheek sped up.

One minute he was holding me, the next we were kissing. My head was saying no, no, no, but my lips were saying yes, yes, yes. "Do you want to—"

I nodded cutting off his vocalization of the question. I cursed myself all the way down the short hall calling myself ten times a fool. When he closed his bedroom door behind us, I made a vow. Today Miles, tomorrow, I'd do the online dating thing.

Tomorrow.

An hour later, I gathered up my clothes and tiptoed to the living room. There I got dressed in my jeans, shearling boots, and an Ohio State hoodie.

I was starving. I'd had nerves for breakfast and sex for lunch. What I wanted was to pack up my shit and flee the scene. I couldn't though. Embarrassingly, I still needed his help. Leaning down, I pulled up my wool socks and padded to the kitchen.

I could count on one hand the number of times I'd been in Miles' apartment. We had always been at mine, so it didn't exactly feel familiar. His kitchen was the same size as mine, but that's where the similarities ended. His had a working fireplace, and lots of upgrades, stone counters, tile backsplash, shiny wood cabinets. Being the mama's boy I knew he was, I knew he'd have more than beer in his kitchen.

I prowled through the cabinets and fridge until I found stuff for an easy one-pot lasagna dish. Living alone for all these years, I'd become the master of the one-pot dish.

In twenty minutes, I'd fried sausage and onions, added a box of tomatoes. I threw in some pasta and water and popped on the lid.

"You let me sleep," Miles said. I nearly jumped out of my socks at the appearance of a nude man in the doorway.

"I was hungry," I deflected. "Why don't you get dressed? It'll be ready in a minute."

I sighed in relief when he disappeared. He was still good looking naked. I didn't need to be induced into a second roll in the hay, when I was already kind of regretting that first one. The timer on the back of the stove beeped. I stirred in some cheese and dished up two plates.

I took them to the dining room. Miles came in with cloth napkins, and utensils.

I held up the navy blue linen. "A paper napkin is fine," I said.

"I don't use paper. My mom always used cloth."

Of course she did. I'm sure Linda Siegel probably laundered them by hand, when she wasn't dishing up healthy, vegetarian, ten-course meals, weaving cloth, or harvesting honey. Instead of blurting out all that judgment, I took the napkin graciously and folded it on my lap.

"Wine?"

I nodded vigorously. I needed that wine more than anything. I had no idea what we were playing at here, but alcohol would surely smooth it all over.

We ate in silence for a few minutes. I didn't say a damned thing for fear of walking on another mine. Miles looked like he was thinking.

"How did Troy Duncan die?"

I swallowed the big cheesy bite I'd taken. "Sepsis, septicemia, septic shock? Something like that. Basically, his colon leaked into his body. From the sound of it, the jail nurses didn't do anything to help him with his bowel movements. They have two weeks from the time a prisoner is admitted to do an evaluation."

"Do you remember Cohen versus Petty?"

"No."

"Intervening cause, superseding cause?" Miles prompted.

I plumbed the depths of my brain trying to remember something from first year Torts. There was a blank space where Torts should have been. "Just spit it out."

"Dinwiddie is saying that your guy died because Marc Baldwin shot him. But if he'd stayed in the hospital, would Duncan have died?"

"Probably not. I think there would have been a heavy rotation of doctors and nurses who would have seen the signs of shock."

"Right. So here's what you do. You'll need to file a motion for leave to amend the complaint."

"But I'm the defendant."

"Doesn't matter. You're going to do a necessary joinder."

I wanted to shout "In plain English," like my clients did. Instead, I waited for the rest.

"You're going to pin the Troy Duncan's death on MetroHealth, the jail, and the sheriff's department. If it weren't for their negligent care, Troy Duncan would have lived."

"Oh, my God. If I do that the focus will totally shift from Baldwin to the city trying to pin it on the county and vice versa."

"Dollars to donuts, you client walks away unscathed."

19

Augustus

January 27, 2006

It was a pretty silent ride most of the way from Campbell's house to Spencer's. I'd picked her up this morning to help tie up loose ends Troy's death had left hanging. One loose end being Campbell herself.

I pulled over near the corner of Superior and something called Robert Lockwood Drive. This neighborhood had made a one hundred eighty degree turn in the forty odd years I'd been in Cleveland. One minute we were an industrial city, the next minute developers were building the Rock and Roll Hall of Fame, knocking down and rebuilding the Browns stadium, and turning old factories into restaurants.

"You okay?" Campbell asked when it became obvious I wasn't moving the car.

"It's hard," I said. I sucked in a breath, let it out through my teeth. Did it again. Then stared my son's mortality in the eye. "It's hard going to the place where your son took his last breath as a free man."

Campbell turned to me, adjusting the white wool beret covering her head.

"It's hard for me too." She laid her hand on my arm. "I want you to know, I always loved him. From as long as I could remember. I loved him."

"Why didn't you guys ever get divorced? Or why didn't you stay together?" I asked not caring about minding my own business for a moment. Countless nights Myrtle and I had stayed up turning these two questions over. We never could come up with a good answer between us.

"It was stupid," Campbell whispered into her scarf. "Do you know how incredibly stupid and insignificant all that seems now?"

"Myrtle and I have always wondered..." why these elementary, middle and high school sweethearts couldn't hold it together.

"There were a few months when we were fighting a lot. There was a guy I'd gone to college with who was pursuing me pretty heavily."

"While you were married?" Campbell had gone away to Lincoln University. Even with her brand new Ford Bronco, she'd only come back a few weekends a year. Troy had been a mess that first year.

"He was an asshole...jerk...sorry—"

"Don't apologize. Death has a way of making cursing feel unimportant. Go on."

"Anyway, I told Troy that we'd gotten married too young, that my parents were right. I told him we needed a break, maybe see other people, figure out if together is what we wanted."

I hit the back of my seat. I'd never known they'd taken a break. Maybe that's why he was so messed up.

"I dated that guy for a minute. But he was as big a jerk as you figured out in ten seconds. Took me a few months though. At the same time, Troy started seeing Lynell. He was going to break it off with her. We were going to get back together and make a real try again. I promised to support him through culinary school. But—"

"Lynell got pregnant," I said, clarity finally coming from a really confusing few years.

"Lynell got pregnant. I thought I could be Jada Pinkett cool about this, you know. Raise a kid that wasn't my own. Be down with a baby mama. But that didn't work for us. When he moved in with her before Ellison was born. I couldn't blame him. He had a family to support. Trying to make it work with them was the right thing to do."

"No divorce?"

"I never wanted it. Neither did he. I think we each had this fantasy that one day we could get back together. Maybe when his kids were older. Maybe because I hadn't met anyone else I wanted to marry. I don't know. I kind of thought we'd always circle back to each other sooner or later."

"Now, you're his next of kin." It was kind of fitting in a way. Campbell had probably been closer to him than any of us ever were. I settled in the seat. Something about her being his surviving wife was just...right.

"Yeah, I know. Let's get over to Spencer's and see what we have to do."

I put the car into drive and made the two turns that put me in front of the restaurant. The owner, Spencer Milburn, had promised to meet us here before the business officially opened for the day.

"There's something I think you should see," the red-eyed Milburn said the minute Campbell and I entered the restaurant. The cavernous room was quiet. The tables were empty, the bar as well. I don't think I'd ever been in a restaurant before it opened. When Troy had worked at the hotel, there's always been someone in the dining room no matter how late or early the hour.

I looked around the space, but didn't see anything that caught my eye.

"What is it?" Campbell asked.

"Come with me," Milburn said. The nervous looking man started walking past the empty tables, past the bar, and through the swinging double doors to the kitchen. We followed close behind.

Five men and women were moving around in controlled chaos. My nose was itching. I rubbed it and blinked several times. I swallowed down the grief because I needed to be strong for everyone, Myrtle, the kids, and now Campbell. Milburn looked both cold and hot at the same time. He didn't take the down jacket hanging next to the computer before he pushed open the back door. I stepped through the small office and out through the opening.

"Oh, my God," I gasped. Never had I expected the display before me. Flowers stood frozen in vases. Small teddy bears and other stuffed animals were tied to an easel where a huge laminated picture of Troy stood. For a long minute, I couldn't place the photograph.

"I think it's his driver's license photo," Milburn said looking everywhere but at us.

Campbell coughed or hiccoughed, then she started crying noisily. I slipped and arm around her. She turned her head into my shoulder.

Hold it together. Hold it together.

"Where did all this come from?"

"I don't know. One day it was a rose, then a carnation. After that, the floodgates opened. Almost every day someone comes by and leaves something, a card, a candle. I just thought you should know that a lot of people are thinking about Troy. I don't have any plans to move it."

If it hadn't been barely above freezing we may have stayed out longer, but I could barely feel my hands as it was. Milburn hustled us back into his office. He had a stack of papers on his desk.

"What's all this?" I asked. I'd only come by for the check. We'd paid Lynell's January mortgage payment and the huge tacked on penalty, but she'd need this for February, probably. I hadn't talked to her about what she'd do after that

"Here's his check," Milburn said handing me a single sheet. It about six hundred dollars. The rest was all tax deductions. Life insurance, health insurance, and the usual city and state stuff. Death was final, taxes weren't. I realized someone would have to file a tax return for him. I looked from Milburn to Campbell and back, ready for the rest.

"What's that?" I pointed to the stack. Even upside down I could read Troy's name and social security number.

"The other is his life insurance policy."

As if her legs had turned to noodles, Campbell plopped down in the single chair in front of the desk. Milburn followed her lead and sat in the rolling chair.

"How much?"

"He did the basic policy, twenty thousand dollars."

I pulled the papers toward me and started flipping. "Who's the beneficiary?"

"He never designated one. So it has to go to his wife. That's what the broker said."

"That's why you asked me to bring Campbell." The puzzle pieces were coming together.

"At the funeral, someone said she was his wife. Troy didn't talk about any of this. I knew he had two kids, but I thought..."

"He was married to someone else. I get it," Campbell said. "Trust me, I get it."

"Well, anyway, here's the policy," Milburn said handing the small stapled stack to Campbell.

"Is that it?" I looked around the tiny room. There were very few personal belongings around here. Nothing of Troy's that I could see.

"He took everything with him when he left that night." Milburn shifted in his chair awkwardly. "He took a uniform with him that was property of Spencer's."

"You'll have to take that up with the police," I was relieved to say. "They kept his property as evidence. I'll put it in a box if we can get it released to us."

"Thanks. Well. I'm sorry for your loss."

"Not your fault."

Milburn stood abruptly. The chair rolled in the small space, banging against a tall bank of metal file cabinets. "I...feel...responsible."

"It's not your fault," I said. The blame squarely lay on the shoulders of one Marc Baldwin.

"Well if any of you or the kids need anything, I'll do what I can to help."

Milburn extended his hand. It was a chef's hand, full of sores and scabbed over parts. Standing, Campbell shook it. "Thanks."

I took the papers from Campbell's other hand and jammed all of them in the breast pocket of my coat. There was a lot to sort out here. We walked to the front door of the restaurant as I tried to figure out how to ask for that money for the kids. But as always Campbell beat me to it.

She paused on the pavement in front of Tenth Avenue.

"Lynell needs that money, doesn't she?"

"Let me see if there's a way you can give it directly to the kids, for college, or something like that."

She nodded. I was confident she'd do the right thing.

"Let's go to the alley again," she said, squaring her shoulders like she was going into battle. "I'd like to see that one more time, if you don't mind."

I followed her around the side of the building trying to ignore my unease. I almost bumped into Campbell when she stopped abruptly. A strange woman stood by the makeshift shrine. For a long moment, she stayed there, unmoving. Her fur-lined hood was buttoned close around her face.

Satisfied with her moment of reflection, she turned toward us. Colorless curls had escaped the hood.

"Sorry, I didn't mean to block you." She blinked back what looked like tears, but could have been her eyes watering in the cold.

"Did you know Troy?" I asked the woman. So many people came and went from restaurants. Half of the pews at his funeral had been filled with those he'd touched at work.

"No...I...uh...are you friends with Troy Duncan?"

"I'm his father, Gus. This is his wife, Campbell."

The woman flapped her hands in her pockets. But she never pulled her right one out. Instead, she nodded. "Nice to meet you. I'm here to meet with Duncan Milburn. I was just...surprised to see this here."

"My Troy touched a lot of lives, I think. A lot more than most people," I said. I was proud that my son could...had been able to get along with anyone from any walk of life. I swallowed and spoke again. "He was a fantastic chef, and a great father as well. He was the wrong person, in the wrong place, at the wrong time, I guess." I don't know how it happened, but those words released something in my chest. It hurt so much, I clutched at my heart through my coat.

"Sir. Mr. Duncan? Are you okay?" The woman in the aubergine coat reached out a hand this time.

"Gus?" Campbell asked, her voice filled with fear.

I gasped one more time, then couldn't hold it in any longer. Goddamnit I was crying. Great gasping sobs erupted from me, and there was nothing I could do to stop it. One moment I was standing, my tears freezing against my face. The next second, I'd crumpled to my knees on the pavement. Cold shot through my corduroy pants, numbing my legs. Campbell knelt next to me, her small arms slipped around me as best they could. The tears were like rain from a summer thunderstorm. Almost as quickly as they came, they left.

I pulled a stiff handkerchief from my pants pocket and dabbed at my face as I stood.

"Sorry you had to see that," I said to no one in particular.

"I think we should get into the car and get on home. I don't want you getting frostbite out here. Myrtle would kill me."

"Or me. You're right, we should get going."

I turned back to the white woman in the long purple coat who was still standing off to one side watching us.

"Sorry. I didn't get your name."

"Oh. Casey. Casey Cort. I should get inside. I'm sure Mr. Milburn is waiting for me."

I looked toward Campbell about to ask her where I'd heard that name before, when it hit me—all at once—like a freight train. I wonder if that's how Troy had felt when the bullet ripped through him.

"Are you the lawyer representing Marc Baldwin?" I asked jabbing a finger toward her.

The woman looked right and left, edging out of the alley.

"Um...yeah...that's me."

"That man killed my son. Shot him in cold blood. And you're on the side of that murderer?" I bellowed.

The woman shrunk into her coat, like a turtle retreating into its shell.

"He hasn't been accused of any crime. I...uh...court rules prevent me from talking to you. I'm sorry for your loss," she said then scurried around the building. Throwing off Campbell' arms, I advanced on the woman. But by the time I got to the front, she'd disappeared through Spencer's front door.

"Don't go in there, Gus. There's nothing to be gained by following her."

"How could she do that? Represent Troy's killer?"

"He has a right."

"What about Troy's constitutional rights to be free of the police?"

"Let's get home. Myrtle's waiting. She said she was going to make fried chicken and biscuits. You and Malik always liked that."

"It was one of Troy's favorites when he was a kid," I said subdued. Anger, sadness, revenge. None of them would bring my Troy back.

"Until he went upscale." Campbell's voice was unnaturally bright. "Do you remember the time he pushed Myrtle out of her own kitchen? She'd been set to make fried fish and hush puppies. An hour later he came out with a platter that looked like the kind of food you only saw on TV."

"Myrtle was spitting mad. But she did come around."

"His hush puppies were good. Creamy on the inside. Especially dipped in that honey butter he made. The catfish was light and super crispy."

"He did clean up the kitchen too. Myrtle didn't have jack to complain about."

"I think she was proud of him. Don't you?" Campbell looped her arm through mine.

"Campbell, she was always proud," I said pulling the papers from my jacket once we were in the truck. I buckled up and started the motor. "Always proud. She didn't know what to do with herself if she wasn't mothering the boys. I think when Troy turned the tables on her like that, she felt kind of useless. She'd always been the one to make them their favorite foods. I think it's when she realized that her little boy was all grown up."

20

Casey

January 27, 2006

I looked at the myriad bottles on the back wall of the bar with a hint of desperation. Having principles is one thing. Defending them to a family with a dead son was something else entirely. I jammed my hands into my pockets warding off the shaking that I knew was likely to follow that encounter back in the alley. It was ironic that I hated confrontation even though that was the very definition of my job.

It took me nearly thirty minutes to get rid of the shakes. Thirty minutes to realize, there was something off with Spencer Milburn. He'd been fidgeting, and sweating and looking as guilty as hell the whole time I'd been asking him questions.

"Are you okay?" I finally asked. Not that I had anything to offer other than nine-one-one.

"I'm fine. I am mighty fine," he said not looking the least bit fine. "Is that all you need?"

"Just a couple more questions," I said. My time was almost up with him. Opening time was just around the corner. I'd promised to be out of his hair long before then, but something wasn't adding up. I couldn't put my finger on the cause, my nervousness or his agitation.

"Have you ever called the police complaining about drug dealing or any other illegal activity in the alley back there or anywhere else in the flats?"

"No. It's usually pretty quiet around here. There are the usual drunks, but as long as they don't loiter too long, I'm all good."

"Have you heard about any illegal activity, like maybe from other bar owners or something like that?"

"We've only been open a few months. I've maybe talked to a handful of other guys around here, the comedy club owner, a couple of the valet services. The rest of the places are corporate chains with corporate drones who don't give a shit about anything but next quarter's stock price."

"Alrighty, then. I'll be going," I said slipping my pen and legal pad into my messenger bag before this devolved into some long anti-corporate diatribe. "If you hear anything, please give me a call." I slipped a business card from the small leather pocket in my bag, and slid the cream-colored stock across the desk.

When Milburn picked up the card, I had to look away. I knew chefs must have burned and cut themselves all the time. Hazards of the job and all that. But Milburn's hands were kind of gross. It looked a lot more like he had some kind of wasting disease than work-related injuries. I closed my mind against judgment. Who knew? Maybe he had

AIDS or something. Maybe opening this restaurant was him fulfilling some lifelong dream as he stared death in the face.

"I'll give you a call," he said. His grin was at once leering and endearing. I'd gotten most of what I wanted, though, so I didn't smile back.

"I'm going to leave through the back door," I said nodding toward the door behind him. "I want to have a last look at that shrine.

"If you're ever in the neighborhood, I'm happy to comp you a drink or two. Your boyfriend even."

"I'm very single," came my automatic response. Sometimes I wished I could think more before I spoke. He was fishing, and I'd just thrown him a nice juicy trout.

"Good to know. Nice meeting you Casey Cort." He gave me a cheery but wobbly salute.

I slipped on my gloves this time. I'd forgotten them in my pockets before and by the time I remembered, they were as cold as the outside air and no good to me.

Milburn shut the door firmly behind me. The noise from the kitchen disappeared and I was bathed in cold, judgmental silence. I looked at the shrine again. Seemed like a lot of people had loved Troy Duncan. His dad and wife, surely. The site of that man falling to his knees on ice-cold pavement would probably haunt me for a good long time.

Death in the abstract was one thing. But in your face grief was something altogether different. Shaking my head clear of that spectacle, I looked around the bricks, gutters and eaves. There weren't any cameras. Milburn had seemed oddly unconcerned about security. I'd thought the owner of a restaurant and bar, that no doubt kept a lot of cash on hand, would be more methodical about how things were handled. My former client, Jarrod Carter had been meticulous about the security of his two restaurants. I know I would be. Money was hard to come by, I tended to keep mine close.

Milburn was probably more like Miles, though. Posh childhood, big ass parental safety net. For them it was all easy come easy go.

I buttoned the coat all the way to my chin, then started walking the neighborhood, such as it was.

Civil wasn't like criminal practice. No one was under any obligation to turn over witness statements to me, if indeed any existed. I turned away, ready to get back to my car. The high was predicted at fifteen degrees. I was certain we'd come nowhere close to that yet. Even the shitty sputtering heat in my Honda would be welcome after this arctic blast. That heat wave from a couple of weeks ago was long gone. It was time to hunker down for a proper Great Lakes winter.

The sound of a door creaking open raised the hairs on the back of my neck. I jumped and turned toward the sound. Some self-defense guru had once said that dangers were best faced head on. In the newly fallen darkness, there wasn't much I could see. The sun was long gone from the sky. I peered at the door and realized it was only a restaurant employee. Probably come out to smoke or dump trash.

"Didn't mean to scare you," he said.

For a fleeting moment, I wondered if this was how Marc Baldwin had felt. Startled, a little out of his element, unsure of what was going to happen next. If I carried a gun, I wonder if I'd have unholstered it by now, ready for whatever might come my way. I didn't think so. I was more a look first, leap later kind of woman. But someone who faced danger every day, that was a different kind of story.

"No problem," I said to the man. "I was just leaving anyway."

"Are you the lawyer for the cop?" he asked in a way that made me think him coming out here wasn't an accident.

I hesitated. I was quickly learning peoples responses were strong one way or another. No one was neutral on the topic of the Troy Duncan shooting.

"Sure. I said. "I was just trying to get a feel for the scene and check to see if anyone saw anything. Did *you* see anything?" Here was his opening. I took a couple of steps toward the building ready to see if he was going to take it.

The man shifted in his starched navy blue kitchen uniform and clogs that didn't quite cover his socks. If I was cold in fur-lined wool, he had to be freezing.

"Look. I'm gonna tell you something that might help your client."

I stepped closer, thankful for the cold. There was little smell coming from the Dumpster next to us.

"I'm listening." I was all ears. Everyone had a lot to say about this case. Little seemed mired in actual facts. Something concrete I could use would be welcome.

"Spencer sometimes sells drugs from the bar."

I leaned forward a bit farther to make sure I was hearing what I thought I'd heard.

"What? Drugs?" I asked. I couldn't quite fit what the man was saying into my overall view of what was going on. What did a little drug dealing have to do with a police shooting. But cases were sometimes like jigsaw puzzles. You always had the corner pieces. The middle was a mystery until it wasn't. I waited for him to fill in a little of that puzzle.

"A little weed, some glass." He shifted from one foot to the other.

"Why are you telling me this?" Motive was sometimes more important than facts.

"The big boss has been snorting and drinking for weeks because he feels guilty. Troy was keeping us afloat. Milburn's going to take us down. I should probably be looking for another job right now."

"Guilty?" I seized on the one word that mattered.

"He was the one doing the deal. There's a big dealer comes by maybe once a week. Supplies some of the club owners. Spencer was getting his when Troy left that night. I went out first. Troy stayed behind to order some stuff and dry his knives, I think. He usually did all that before closing up."

"It's how he finances this place?" I said. I knew better than to jump to conclusions when talking to witnesses, but some of the middle of the puzzle was fitting together.

The man nodded. "We're not moving enough food to pay the bills."

"I thought he was rich." Milburn had said as much when I asked him about how he'd opened a restaurant. He was my age, and not the kind of big time chef like Bobby Flay where investors were willing to throw their money behind.

"Might be that too. I've said my piece. I have to get back to work. Maybe things will pick up. Don't know."

"Time will tell," I said. Awkwardly, I tried to unclasp my bag, but my hands were too stiff to move.

"I don't need any card or anything. I got your name."

"I didn't get yours."

"That's okay," he said and shut the door behind him. I looked at the smooth metal. There wasn't even a knob on this side. Just a keyhole.

I spun around again looking at all the doors and awnings. I'd started at two and had covered all of the buildings. No one had a camera or a clue. I liked to give a judge and jury as many facts as possible. People were all too quick to fill a vacuum with their own prejudices. This was good, though. Actual drug dealing backed up Baldwin. He didn't look like a cop gone rogue.

With renewed energy, I took another look around. The alley backed up on a parking lot that wasn't open to the public. I stalked to the lot and looked more closely at the building. It wasn't a bar or a new loft. It was a business. I walked around the entire block until I got to the front. The letters KJN were plastered to the top floor of the building. KJN were the initials of one of the three top accounting firms in the country, Keller Jordan Nash.

Other than tabulate votes for awards shows, I had no idea what these firms did. But this was one of the few who'd survived the Enron scandal. If the secrecy of Oscar voting told me anything, it was that Keller Jordan Nash was the kind of place that surrounded itself with cameras and security.

On a hunch, I walked up to the security guard manning the front desk. He pulled a black ski cap off his head. Probably wasn't supposed to wear it inside, but the lobby was anything but warm.

"I'm Casey Cort. I'm an attorney investigating the Troy Duncan shooting."

"How can I help you ma'am?"

"Do you have security cameras?" I asked. No reason to beat around the bush. If I didn't get a yes now, I would get a subpoena later.

"Of course." The balding man looked at me like I was little touched in the head. I'm guessing he'd be surprised that no one else thought they were important in this neighborhood.

"Can I talk to head of security?" I said. Straight to the top always saved time.

"Help yourself," the bald man said. "There he is right now."

I ran up to the man who looked like he'd had a turn at some vending machines. "I'm about to eat my lunch," he said. A sandwich cut in triangles and encased in plastic was in one of his hands, a soda and bag of chips in the other. I looked from the food to the face. Something about him was dead familiar. I flipped through my mental Rolodex. It wasn't as if I had a long list of middle-aged black men in my life. I looked at the patch on his left breast pocket for a clue. Grant.

Fuck me.

It was Keith Grant.

Little more than three years ago, I'd stood in a courtroom and watched as this man found out his daughter wasn't his biologically. I'd stood there while my client had refused to name the girl's real father. I'd stood there while the system circled the wagons and took the girl he'd thought was his daughter of thirteen years from him, and tossed her back to the foster care system that had abused her. I thought he'd been a security guard somewhere else. But of course he could be here. People switched jobs all the time.

Shit. Shit. Shit.

If he recognized me, there was no telling where this would go. I had no idea how long I'd been quiet.

Loudly, I said, "Do you have cameras that point..." I spun around trying to get my bearings. "Southwest?" I hoped my voice covered up my nerves.

The security chief sighed. "Why don't you follow me."

Sometimes attorney was the oddest job in the world. One minute I was holed up in the county library trying to find the magic legal bullet that would help me win a case, but those didn't exist outside the movies. In the next moments, I was walking through some shitty neighborhood recreating the scene of a crime. Now I was interrupting Keith Grant's dinner looking for videotape and hoping beyond all hope he didn't recognize me.

The long hall ended at door labeled "Security."

"Let me hold that for you," I offered when Grant couldn't handle the keys and door and dinner. He gave me his food, then unlocked the door.

"Ladies first." He held open the door. I was happy to walk ahead of him. The less he saw of my face, the less likely he'd be to recognize me. I'd been shit at protecting his daughter from the system. Guilt I'd long buried, started to eat away at my stomach. I closed my eyes for a long second, opened them, then took in the room around me.

I'm not sure what I'd been expecting. Actually I knew exactly what I'd thought was behind the door, a small metal desk, and a 1970s close circuit monitor. This was one hundred percent high tech. The security office was easily the size of my living room. Flat screen monitors covered three walls. There had to be at least fifteen screens. They displayed multiple angles inside and outside the building in full color.

"Where can I put this?" I said my back to Grant. I peeked out of the side of my hood to catch his answer.

"Over there." He pointed to the conference table in the middle of the room. Carefully, I placed the vending machine food on the fake wooden tabletop. "What are you looking for?"

"Video of the alley southwest of your building. From December twenty-eight." The tightness I hadn't noticed in my chest eased. He didn't have a clue who I was. I thanked God for losing twenty pounds and Canada for keeping Cleveland cold enough that I needed an enormous coat.

"What time?" he asked hunt-peck typing into a keyboard and peering at smaller monitor I hadn't noticed during my initial inspection of the office.

"Maybe eight o'clock to about midnight," I said. My head shifted from recognition panic mode to work mode.

"That's a lot of footage. What are you looking for specifically?"

This was always the make or break moment. Lawyers were not something people were generally neutral about. Keith Grant was probably not on the fence for sure. Police shootings even less so. But not laying your cards on the table always got you in trouble. Always. Not to mention that Dinwiddie had represented Grant. I had nothing or everything to lose.

Oh God. Oh God. Oh God.

"I'm investigating the Marc Baldwin shooting of Troy Duncan," I said like I was talking about the Indians' box score. "Were you here that night?"

He sat in one of the three black office chairs and the room and leaned way back.

"Got enough seniority that I have the holidays off now. Left here before Christmas and came back after New Year's."

"Who would have been here?"

Grant turned back to the computer and typed a few more keys. I tried not to shift in impatience as he hunted for the keys he needed and pecked out words. He gave me a name. Rather than take off any of my outerwear, and fish for pen and paper, possibly revealing myself, I committed the name to memory.

"Do you have tape from that time?"

"There's no tape." He laughed. "An outfit like this is all digital. They store everything in a computer somewhere. Let me see."

He hunted, pecked, and typed some more. "Got it. I'm going to eat dinner. And I don't think you want to sit here for the next four hours looking at a parking lot. You got a way for me to download this?"

"How big a file would it be?"

I started to panic. I had a willing witness who was going to happily give me what I needed, probably in violation of company policy. A subpoena might work, but I was pretty sure KJN would file a motion to quash and out lawyer me in a hot minute. If I didn't get these files today, I'd never get them.

"About five gigabytes."

My mind ran through the myriad of ways to get data from one place to another and not one was feasible. I'd gotten a free USB drive from Lulu's firm. I'd carried the adoption cases we were working on the little stick, but it was a half a gig, tops. Tape backup drives probably didn't exist anymore and entire hard drives weren't portable. My heartbeat sped up, and sweat trickled everywhere. For a second, I considered unbuttoning my coat then thought better of it.

"Do you have a Zip drive here?" I'd gotten the external storage system for my files about a year ago.

"It would take maybe forty or fifty of those things."

"Can you burn it on a disk? Like a CD?"

"Give me a few minutes. Take a seat. You hungry?"

"I'll run out to the vending machines if you don't mind." I scurried out of the room, grateful for the break. The less time Keith Grant spent with me, the less time he'd have to figure out who in the hell I was.

I wasn't the least bit hungry, but I stuck quarters into the vending machine anyway. I took the bag of cheddar fries and popped it open. Easing back my hood, I crunched through a few. The corn or potato or whatever it was did a great deal to ease my nerves. With each bite, I didn't have to think about Marc Baldwin, Miles Siegel, Spencer Milburn, or Keith Grant. Not for the first time, I vowed to change a lot about my life. I didn't like where I was, and I was the only person who had the ability to change it. At least that was what the afternoon talk show hosts would probably say if I were one of the desperate guests filling their seats.

After I finished the snack, I wiped my mouth as best I could with a wadded tissue from my pocket then checked my watch. Grant had a good half hour to eat his lunch and burn my disks. I took myself down the hall and knocked on the door.

I stepped in when he opened up. Quickly, he shut the door behind me. One of those old interoffice envelopes was now on the conference table where the food had been. The heat ground on and suddenly hair blew about my face. My hood. I'd forgotten to cinch it back up while I was waiting. I stood stock-still. If my cover was blown, there wasn't a single thing I could do.

"Is that envelope for me?"

"It has all the video on it. Four hours. There are about six disks in there."

"I can't thank you enough," I enthused.

Grant picked up the envelope. It swung between his thumb and forefinger. I reached out to grab it, but he pulled it away.

Uh, oh.

"Casey Cort, I have a couple questions of my own."

"You know who I am." I swallowed down the cheddar fries that threatened to come up all over the shiny linoleum floor.

"The hood was not a great disguise. I knew who you were the minute you walked up to the front desk."

I held back saying I was sorry. I didn't have anything to be sorry for. I hadn't lied to him for years about paternity. I hadn't stolen the girl he'd always thought of as his and hidden her away.

"What can I tell you? I don't know anything more than you."

"Do you know who Olivia's real father is?"

"In the eyes of the law, you were her real father. In her mind, I'm sure she thinks of you as Dad."

"You're dodging the question."

"I'm not breaking confidentiality to tell you that Sheila never told me a thing. I suspect she's taking that secret to the grave."

"Where are they?" He meant his ex-wife and the girl he'd thought his daughter. They absconded the jurisdiction quicker than I could file and argue my appeal of the case that would have likely turned over custody back to Judge Grant.

"I have no idea."

"Sheila never contacted you?"

"Not once," I said truthfully. I had a really good idea of where she was, but I couldn't see what would be gained from revealing my speculation to Keith Grant. Not a single reason to share. Being a lawyer had turned me into a vault. This Grant did not have the key or combination.

"Take this," he said. He handed me the envelope. I unbuckled my bag and jammed it in.

"Thank you."

"I trust you'll do the right thing," he said turning away from me and toward the bank of monitors. I followed his gaze and saw nothing more than a janitor pushing a bucket of water.

"I'll do my best." I let myself out.

While I warmed up my car to the point where I could touch the steering wheel without worry of frostbite, I pulled out the little cell I'd told myself was essential to practice, but was probably a luxury I couldn't afford. Marc Baldwin answered on the first ring. For a moment, I couldn't hear him over the blare of a television and the loud voices of what I assume were his kids.

"Casey Cort," I announced.

"Any news?"

"Not on the lawsuit, specifically. But I wanted to let you know I have an as yet unconfirmed source who says that Milburn is dealing out of the restaurant. He was probably getting a…delivery…when you wandered into the alley."

"I'll check into that," Baldwin said. That was what I was hoping he would say. I assumed when I hung up seconds later that he would get some incontrovertible evidence via his police contacts, that there was dealing that night. Even if it didn't involve Troy Duncan, it gave Baldwin further ammunition.

The drive home was long and slow. The Rapid wasn't that warm in winter, but my ancient Honda was colder. I rarely drove to work, but given today's legwork, I didn't want to die of hypothermia along the way.

The phone rang as I glided to a stop in front of my building. I looked at the caller ID. It wasn't Baldwin or a Private Number, which was Baldwin's home. Since I'd left my cards in about a thousand places over the last couple of weeks, it could be anyone. I dropped everything to fish out the bleating gadget that had fallen between the seat and center console.

The number looked both familiar and not at the same time. I was too tired to try to figure it out. Instead, I answered as I stepped from the car.

"Casey Cort. How can I help you?"

"Spencer Milburn." I'd heard that tone of voice a hundred times before. Something told me, he wasn't asking for a date.

21

Marc

January 27, 2006

Not that I'd thought it for more than a second, but Casey Cort's call couldn't have come at a better time. I wasn't crazy. Not in the least bit. Milburn was both restaurant owner and small-time dealer. Made a lot of sense.

"Why do you have your coat on?" Jan asked coming up on me as I stood with my hand on the front door knob.

"Gonna run down to the Zone Car. They're having a last minute retirement party and I wanted to pay my respects." It was all a lie. But the bar required a cop's ID to get in, so she'd never show up.

"Did you buy a card?"

"It's not that kind of thing. Maybe there'll be something more formal later. I'll let you know if we need a card and gift then. Okay?"

"Don't drink too much. A DUI now would be a huge mistake."

I nodded before I blew up at her. We'd been in close quarters too damn long. I headed out the door and jumped into the car I'd left warming up in the driveway. If I could get a bead on Milburn's dealer, it would go a long way toward getting me the hell out of my house and back to work.

The part about the Zone Car was only half a lie. I was headed there, not to raise a glass to retirement, or even to raise a glass at all. I needed the help of someone who wasn't on leave. Dollars to free donuts, Neil Walsh was keeping a barstool warm.

"Walsh!" I called out to one of the few narcotics detectives I knew personally. As expected, he was there on a Friday night.

"Fucking A. It's none other than Marc Baldwin. Man oh man, you're a site for sore eyes. Department brass practically has you buried under the jail. You ain't even riding a desk."

"Can we talk?" I tilted my head toward the private room in the back that sometimes hosted a poker game for the white cops or dominoes for the blacks.

"Why not? These guys are skipping down memory lane. Ain't a place I want to go today."

I put my untouched beer on the table once Walsh closed the door.

"How are you holding up?" he asked after he'd drained his own stein.

"Going out of my God damn mind. I can only fuck my wife so many times. Plus I can't stand all the self-help bullshit she watches in the afternoon."

"You're not gonna let Oprah or Dr. Phil make over your life?"

"Shit no. I need to get back to work. The brass is dragging their feet like they're up to their necks in quicksand."

"What do you need?"

Relief flooded my brain. Walsh was in.

"My lawyer's been poking around a little bit. She found out the guy who owned the restaurant that Duncan worked in, is a low level drug dealer."

"Out of the back of his place?" he asked, his tone doubtful.

"No way. He sells from behind the bar." We both knew that coming and going in the alley would eventually arouse suspicion. No one would suspect a bartender. Shit, it was always the bartender. There were too many in town to shake down, though.

"What are you gonna do? You want us to bust him?"

"That's what I first thought. But while I was on my way down here, I figured it might be better all around if you can kill two birds with one stone." Get both the dealer and his supplier.

"Let's go check it out," Walsh said.

I only hesitated for a second. Took a fortifying sip of beer, plunking the nearly full glass on the table. Then I zipped up my coat. No doubt Casey Cort and Captain Todd and even Jan would tell me to stay my ass at home. But so far, that hadn't gotten me shit, but a sore butt from sitting on my own couch.

The drive from West Fifty-eighth to West Tenth was less than ten minutes by my watch. I didn't ask Walsh why he hadn't turned in his undercover car for his civilian ride. I just hunkered down in the Nissan SUV keeping as warm as possible. Despite the security gate at KJN, Walsh swiped a keycard and drove into the parking lot.

It gave a perfect view of the back of Spencer's.

"You got binoculars?" I asked.

"Under the seat," Walsh answered. He already had his field glasses up to his eyes.

I took the spare pair and peered out. Took only a second to get my bearings before I saw everything laid out before me. Spencer's back door, the Dumpster to the right, the alley's exit to the left. The bright lights and police tape that had decorated the scene when I was last over there were long gone. In its place was some kind of mini shrine to Troy Duncan. I had no memory of how these things had popped up. Twenty years ago, someone would get shot or killed in an smash up, a cleanup crew came in and did their thing, then people moved on. Nowadays every car accident and death was marked with teddy bears and flowers.

R.I.P. the poster board above Troy's picture read.

"Today is your very lucky day," Walsh said.

I swung the binoculars from the picture of Duncan to the back door of Spencer's. I refocused on the sliver of light spilling from the restaurant's delivery door. A huge pickle can propped open the back door. A man who I guessed was Milburn was standing by the door, cigarette in hand, cooling his jets. Normally, I'd discount a smoker. They would do nearly anything to service their habit. But near freezing temperatures made that addiction seem plain deadly especially for a restaurant owner who could probably smoke in his office undetected by the health inspectors.

"What are you going to do?" I asked when Milburn was joined by a couple of tweakers.

"Calling backup now," he said lifting the radio concealed in the console. "You stay put." The narcotics officer jumped from the vehicle and headed over to the alley.

Walsh didn't have to tell me twice. I couldn't think of a single solitary reason to leave the warmth of the Armada. Not a minute later, a patrol car screamed on the scene, lights blazing and sirens wailing. I hoisted my binoculars to watch the arrest and round up.

The man I thought to be Milburn and another two skinny looking white guys were cooling their heels in the back of three different patrol cars after all was said and done.

Walsh was back in the car in a half hour. He turned the lights back on and drove over to the station.

"I'll hop on up to the video booth," I said. The booth was where we watched suspect interrogations if we were so inclined. I usually didn't. I liked to drop off suspects, and leave it to the detectives to sort out. The beat was where I belonged, not holed up in one room or another with a perp on the wrong side of the law. But tonight, I was supremely interested in what was about to go down.

Spencer Milburn was up first. Not surprising. He had the most to lose.

"Milburn. You're looking a little shaky today. How are you doing?" Walsh asked.

"Fine," he answered not looking the least bit fine. His hands shook. He looked down and as if he realized that gave him away, he laid one over the other. Seconds later he was picking at his skin, opening a sore. I looked away in disgust. "Do I need a lawyer?" I heard him ask.

"No, don't think so," Walsh said. "Do you think you need a lawyer?"

Milburn shook the cuffed wrists that lay on the table. "Something tells me that these plus you all reading my rights means I'm under arrest."

"We need to straighten out a couple of things. I'm thinking you can help."

"What am I under arrest for again?"

"Possession of a controlled substance."

"You found drugs in the bar? I'm going to have to conduct an internal investigation, root out the bad seed. I will probably have to fire somebody."

"You're a comedian. Maybe you should get a second job at the club down the street."

"Maybe," Milburn said slouching as far as the shackles would allow.

"Sit up!" Walsh ordered. "We're also looking at a trafficking charge. Those two guys we picked up behind Spencer's look like they want to tell us about your whole meth operation."

"What kind of time does that carry?"

"You could do a dime down in Mansfield for that one."

"A dime?"

"Ten years."

"Need that lawyer now." Milburn stopped picking at his skin. Instead, he pulled out a business card from his pocket and tapped it on the table. The tap-tap-tap was right above the microphone concealed under the wood. The officer listening to the recording pulled off his headphones. The tapping annoyed the hell out of Walsh in ten seconds flat.

"Fine."

I stepped away to get some coffee from the machine at the end of the hall. I pressed buttons for creamer and sugar. I was going to need all the help I could get to stay alert and plugged in. Assuming his lawyer didn't put a wrench in the works, Milburn had the key to my freedom. I cribbed a couple of day old donuts from the small copy room. Didn't even feel too bad. Jan's cooking had slimmed me down right quick. It had been the easiest ten pounds I'd ever lost.

"Lawyer's here," the booth attendant called down the hall.

Brushing off the crumbs, I joined him in the too hot room. There were a few more guys inside and I had to pull out a rolling stool from the corner. Took me a minute to sit without falling and find a space where I could see the monitor.

"There's no sound," someone called out.

"Lawyer's in there. We'll turn it back on when she calls Walsh back in.

"She?" someone questioned.

"I thought he had money. He didn't get one of the big dogs?" another asked.

The booth operator let out a piercing whistle.

"Walsh? They're ready for you to go back in. The rest of you can stay if you can be quiet. I swear you're like a bunch of second graders. I actually need to hear what's going on to make sure we're recording everything. Got it?"

A couple of guys who knew they couldn't keep their commentary to themselves elected to leave the room. The temperature immediately dropped a couple of degrees and I could move from the rolling hazard on wheels to a better chair. I started at the screen.

Walsh was removing Milburn's handcuffs under his lawyer's watchful eye. He said something and both Milburn and the lawyer looked up at the screen.

"Jesus fucking Christ!" I jumped and the seat rolled behind me hitting a metal shelf. A few CD cases hit the floor with a crash.

"Baldwin! What did I just say? You of all people—"

"That's *my* lawyer," I shouted.

"What do you mean? Milburn's got a union rep? I don't recognize her. I didn't think they had chicks over there."

I didn't have time to explain. I had to run down there and fix it now before anything happened. Before Casey ruined my play. It took precious seconds longer to get downstairs than I wanted. I'd had to run to the end of the hall, take the stairs, then run all the way back to the same end.

I barreled through the door. "You can't represent Milburn! There's a conflict," I shouted to everyone in the room. Slowly, it became clear that there were more people in the room than I'd thought. Sure, I'd known about Walsh, and Milburn, and Casey Cort. But Captain Todd had been holding up a corner of the room outside of the camera's view.

Todd stepped forward and pulled me from the interrogation room. His viselike grip gave me no room to maneuver. He must have been hell on suspects back in his day.

"What in the hell are you doing in the station? Do you have a crime to report?"

"I'm here to watch Milburn."

"Do you understand the meaning of administrative leave?"

"He's the key. Casey Cort's going to fuck this all up if she stays in there!"

I pulled toward the door, not that it made a bit of difference.

"How do you know the name of the lawyer?"

"She's my lawyer. She's representing me in Troy Duncan's suit against the department and the city."

"She's a criminal lawyer?"

"Both. I guess. I don't know."

"What in the hell is she doing in there?"

"She's the one who tipped me to Milburn and his buddies. Best I can figure, she gave him a card when she paid a visit. It's the first lawyer he thought of."

"This is one hundred percent royally fucked. Only you Baldwin. I swear it's like you have a raincloud over your head. Nope that's not it. You're like Pigpen with a cloud of dirt and shit following you."

"What about the conflict?"

"What's this conflict you keep talking about?"

"How can she represent me and Milburn?"

"Is Milburn being arrested for shooting Troy Duncan?"

"No?"

"I'm not sure I see the conflict. Doesn't matter. Either way you need to get the hell out of here. If it leaks out that you're interfering with the investigation of your own case, you're toast. Go home. Fuck your wife. Play with your kids. Get a hobby. But whatever you do, do not show your face in any police station until I personally tell you that you can. Got it?"

"Crystal clear."

22

Casey

January 28, 2006

I sipped at my third glass of wine. It was before five o'clock, but it had been wine o'clock since the moment I got up.

For the life of me, I couldn't figure out how I could have played last night any better. Well, if I hadn't answered the phone, all would have been fine. But I did answer the phone, and I did turn around and take my car back downtown.

Maybe the mistake had been calling Baldwin. I had been almost one hundred percent sure my tipoff would lead to the arrest of Milburn. And the arrest of Milburn would lead to the conclusion that Baldwin hadn't been tilting at windmills.

If Milburn hadn't been drug dealing, and if the county hospital system hadn't denied Duncan care, then except for the gunshot wound blowing a hole through his digestive track and the resulting paralysis because of the bullet lodged in his spine, all would have been okay. I looked in the mirror by my back door. Nope, even I wasn't convinced. I'd have to work on that face before a judge or jury saw it. Surely, it would look more convincing without a white wine glass hovering at my lips.

I needed to get my mind off Milburn. I'd talked them out of the aggravated trafficking charge before I'd tentatively agreed to his cooperation and turned him over to one of the high powered defense attorneys I'd met in the courthouse a few months ago. I was pretty sure that attorney wouldn't reciprocate. Whatever. I didn't want him to refer anyone back because I was getting out of the criminal racket. In a minute, a second, a year. It would probably be a long year between Baldwin, Milburn, and the bliss of non-adversarial adoption practice, though.

Fortified by three glasses of wine, I went back into the living room and opened my bag. I shook the CDs from the envelope and on to the floor next to the prefabricated entertainment center in the corner of my living room. I wanted to replace it with those super nice things you see in Pottery Barn catalogs, but—money or lack thereof to be exact.

Dad had replaced my outdated VCR with a DVD player this Christmas. Its shiny slickness was in sharp contrast to the bulky fiberboard. Frustrated by crappy life decisions and being perennially broke, I jammed at the buttons until the unit turned on and the plastic tray glided out. I stuck in the disk Grant had labeled number one and walked myself and two remote controls back to the futon.

Took me a good couple of minutes to navigate through both the TV and DVD menus. The DVD had been a great gesture from my parents, but I wasn't a regular movie viewer. I'd been weaned from Hollywood entertainment in those leaner years when I didn't have the disposable income for regular video rental nights.

I pressed play. The disk spun, then nothing. I got up and searched the storage space under the TV. I could have sworn my dad said this would play anything. I ejected the CD and stuck in my favorite Alanis Morisette CD. "All I Really Want" blared from the TV. Assured the damned thing worked, I switched the CDs. Again, nothing.

Fuck.

This day was going from weird to worse. I put Alanis back in and turned up the TV loud. I was halfway through a duet version of "You Oughta Know" when the banging started on my door. Immediately, I hit mute. Slowly, I made my way over to the door and pulled it open to face whichever angry neighbor happened to be standing there. The ready apology died on my lips.

"I hope you weren't singing about me," Miles said. He stood there all buttoned up in a coat, hat, and gloves, work bag slung across his body.

I thought: *What are you doing here.* That seemed rude to say out loud. So I just pulled back the door wide. He stepped in like he'd been here yesterday and not fourteen months ago.

"You didn't answer your phone."

"You want some wine?" I asked retreating to the living room and lifting the nearly empty bottle from the steamer trunk I used as a coffee table.

"Is there any left?" When I didn't answer, Miles hung up his coat, hat, and bag, then said, "I'll get my own glass." Clearly the phrase, make yourself at home would be lost on him. He was already more comfortable than most guests.

I'd poured myself a very imprudent fourth glass by the time Miles came back for his. He emptied the bottle. He looked from me to the blue screen casting a pall through the room.

"Did you drink that entire bottle? It's only three thirty," Miles said looking at his expensive designer watch.

"I'm well aware of the time. I had a shitty night."

"Want to talk about it?"

I shook my head. His advice would probably be helpful, but I wasn't ready to share my latest humiliation with the public quite yet.

"Why are you watching a blank screen?"

"I was trying to get those CDs on the floor to play. But it's not working."

Miles walked to the corner of the room where all the doors of the entertainment center stood open in defeat.

"Are these the disks?"

"Yeah, those."

"They're burned."

I jumped back like the television was combustible. I peered from top to bottom looking for smoke. The telltale smell of burning plastic was absent from my living room.

"What? I haven't done anything to set them on fire. They were fine on the way home. It's too freaking cold outside for anything to burn. Maybe the new DVD player overheated?" I couldn't remember if or where I had an extinguisher. I was thinking one had come with the apartment somewhere. I was *not* sober enough for a fire.

A laugh escaped from behind the hand Miles had clamped over his mouth. "I mean that they were burned…made by a computer, not in a factory like Alanis here."

My relief was palpable. I wouldn't have to add burning down a Shaker Square pre-war building to my list of recent blunders.

"Yes. I saw the guy make them the other night. What does that have to do with anything?"

"Not all DVD players can play burned CDs. More expensive units usually have that capa—"

"Oh, God. If this is going to be another I have more money than you discussion? Can we cap it now?"

"I wasn't. I'm sorry. I came here to apologize for being insensitive the other day. I'm back at it, huh?"

"Not everyone grows up in a family with a big house, and money, and top flight schooling. I'm not saying woe is me. Except for the loans, I'm fine. What I'm saying is that you act like your life experience is the majority one and it's not even close."

"You think we're different? Your parents are married. My parents are married. You went to college and law school. I went to college and law school."

"You're kind of right. I mean to the rest of the world, we're probably more similar than different. But here, between us, it's night and day. You could probably have any job you want anywhere in the country you want. A surprising number of people didn't hold open the door for this Cleveland Marshall grad."

"Have you thought of getting a job at small firm and working your way up? Getting your foot in the door that way?"

I tried not to be angry at his suggestion. Men had that problem-solving gene they couldn't turn off. My father had made many of the same suggestions after I passed the bar, but was still *persona non grata* in Cleveland's legal circles. I waved my flat hand in front of my neck in a cut-it motion.

"The last thing I want to talk about on a Saturday night is my career. I just want to watch these CDs."

"I have my laptop here. Want to try that?" Miles took the hint, but the problem-solving gene snuck through. I was grateful this time. Sometimes a penis and a man brain were good things. Not always. But sometimes. I nodded my thanks.

"Finally a solution to a problem I actually have."

Miles didn't take the bait. Instead, he set up the portable computer on my coffee table and popped in the first CD I handed him. He clicked a few keys, and a grainy picture came up on the small screen. A date remained constant in the upper right hand corner. A time code whirred in the lower right hand corner.

"What are we watching?" Miles hunched forward on the futon.

"Security video."

"How many hours do you have?"

"Maybe four. That's what Grant gave me."

"Grant, who?"

"The security guard from KJN," I said then leaned a little farther forward on my seat. I could just make out figures walking to and from their cars. I scrutinized the screen.

"There!" I pointed. Miles leaned forward as well. Just on the left side of the screen, I could see the Spencer's blue awning. The white piping on the bottom was blowing slightly in the breeze. A light came on, and the camera took a moment to adjust. Someone had exited the restaurant, tossed a bag in the dumpster and gone back in. A few seconds later, the light went out.

"That's an automatic security light," Miles said.

"Got that. So the time stamp says eight eleven right?" I rose from the futon and walked from the living room.

"Where are you going?"

"I need the statement that goes along with this."

"Nothing happened," he said when I came back. He'd unlaced is Timberland boots and placed them next to mine on a rug by the door. The sock on his feet looked hand knit. I resisted asking if his mother had whipped those up for him. Instead, I parked myself on the cushion and placed the heavy file on my lap.

"I didn't think I'd miss anything. Parking lots, alleys, and Dumpsters are usually pretty quiet. Especially in the winter. Anyway..." I flipped through my Marc Baldwin folder, thicker than most in my office, and found the initial statement he'd given to his boss the night of the shooting.

"It says here that dispatch got a call at twenty forty-five. Can you fast forward it to eight thirty?"

Miles fiddled with a few buttons. "This disk ends at five after eight," he said. He ejected then queued up the second disk I handed him. Then he pressed the spacebar, pausing the action.

"What?" I swiveled my head his way.

"Did you think I was a total asshole the entire time we were together?"

"I have no idea what you mean," I said feigning misunderstanding.

"Casey." His two-syllable drawn out pronunciation of my name let me know he wasn't buying what I was selling.

"What? What do you want me to say?"

"Last week you made that crack about first versus fourth tier. You did it again tonight. Did I come off as some Ivy League asshat lording his school over everyone?"

"That seems like it may be an accurate self assessment. Run with that."

"Are you serious? What was it that you liked about me?"

I didn't ever want to have this conversation ever. But it looked like we were having it now. I finished my fourth glass of wine wishing for a fifth. *In vino veritas* and all that.

"What I loved about you Miles was that you were kind, and honest, and you believed in what you were doing. You wanted to get married, have a partnership. It was kind of a perfect package," I babbled.

"Everyone has flaws. So yours included obliviousness to the plight of others who didn't grow up like you. Maybe I thought you'd grow up a little. Mature. I was willing to make that leap. Plus, you weren't exactly chasing prostitutes. That was a bonus." I stopped talking for a long time, looking out at bare treetops outside my living room windows. I turned back. Looked him in the eye. "You were my Cleveland Heights."

"What does that mean?"

"I've kind of had a minute to think about stuff, you know. Lulu signed me up for eHarmony and I kind of had to figure out what my own faults were. I seem to have a thing for guys above my level."

"Level?"

"Pay grade? Whatever. I chase rich guys." It was a bit liberating to admit that out loud. It was probably what had me running to Milburn last night against my better judgment.

"Maybe I have some damsel in distress fantasy. Somewhere deep in my brain I must think some guy can rescue me from my debt, from my problems, from this perfectly lovely pre-war apartment and move me to that biggest house on Lake Avenue or Shaker Boulevard. I don't know. I haven't figured it all out yet. But I walked eyes wide open into the situation with you and Tom. I learned *something*. So the whole thing wasn't a total disaster."

"That's some post mortem." I could tell he didn't take kindly to being compared to my prostitute-chasing, corrupted-family ex.

"I'm not without a thought in my head, Miles. And you're really hot. So there's that. Maybe all those hormones flooding my brain stopped me from thinking."

"You're dating?" Miles asked with a hint of jealousy in his voice. Hot rich guy did not have a thing to be jealous about. He'd had a girlfriend when I met him. He'd have another in the next few months if he so much as went outside for longer than the time it took to get from car to door.

"I'm thinking about it. The online profile for this one site is taking forever to complete, though. I don't have a computer at home, so I can only work on it between court and clients."

"I'm not dating."

"I'm sure you won't have any problem when you decide to step out." I mimicked his actions, pressing the spacebar. The video started again. The KJN parking lot was empty and quiet. My mind filled the darkness with bogeymen.

"Why do you think KJN has a camera back here? What—"

Miles hit the computer again freezing the picture.

"Casey…"

I stood suddenly very nervous. "Do you want more wine?"

"I want you to sit down."

I plopped down next to him, far too close for comfort. "Ah, Case," he said, his lips far too near for my own good.

"Miles, this is a bad, bad idea."

"I like bad ideas," he whispered. I closed my eyes and turned my head into the hand he'd used to frame one side of my face. My stomach got all twisty and my head got all floaty. I wanted to blame it on four glasses of wine in an hour, but if I were being honest with myself, I couldn't pin the blame on alcohol.

Not the kiss, nor me pulling off his sweater. Neither of those were about wine. Not me nude under him on my futon. That wasn't wine either. It was old love, or new lust, or something I wasn't quite ready to try to understand.

Afterwards, I wanted distance, but I needed his computer. I wasn't exactly in a position to ask Miles to leave after he came back from the bathroom. Silently, I handed him his clothes and took mine to my bedroom. I tossed them into the hamper then took myself to the one bathroom in the apartment.

Me and my nowhere color hair and no particular color eyes stared back at me from the medicine cabinet. I had no idea what I was doing. Miles had dumped me. I knew because I was oh-so-familiar with the dumping bit. Tom had done it. I was always the dumpee. Probably a year's worth of therapy in that. I jumped in the shower to rinse off and wrapped myself in pajamas and my fuzzy bathrobe when I was done.

"I got myself some dessert and a glass of milk. Hope you don't mind," a fully dressed Miles said.

"Strudel?"

"I did love it last year."

"Have at it." It had been in the fridge a few weeks. The last thing my hips needed was more dessert. But I didn't want to hurt my mother's feelings by returning a half-eaten pan. My neighbors Jason and Greg had stopped my hospitality at a single pan.

"Press play. I forgot socks."

"I could rub your feet."

"Okay. That's weird. My mom gave me a six-pack of wool socks for Christmas." It took me a good five minutes to free a pair of socks from the cardboard, adhesive, and plastic stays.

"Casey! You're going to need to rewind," Miles called out.

Feet fully covered, I ran back to the living room. "What did I miss?"

"What are we watching?" His question and face were wary.

"It's video from the Troy Duncan shooting."

Miles dropped his fork and plate on the floor next to the futon. I hit the spacebar again.

It was grainy black darkness. Then the light went on over the Spencer's awning. Expecting someone to dump trash again, I was surprised that the person who came out appeared to be empty handed. No trash? Maybe they would smoke, though I had to say that would have to be one hell of a habit to go outside and stand next to rotting food.

Another two people came from the west side of the alley. The light over the back of the restaurant went out and I couldn't see much. The kitchen door opened again a couple of minutes later. The light came on and two or three people came out. They talked for a minute, kind of looked like goodbye, then went their separate ways.

"What's that?"

"Spencer Milburn let everyone go early. Slow night. Wanted to cut staffing costs."

"Where's Duncan?"

"He stayed late to wash his knives, clean up, and complete inventory. There were First Night specials planned."

The light switched off again.

On.

This time it looked like someone was going back into the restaurant. The other two people who'd been behind the dumpster scattered like cockroaches.

"Those are drug dealers," I pointed. Those were likely the guys from last night. The dealers up from Geauga County where, according to Milburn, they had a meth lab.

"You believe his story?" Miles' exaggerated cough told me he didn't put much stock in it. I may have agreed with him yesterday.

"I met the drug dealers last night. Matter of fact, one of them called me down to the justice center to represent him."

"Why you?"

"Because I'd given Spencer Milburn my card not three hours earlier."

"Shit. Is that a conflict?"

"Who in the hell knows? I didn't have time to do research on that from the front seat of my Honda. Instead, Baldwin comes charging into the room yelling about how I was *his* lawyer."

"What was he doing downtown? Have they allowed him in on their investigation of him?"

"He probably got a heads up on the arrest." It was a non-answer that didn't even hint at the complicated problem I'd made worse by trying to make it better.

"You should have called me."

"To do what? That would have been like calling Tom. They did *not* need a prosecutor in that room. I handled it, okay. Referred the case out right there. Problems solved."

It was another two or three minutes before the light came on again in the video focusing our attention somewhere other than bickering. I slipped from the futon to the floor. I needed to see this up close.

"Your hair is in the way."

I shifted sideways landing on my hip, but out of Miles line of sight. On screen, the door opened, and a man came out. I couldn't see much because he was in all black. But dollars to donuts, it was Duncan. He doubled back shoving the door closed with this foot. Then the man paused, glanced toward the dumpster then glanced back. He pulled up his hood and shrugged his shoulders. He had a small bag on one side and a duffle on the other. His movements were slow.

"I think he's cold," I said.

"Looks like he hears something to me," Miles responded.

I blinked. My eyes were watering from staring so hard. I wished for night vision goggles on KJN's camera or some kind of tuning button to make this clearer.

Another man walked into the frame. From the bulk of his clothes and the shape of his hat, I was guessing it was Baldwin. The futon creaked as Miles leaned forward as well. In what looked like a split second, Duncan hesitated, his steps faltering. Then he reached into his pocket. The flash must have been the gun firing, then Duncan crumpled to the ground. Not pitch back and fall like the movies, but folds like a cheap suit.

"Play that again."

Miles got down on his knees next to me, fiddled with the laptop's controls, and the video started again.

I watched Baldwin this go round. He walked toward the alley, pulled his gun from the holster. I think his mouth moved. He fired. My neck snapped as I swiveled back to Duncan. But he was already on the ground. I looked all around the screen. Where's Darlene Webb? Where are the drug dealers?

The counter on the bottom of the screen continued its endless scroll. A man broke from the knot of people waiting for the Rapid. It was the first time I'd consciously noticed them. They'd been blobs of light on the screen before. It looked like the man was saying something to Baldwin. The cop turned in his general direction with his gun hand still extended. The man shrunk back and melted back into the crowd.

Baldwin turned his head toward his left shoulder away from the camera. Seconds later, a car pulled up. From the blazing headlights and pulsing sirens, it was no leap to guess that was the police car he'd probably been in with his partner. Another officer jumped out. Webb, I guessed because this person was a lot smaller even with the bulk of winter clothing and equipment belt. The two exchanged words. Webb went to the trunk of the car and got out something. More cars pulled up making a square around Duncan's body. The lights made everything clearer. But I could no longer see Duncan.

The police shifted around, looked at what I assumed was Duncan, looked at each other. An ambulance came onto the scene from the opposite direction. Two EMTs pulled a stretcher from the back. Minutes passed before Duncan was loaded and rolling toward the back of the ambulance. Baldwin broke from the knot of officers and sprinted toward the van. The EMTs closed the doors and Baldwin walked back slowly. I clicked on the button Miles had used before. The video froze.

"How did you get footage of the Troy Duncan shooting?"

"I asked nicely."

"What did that look like to you?"

I didn't answer. There was no right answer. I could see a judge, the jury, and the public interpret that ten minutes of video in a lot of different ways, few of them favorable to Baldwin.

"Casey?"

"I don't know, Miles."

"Yes, you do."

"Since you're so sure. What did it look like to you?"

"It looked like a cowboy cop shot a black man in cold blood."

"There's no audio. We couldn't hear Baldwin shout police or stop or get down."

Miles shifted onto the floor next to me and rewound the video. "The time stamp there is twenty fifty-six, forty-three." He clicked a double arrow on the video viewer. He stopped when Duncan fell to the ground. "Twenty fifty-seven oh two. At most nineteen seconds. Do you really think Baldwin had time to say all that he claimed?"

"That's something for a jury to consider."

"That's it? Isn't Troy Duncan owed something more?"

"Thanks for your computer. We've already had this fight and broke up, so we don't have to do this again." I peered on the side of the computer and pressed a button. Fortunately, it was the right one. A plastic tray slid open noisily. I collected the disk and inserted it into a plastic sleeve.

Miles stood and took his plate and glass to my kitchen. I'd closed the top of the computer and slipped it back into his bag by the time he came back to the living room.

"What now?"

"Now? Now I take two aspirin with a glass of water and go to bed. You go home and do whatever you like. I wish you a good rest of the weekend."

I walked to the kitchen to get the aforementioned water and pills. A bottle of wine had been easier on my liver in my twenties. Now I prayed to wake up with nothing more than a little headache and cotton mouth. I didn't have the energy for full-blown hangovers.

"We need to talk about this," Miles said from the dining room.

I turned and dropped the pill bottle on the counter with a clatter. I held up my finger as I swallowed the pills and most of the water.

"This is exhausting. My job. My responsibilities. I can't add you to the mix right now. Maybe I'm stupid, but I'm still looking for that white knight. Someone to support me, help me, and love me."

"I love you, Casey. That's what I've figured out between last fall and tonight. I love you. I want to try to make us work."

My head was going to explode, and not from wine. "I don't have the capacity for this now, Miles. I really don't. Marc Baldwin probably lied to me, his chief, himself. I don't know. He thinks he was justified in his shooting of Troy Duncan. Maybe he was. Probably not. I have to deal with that personally before I prep him for deposition on Monday. Because despite what you think of me, I do have a strong sense of personal morality, and do you know what that's gotten me? Here. Doing these cases. Now. I was all moral and ethical through and through. Do you know what I found out?

"I'm the only one. The Strohmeyers aren't moral. The Brodys aren't ethical. Jarrod Carter locked women in a container and sold them to the highest bidder by the hour. Baldwin's a murderer. So I'm going to step up to the plate, take my medicine, and do what I'm constitutionally obligated to do. Do what I signed a retainer agreement promising to do. I'm going to go into court and defend my client as best I can. That's it. There's no gray area. My personal feelings are not involved. This, Miles. This is who I am now. Who I am is going to bed. Please let yourself out."

23

Marc

January 30, 2006

"I want to show you something," Casey Cort said the minute I walked into her office. I didn't get a chance to ask her about the Milburn situation or tell her that I might be in more trouble than I was before. Her facial expression didn't invite chitchat.

I closed the door behind me. Casey turned her back swiveling in her chair to press a few buttons on her computer. A grainy image of what looked like a parking lot came up on the screen. Satisfied, she stood and walked to my side of her desk. She sat in the chair next to mine, and rested her chin in her hands.

I scanned the screen trying to get a sense of time and place. When a light came on, I saw that I was watching the alley behind Spencer's. My stomach knotted. The entire night unfolded before my eyes. When all the cop cars pulled up and obliterated the scene, Casey rose and stopped the video.

"How long was it?"

She didn't pretend to misunderstand. "Nineteen seconds."

"Seemed longer."

"I'm sure somewhere in your training you learned that events can seem slow when you're in the middle of them, but later the true time and split second judgments are all other people see."

"What happens now?"

"You and I need to decide what we're going to do."

"About the tape or Milburn?"

"Is there any further disciplinary action against you?"

"I don't think so. The captain was pretty pissed, though."

"I was not planning on representing Milburn for more than a night. But you acted a little faster than I anticipated. I figured if I was there, I could control the situation, maybe get him to admit to buying the night of the shooting in exchange for leniency on the other. You kind of blew that when you stormed into the room. This situation between you and me can't work if you don't let me do my job. Understand?"

I nodded vigorously. She'd done me a huge favor by dropping the dime on Milburn. "I was caught off guard."

"You cannot for any reason go off like a loose cannon. If tape from that night surfaces, it's not going to help this case here."

"Do we have to turn the other tape over to Dinwiddie?" I asked. Video wasn't looking like it was my friend.

"This isn't a criminal case. You didn't shoot the video. It's not exculpatory evidence, per se. I think we can make an argument, if it comes down to it, that we don't have to give Dinwiddie anything."

"Okay. What's the strategy?"

"We're going to prepare you for deposition like we've discussed. You're going to stick with your story, exactly. That's it. If we can pin Troy Duncan's death on the way the jail bungled his medical care, then you win. If we can pin the drug dealing on Milburn, you win.

"You merely injured a man in the line of duty. Milburn started the chain of events. But it was the county's carelessness that did him in. It's called superseding cause, and it's going to win you the case. I think we push for a quick settlement, getting the county to pay, and clearing you of wrongdoing. Then work on reinstatement. You with me?"

"Absolutely," I said. Clearing me of wrongdoing was what I needed. "All I want is to get back to work."

"Then I think *we* need to get to work."

We worked for a good three solid hours before my hunger got the best of me. When I had breakfast with the guys, I always had the special of the day. It was guaranteed to keep me going for hours. Jan's toaster bagels did not hit the spot. The loud stomach rumble gave me away. It was the last straw for my concentration.

"I hate to stop you, but—"

"I heard it. What do you like, Chinese, sandwiches, Italian?"

"Sandwiches would be fine. Roast beef if you have it."

The lawyer excused herself. Ten minutes later her assistant, a Puerto Rican woman brought in a sandwich and a bottle of raspberry Snapple.

"Where's Casey?"

"She's on the phone. She'll be back in a minute."

I looked around the room at the steel gray phone on her desk. A tiny light bar glowed solid red. She must have muted the phone during our meeting. A minute stretched into ten.

When Cort came back, she was carrying an uneaten salad in her hand. She set the food on the windowsill. Her face, when it turned to me, was grim.

"Captain Todd?"

She shook her head so slowly. It was somehow worse than a slap in the face from the brass.

"The Cuyahoga County grand jury has summoned you to testify. They're conducting a criminal investigation into the death of Troy Duncan."

"Criminal? Me?" I'd always been on the right side of the law. "What does that mean? What would they charge me with?"

"Murder, manslaughter, assault with a deadly weapon to start."

"To start? But I didn't do anything wrong. I'm a God damn police officer for fuck's sake. I have the God-given right to carry a weapon and keep the peace. Troy Duncan might come across all innocent, but he was there right along with the drug dealers. What kind of innocent man reaches into his pocket in the face of an officer with a weapon? That's just plain stupid."

"We live in a society where people aren't shot for being stupid."

"What about my Fifth Amendment rights? Do I have to testify in front of the grand jury? Who goes shows up to the hanging and lets someone put a noose around their neck?"

"Defendants are generally not summoned to the grand jury. But in your case, you're one of very few people who can testify as to what happened. They don't have the videotape."

"So if I ignore the summons what happens?" Suddenly hiding at home on leave was very appealing. Even toaster pastries were looking good.

"There's no way *you* can ignore the summons. You do not want a bench warrant."

"What do I say?"

"You plead the Fifth."

"Then they'll think I'm lying."

"Then you stay that much further out of jail. Don't bring rope to your own hanging."

"Fuck. When do we have to go?"

"Tomorrow. We'll kick the deposition. Criminal always comes before civil."

"Fine." I was starting to get used to feeling like a pinball. "what now?"

"Now you go home and get a good night's sleep. Is there anything you haven't told me that's germane to this case, I should know?"

"No. You know everything you need to know."

Casey Cort looked at me queerly, but let me go after I finished my sandwich.

All the way home, something gnawed at me. I couldn't put a finger on what it was, but something about this whole thing wasn't sitting right.

"How was it?" Jan asked when I walked in the door. She was reading a magazine at the table. The kids were pretending to do homework. I poked my head into the kitchen. Nodded to myself. It was what I suspected. The timer on the stove glowed blue as the seconds counted down. She'd promised them game time if they did homework for an hour. On impulse, I pushed the button turning off the timer.

Shrugging off my coat, I hung it on the back of the chair.

"Family meeting," I said loud enough to get everyone's attention. Michael, Donna, and Jan looked at me warily. I no longer hung the moon for any of them.

"Do you think this is a good idea, Marc?"

"Donna, why is Daddy home all day?" I asked my littlest. She hadn't learned to filter her thoughts yet. She would tell the bald truth if you asked her.

"You shot a man who didn't have a gun. Everyone says you killed him because he was black."

"Michael?"

"You *thought* the guy was armed, but he wasn't. So you shot and killed an unarmed man. Police do that all the time, so you'll get off, but it will be a while."

I looked across the table at my wife, deliberately raising an eyebrow. Jan liked to pretend the kids lived in a bubble here in Westlake. She's always acted like sending them to St. Raphael would somehow protect them from the world. But they knew as much if not more than everyone else. This little demonstration proved that.

"Fine they can stay. What do you want to say Marc?" She wasn't doing the best job at controlling her anger.

"I've been summoned to testify in front of the grand jury tomorrow."

Jan's gasp probably put the fear of God into the kids. Maybe I should have called her first to warn her.

"Mommy what does that mean?"

"It means, Donna, that the prosecutor thinks he committed a crime. That means Daddy could go to jail."

"For how long?"

"Forever, honey."

"Jan. Stop. It's just an investigation into Duncan's death. There's no way Lori Pope could get away with doing anything different. Like everyone else around here, she has a political career to protect. Donna, Michael, I'll be fine."

"How can you say that? How many times have you told me the bozos over there would indict a ham sandwich?"

Probably a thousand times over the years. I think the county hadn't indicted one of my suspects maybe once or twice in my years on the job.

"I don't actually have to say anything anyway. My lawyer says I can plead the Fifth."

"What do you mean?" Jan asked. "You'll be under oath."

"What's the Fifth, Daddy?" Donna asked.

"The Fifth Amendment to the Constitution honey. No one can require you to incriminate yourself?"

"Incriminate?" Donna asked. She mimicked me exactly.

"It means that if I did something wrong, I don't have to walk myself into jail."

"Did you do something wrong?" That was Michael. He didn't say much, but I'd made the mistake one too many times of confusing silence with deaf ears.

"No. I didn't do a thing wrong. Everything I did was within the law and justified by the badge."

"Then why would you take the Fifth Amendment?" Michael's eyes were full of judgment. He saw everything in terms of bad or good, right or wrong. It's why I think he loved those video games. There wasn't any gray in those electronic worlds. Good guys got bad guys. The more you killed, the higher your score.

"Because not everyone sees things the same. What one person believes is okay, another doesn't. That's kind of how our jury system works. It allows twelve average people to decide what is good or bad for our city or country."

"Daddy. I think you should tell the truth," Donna interjected.

"Do you Pumpkin?"

"You're not a ham sandwich. No one will blame you for doing the right thing."

Even Jan had to smile at that one. It was something I said to the kids at least once a week. She'd repeated that back to me exactly. Kids. You had to appreciate their wisdom.

"You're right, Donna. You're one hundred percent right."

24

Casey

January 31, 2006

Marc Baldwin had taken my suggestion. He walked through the halls of the Justice Center in full dress uniform. It was a fantastic display of authority. If the situation hadn't been so serious, I would have clapped my hands with glee. I was two for two in the client appearance game. They were finally listening to me.

"We're scheduled for four o'clock. You're the last witness," I announced in lieu of a greeting.

"Why last?"

"To give the appearance of fairness," I said. It was my best guess. None of my clients had ever been invited to give testimony before their indictment. I always met them after they had that damning piece of paper in their hands. Baldwin was getting the top shelf treatment afforded to few others. I didn't say any of that, of course. He would not be grateful for the special consideration.

"I made a decision last night," Baldwin announced while tucking his hat under his left arm.

"What did you decide?" Client decisions were never good. I was about to be ambushed. As best I could, I braced myself.

"I'm not taking the Fifth. My nine-year-old daughter—her name is Donna. Did I tell you that? My older one is Michael. They're in third and sixth grade at St. Raphael. My Donna said that 'no one will blame you for doing the right thing.' I did the right thing back there in that alley that night. All this second guessing is after the fact. Not one of the people standing in judgment has been in uniform. Been scared for their life. Been in a dark alley facing 'them or me' decisions."

"You understand the implications?" I asked, though I knew he couldn't. Clients believed in the justice system at the most inopportune times. "You need to understand that if your testimony puts you in the cross hairs of the law, there's little I can do to protect you."

"That was my mistake from the beginning. Thinking I needed anyone's protection."

I cursed myself for the way I'd handled things yesterday. Maybe I'd been way too ra-ra about his chances of prevailing. I'd tried taking a page from the playbook of the big name lawyers in town who always told their clients they were going to win, no matter how improbable that was. I'd gone from confident to swagger. It was about to bite me in the ass. The door marked by the grand jury sign at the end of the hall, opened.

"We're ready for you Sergeant Baldwin," a voice said from behind the door. The prosecutor emerged. It was Nicole Long, the prosecutor I'd encountered on one of Jarrod Carter's two cases last year. I'd won the case against her, probably knocking her ninety-eight percent win ratio down to ninety-seven.

"Ms. Long." I didn't extend my hand.

"Ms. Cort." She didn't either. "Do you understand your role here today?"

"Observation only," I said. The prosecutor I'd spoken with on the phone yesterday when Baldwin had been in my office had hit hard on that fact quite a few times in the ten-minute call.

"Come in, then."

I walked into a room I'd never seen before, and would probably never see again. For all the power the people in there wielded, the room was seriously unremarkable. I'm not sure what I expected from the bland 1970s building, but this wasn't it. Nine nondescript folks from the county sat in padded chairs surrounding a white melamine table. A tiny sprite of a court reporter sat in the corner, the little stenotype machine braced between her legs.

They wore badges that probably got them by security, but little else. Maybe a free lunch too.

Long turned to the jurors. Like obedient students in a classroom, they swiveled their faces to her.

"Marc Baldwin is our last witness in this case. He's here to answer any questions you may have about the Troy Duncan shooting. I have to inform you that any conversations he's had with his attorney, Ms. Cort there, are confidential. You can't ask him what he told her or what she told him. Let's swear Mr. Baldwin in."

Baldwin took an empty seat at the front of the room. A clerk asked Baldwin to raise his right hand. I watched yet another client swear to tell the truth all the time wondering if they'd hold true to the promise.

"Please introduce yourself," Long said. "Tell us where you work and your rank."

Baldwin spoke and spelled his name for the record. "I'm a Sergeant in the Cleveland Police Department."

"How long have you worked for the CPD?"

"Twenty-two years."

"Have you appeared before a Grand Jury before?"

"Yes. No. Not as the defendant. I've testified trying to get someone indicted."

"Sergeant Baldwin. There's no need to hurry. You can take the time to think about your answers. Now, do you know any of the nine jurors here today?"

Baldwin took a hard look around the room, meeting the eyes of several people in the room. "No. Not a one."

"What's your work status right now?"

"I'm on administrative leave pending the outcome of the department's investigation of this case."

"Did you come here voluntarily today? Is anyone forcing you to testify before the grand jury?"

"Nope. I'm here to tell the truth."

"And you understand that you can consult with your attorney at any time. Just ask and we'll stop the proceedings so you two can have a discussion outside. Okay?"

Baldwin nodded in such a way that I knew he wouldn't take that offer. Cocky cop confidence.

"Everyone knows why we're here today in this unusual circumstance, so let's get to it," Long said to the group. They nodded with familiarity. "Were you working in your capacity as a Cleveland police officer on the evening of December twenty-eighth?"

"Yes I was. Darlene Webb and I—my partner and I—were working the second shift."

"How long is that?"

"Three to eleven."

"Did anything unusual happen in the first hours of your shift?"

"Nothing out of the ordinary. More domestic disturbances than usual, because of the holidays and more people being off work, but less other call outs. Too cold for the snatch and grab." Baldwin smiled at the group. A couple of jurors nodded in acknowledgment. The rest sat stone-faced.

"What brought you to the area near the flats that day?"

"Domestic abuse call from the Bradley building on West Sixth."

"Did you make an arrest?"

"Nah. The guy didn't live there. We suggested he go home and that the woman who was on the lease lock the doors. He didn't have a key."

"What was your next call?"

"Right after we got downstairs and back in the car, dispatch radioed there was a complaint of drug activity in the alley that ran behind West Tenth Street. I was driving, so Darlene said we'd take the call."

"What time did you get to the Flats?"

"Twenty-about eight forty-five. It was less than five minutes from the loft."

"Were you dressed like you are today?"

"No. Not the dress blues. I was wearing the standard uniform, navy shirt and pants. In the winter, we can wear a ski cap instead of the peaked cap, so I had that on. I also had on a department issue winter coat and. It was maybe thirty degrees outside."

"Are your coat and hat clearly marked?"

"They all have the triangle shaped patch with gold lettering that mark us as police officers."

"What kind of car were you driving?"

"Police interceptor."

"Is that the well marked black and white vehicle people would be familiar seeing around Cleveland?"

"Yes."

"Did you drive that car to the alley?"

"No. I told Darlene to park on the street. If you show up in an alley with lights and sirens, the druggies will scatter like rats. You can't arrest anyone, and they come back the minute you pull away. I approached on foot in order to investigate the level of crime, and possibly make an arrest of the dealer."

I watched the interplay closely. Baldwin was good. The years of testifying in court served him well now. I wished half my clients were this practiced and comfortable. Even when they were truthful, many came off as liars.

"Were you fully armed that day?" Long said after consulting her yellow legal pad, flipping through a few pages, then flipping it to the front again. "Let me ask that another way. What did you have on you?"

"On my belt, I have my weapon, an extra magazine, a stun gun, cuffs, a night stick, and my radio. The radio has a hand mic that's pinned to my right shoulder."

"Were you wearing an ear piece?"

"It's not required. No."

"How did you approach the alley?"

"I came around from Front Avenue. Between the underpass, empty buildings, and the train tracks, there are a lot of places for people to hide in that area. I came from the side that gave me a ready exit in case I came upon a situation that was unsafe.

"What would you consider unsafe?"

"If they had greater firepower than the two of us. We'd need backup if something like that happened."

"What did you see?"

"The alley was dark. I saw what looked like a clump of people. A couple of dumpsters were back there. There were also back doors to the businesses, but none of them were open."

"The doors or the businesses."

"The doors. Sorry. From our drive by the front, it looked like most businesses were open. Some were more busy than others. The restaurant in front...Spencer's if I remember correctly...had a lot of lights on, but not a lot of people inside."

"What happened when you approached the alley alone?"

"I saw a group of people, like I said, kind of huddled around the dumpster. I thought it might be smokers, but dismissed that because it was freezing cold, and I didn't see any of the glowing tips you usually see when smokers are around."

"What happened next?"

"I yelled to them that I was the police, that they needed to come out. Most of them ran away."

"Did you alert your partner to chase the ones who fled?"

"There wasn't time, because one man didn't run. Instead, he approached me quickly, in an intimidating manner."

"Did you identify yourself or tell him to stop?"

"I did. Several times. I said 'Stop' and 'Police' a few times, but he didn't stop."

"Did you unholster your weapon?"

"I did and ordered him to stop again. He continued approaching. I noticed he had what looked like a short barrel shotgun under his arm. Then he reached his hand into his pocket. Assuming he was going for a weapon, I pulled the trigger."

"Did you have to move the safety or anything?" One juror, an older white woman asked.

"The Glock doesn't have a safety."

"Is that a special police gun?"

"No. But a lot of departments use it. The trigger has a little harder pull than the other Glocks."

"What was the guy wearing?" was the woman's follow up question.

"All black, or something almost as dark," Baldwin answered. He nodded his head like he was confirming what he remembered. "His jacket was black. He had his hood over his head. His pants were dark too."

Nicole Long cast her eye over the jurors. When no one asked any further questions, she looked down at her notes.

"To circle back, you're in the alley behind the buildings on West Tenth Street. Troy Duncan is approaching you with his hand in his pocket."

"Right, so I tell him to stop. He doesn't. I aimed my service weapon and fired."

"Where did you aim?"

"In the academy, we're trained to aim for the largest part of the body we can see. For him, it was his torso."

"Where did the bullet hit him?"

"I think his gut or maybe a little bit lower. Shooting at a moving target is harder than it looks on TV." Baldwin's small smile at his joke didn't land. If we'd been in a regular courtroom, I'd have kicked him under counsel table.

"Did he fall to the ground?"

"Yes. Right away. With the threat gone, I radioed for my partner."

"Did she come right away?"

"She drove around the corner and parked a few feet from the perp. I asked her to radio for backup, to tell them that we had a shots fired/man down call. She did."

"How many shots did you fire?"

"One, maybe two. He was close, and coming at me, and I just wanted to make him stop if he wasn't going to obey."

"And it was him coming at you, and reaching in his pocket that made you think you had to shoot him?"

"Him moving aggressively, looking mean and menacing, and reaching for something that could have been a weapon is what made the difference between me using other methods to subdue him and me being authorized to use force."

"Did an ambulance eventually come?"

"Yes."

"Did you have any interaction with the EMTs?"

"I did run over to the ambulance to check on the perp. They let me know he was alive. They did some stuff to him, like cut off his clothes, and put a collar around his neck. Then they drove off."

"Did you talk to anyone after that?"

"I gave the CPD brass on the scene a rundown of what happened. They directed me to go back to the station so I could make a written statement while my memory was fresh."

"Thank you, Sergeant Baldwin. Do the jurors have any questions?"

"Have you ever had any other incident that may be considered excessive force?"

Sweat prickled my skin: on my neck, under my arms, between my breasts. A room that had been cool a moment before heated up. At that moment, I wanted to kick myself ten times over. I was learning to be a better lawyer. But I wasn't learning fast enough. For all the questions I'd learned to ask clients, children they didn't mention, felony convictions they'd forgotten, I'd never asked the one question a grand juror had thought to ask after knowing him for all of an hour.

Silence hung heavy in the room. Baldwin shifted in his chair. I was in this room as a courtesy, so I didn't pull the itchy wool collar of my suit jacket away from my neck. One wrong turn on my part and I was toast. I glared at Baldwin the best I could without looking like I was signaling to him. After his eyes swiveled everywhere, they finally connected with mine. I gave a slight tilt to my head, jerking it toward the door on the left. He needed to tell Long if he wanted out. If he needed consultation with his attorney. Now was the time to do it.

Baldwin broke our stare. Damn. Damn. Damn. He looked at the juror head on.

"Yes. I was cited for one other instance of excessive force."

Long bent her neck from one side to the other then looked at the juror who'd asked the bombshell question.

"What happened in that case?" the juror continued.

Baldwin didn't meet anyone's eyes then. I wanted to think it was because he was dredging up the far past, not because he was about to lay something heavy on all of us.

"There was an officer-involved shooting on the eastside early in my career. I think it was nineteen eighty-five or thereabouts."

Baldwin stopped speaking, failing to elaborate further.

"What happened in nineteen eighty-five?" another juror finally asked. From all the chair rolling and seat shifting, she wasn't the only person who was waiting for an answer. I bowed my head ready to listen. But I kept my neck bent and eyes lowered because I wasn't sure I was ready to control my reaction to whatever story he was going to tell.

"My partner and I were patrolling. We were on Outhwaite Avenue when we got a call that an armed man had just robbed a Rib King. It's a local fast food restaurant on Woodland between East Fifty-fifth and East Fifty-ninth. At that time, a lot of the local drug and crime activity came from folks living in CMHA housing. The King-Kennedy towers were right around the corner.

King-Kennedy was Cleveland's answer to Cabrini Green.

"We turned right, heading southbound on Fifty-ninth to try to intercept the suspect. Before we could get to Woodland a man ambushed us from Halnorth Court. We pulled up to block the street and saw a man running toward us. It scared the crap out of me. Up until then, I'd been on the job all of two years and no suspect had ever run right at me. Run away, sure, run at me? Never.

"This guy keeps coming, and he's got his hand at his waist. My partner shouts that he's probably the suspect. He fit the description. Black man, medium height, black jacket. Crack junkies and drug dealers were a huge problem at that time. I figured he was a junky who'd robbed Rib King to support his habit. There were so many of those back then, junkies, not Rib Kings."

The jurors didn't laugh at Baldwin's joke. The only people who told jokes in court were judges. My client had to know that. Silent as a statue I sat.

He continued. "Anyway, seeing a big man drugged out of his mind running at me had me pulling my weapon. My partner jumped out of the passenger side of the car. Right then I heard shots and fearing for my life and that of my partner, I shot at Blount. That was the guy's name Marcellus Blount. He was pronounced dead at the scene."

"Where was the excessive force?"

"There wasn't any, really. But the *Plain Dealer* called it that. A couple of things happened that turned that case against us. For one the Supreme Court came down with a ruling that no longer allowed cops to shoot fleeing suspects. It wasn't exactly what happened to us, but the department was on high alert about the shooting of felony suspects. The second thing was that Blount wasn't the guy who robbed the rib place. He fit the description. Some people said later that he had been out running. The thing he was messing with at his waist was a black clip on Walkman. The shots I'd heard fired were from my partner and not the suspect."

"Were charges filed?"

"Nope. An officer who has a reasonable fear of death or imminent bodily harm isn't guilty of wrongdoing. My partner and I were on leave for about a week before we were cleared for duty. Department brass said the shooting was justified. But...the department did stick a disciplinary note in my file for a couple of things I did that didn't follow procedure."

Not a chair moved. Everyone was still for a long moment before Long walked back and forth across the room, laying her legal pad on a table.

"Any other questions about the *Troy Duncan* shooting?" she prompted the grand jury.

The sea of heads shook back and forth.

"Thank you, Sergeant Baldwin for your honest and forthcoming testimony today. You're excused."

Taking the cue, I leapt to my feet, grabbed my bag and my client, and herded us out the door as fast at my Cuban heels would take us.

"What the fuck was that? I asked you no less than ten times if there was anything that might impact your case. You told me a lot of shit, but Marcellus Blount wasn't in there."

"It was an open and shut case. Did you see any of that in my record?"

"There was a note about you discharging your weapon in June of eighty-five, that's all"

"That would be it."

"Killing an unarmed man on the streets of Cleveland more than once is worlds away from a weapons discharge."

Baldwin shrugged. I was standing next to a man who'd killed two different people, at least, and all he could do was shrug. I wanted to kick him hard in the shins. Maybe then he'd feel a tiny sliver of the pain he'd heaped on others.

"I have to get going. I have other cases to work on," I said moving down the hall at a pretty fast clip.

His long legs ate up the distance. I was unable to outpace him in the carpeted hallway of the Justice Center.

"When will the grand jury issue a decision?"

"Could be anytime," I said as I jabbed at the elevator button. I hated the ancient elevators. They moved at a snail's pace, and nearly half the time they were filled to capacity. It could take a good fifteen minutes to get up or downstairs in this building. Today I was not looking forward to that wait. I wanted to be as far away from this killer as possible.

25

Casey

February 3, 2006

"Are you scared?"

After Baldwin's testimony, I was hellishly scared of a run-in with the CPD, and I wasn't a black man in Cleveland. I have no idea how Miles' mother ever let him leave the house. If he were my son, I'd have locked him in his room forever.

"Of what? You? Commitment? A riot?" Miles stood on the inside of my front door, the buttons of his black anorak undone, but the zipper was still zipped. He was half smiling. I definitely was not.

"Of being shot. Of fitting the profile. Of being in the wrong place at the wrong time?" I tucked my shaking hands into the kangaroo pocket of my OSU sweatshirt. Miles sighed, unzipping his coat slowly. He took his time lifting the messenger bag strap over his head, then hanging the heavy wool garment on the coat rack by the door. He even stopped to pet Simba, who twirled between his legs.

"What happened, Casey?"

"He did it before." From Miles' slow blink, I knew I didn't need to name my client. "The kid's name was Marcellus Blount. He was jogging. Baldwin and his partner thought his Walkman was a gun. Or they said that. Who knows what they thought?"

I tried, but I couldn't stop myself from talking.

"Do you know my parents bought me a Walkman for my fourteenth birthday? I listened to music on it every day on my way to and from school. Never did I worry about a cop mistaking it for a gun and getting shot because of that mistake or the cops not being charged with anything if they mistakenly killed me."

Miles stepped forward and wrapped cold arms around me. I didn't care because I was already cold to my bones.

"You've got to stop doing this," I said into his chest.

"Doing what?" He was stroking my hair in a way that was distracting me from the hearing, his unannounced visit. I stepped back, putting needed space between us.

"Showing up. You have a phone. It never leaves your right hand. Use it."

Self-conscious, Miles shoved his Blackberry deeper into the pocket of his slacks.

"Would you let me in if I called?"

"Probably not." That was a lie. But I needed some plausible deniability.

"That's why I didn't call."

"You're here. Now what?" I asked. This circular discussion about protocol wasn't going anywhere. I stepped out of his embrace.

"Did you see that group of protestors?"

"The ones I had to wade through to get to my train the other day? Those people?"

"Despite the winter weather, or maybe because of its unseasonable warmth, the protestors are still out there. I came here because I'm worried about you. I don't know what will happen to the city if Baldwin isn't indicted. That Marcellus Blount kid was on a protestor's sign. His name and picture and a long list of others who were killed by police without any kind of charges being brought against the cops. If someone links Blount and Baldwin, I think that could be the match on the powder keg."

"Crap." That didn't sound good. I wasn't naive enough to think there wasn't a breaking point. I feared this was it.

I unearthed the remote from its hiding place under the cat, and flipped the TV on. The anchors at Channel Five were hard at work. It was one special report after another these days.

"Police in riot gear have surrounded Public Square," the anchor said. "City officials are trying to calm the crowd before a riot breaks out. Our man Rick McDaniel is on the scene. Rick?"

Rick stood outside a group of protestors. I only half wondered where in the hell he'd gotten a flak jacket. It was a most excellent prop, but overkill for downtown Cleveland.

"It's chaos here. On Tuesday police officers Darlene Webb and Marc Baldwin appeared before the Cuyahoga County Grand Jury to answer for their role in the Troy Duncan shooting."

Tape rolled showing Darlene and her police union lawyers leaving earlier on Tuesday morning. It switched to me trying to hustle Baldwin through the crowd. I hadn't thought to order a car as a way to safeguard us. Fortunately, a few of his police buddies had planned ahead. The tape ended with Marc and another officer shoving me into a large black and white SUV before lights, sirens, and the threat of bodily harm dispersed the angry mob enough to drive.

"When will the grand jury reach a decision, Rick?"

"A spokeswoman for Lori Pope and the Cuyahoga County Prosecutor's Office have told us that Sergeant Marc Baldwin was the last witness to testify. The grand jury will either indict or send down a no bill in the next few days. Our legal experts say it will probably be Monday."

"Thanks Rick. We will be sure to alert viewers as soon as a decision comes down."

I hit mute. My eyes met Miles'.

"That's hairy," I said. I'd kind of thought the crowd would go away once we'd left. The fact that they were lingering three days later and well past sunset made me a little bit worried, not so much for myself, but for the city. Lightening my case load had meant I'd been working from home for the last couple of days and not sitting in my office on Public Square. I'd gone home. I'd wrongly assumed everyone else had done the same, to try to occupy themselves until the grand jury made a decision.

"It's only liable to get hairier." Miles' voice was ominous.

"Spill it," I snapped. I didn't have time for guessing games.

It was a true testament that Miles only hesitated a second. Maybe he was maturing.

"The Department of Justice is opening an investigation into the Duncan shooting."

"Because the attorney general thinks the grand jury is going to hand down a no bill."

"Don't you?"

"If Baldwin were any other client, I'd say the chances were ninety-nine percent in favor of indictment. Ham sandwich theory and all that. But for Baldwin I'd say the odds are fifty-fifty."

"This case is on the DOJ's radar now," Miles said as if that changed the fundamentals of the equation.

"Because of the potential for a rust belt riot?" I asked using the term Channel Five had coined.

"Because Reverent Wilkinson was in D.C. last week pleading the Duncans' case."

"Are you going to tell them about the videotape?" I couldn't see a way that I'd be disbarred for withholding it. Technically I hadn't even withheld it yet. But I was quickly running out of time before I'd be required to turn over my discovery. If the tape got out after that deadline, I'd be tried and convicted in the headlines, if not the courts.

"I'm not on the case. Rachel Schaefer is. She has the plum assignment of being the local attorney. She's going to work hand in hand with the Civil Rights Division's Special Litigation Section."

I only nodded. I had not been the biggest fan of Schaefer. She was the kind of attorney I'd grown to hate—a true believer. She saw cases in black and white, win or lose. She wanted to put every black hat behind bars then swan around in her white one.

"Toledo got me a better caliber of cases," Miles said. "But I don't think Chas is ready to let me partner on this one."

"And of course, you can't share the progress of an ongoing investigation."

"Of course. But the AG will hold a press conference with the U.S. Attorney and make the announcement tomorrow."

"Thanks for telling me what you could at least. Will my client get a target letter?"

"Probably not. I've asked Lou Valdespino to keep an eye out for you." He'd changed the subject so fast I was surprised I hadn't gotten whiplash.

"For me? I haven't shot anyone." I was more afraid for Miles than I was for myself.

"But you're representing someone who did. After a decision comes down, everyone in Cleveland will know who you are, and a lot of people won't like it."

"I'm unlisted. The Ohio Supreme Court only has my Illuminating Company Building address."

"You take the train and walk home. You're becoming a public figure who's always out in public. That makes you vulnerable. I'd encourage you to drive more, but that car breaking down in the middle of nowhere would be even worse."

"Thanks. I guess." I didn't call him out for trying to protect me on the one hand and insulting my shitbox car on the other.

Miles stood in my doorway. He shifted from foot to foot. I'd always talked way too much, which had done me no favors in life, so I didn't say a damned thing. I waited.

"I have something I want to say to you."

I didn't tell him how unsurprising that was. That he'd had all the telltale signs of a man with something on his mind from the moment he'd stepped over the threshold.

"I think we should get back together."

The funny thing is, I didn't see *that* coming. Probably there were a hundred signs, starting with him showing up to my apartment unannounced, and the sex we definitely shouldn't have had. But I was as shocked as the time this happened a year and a half ago with Tom Brody.

"So this is my life," I said to myself more than him. "Dump me. Get back together. Please tell me you don't want me to be your beard."

"God no, Casey. I'd say that our chemistry is solid."

I turned toward the windows. Anything to take a breath, a moment away from the reality of Miles. I didn't want to want him. But I did. I wanted to grab hold of the promise in his eyes with both hands and never let go. I resisted the temptation. Because I know how this ended. How many times did I have to face this same damn decision? They said that the definition of crazy was doing the same thing over and over, but expecting a different result.

I wasn't crazy.

Not a single bit.

"Please go home, Miles."

"Is that a yes or a no?"

"We're on opposite sides of a case."

"Unless one of us makes a career change, we'll always be on opposite sides during the day. But I want us to be on the same side at night."

I looked into his brown eyes. I could fall into them. I hadn't been lying when I told him he was hot. From his tan skin, to his curly hair, to...well...to the rest of him, I was attracted like iron filings to a magnet. But I wasn't as dumb as a handful of metal shavings.

"Go home," I said.

"Casey?"

"Later. We can talk about this later. You really hurt me last year. You can't just talk or kiss your way out of that."

"Gotcha."

"I think I need to work tonight. Figure out how to get my client out of the ten different jams he's in. This. You. It's all too much now.

"Okay?

"Later. Not now."

26

Augustus

February 4, 2006

Dinwiddie's diminutive size did not make our small living room look any larger. The small man shifted impatiently from foot to foot.

"Do you want a cup of coffee or tea?" Myrtle asked from the dining alcove, where she was sipping at her morning cup of caffeine. It had been years since my wife used coffee and tea to wake herself up in the morning. When the boys had been old enough to put themselves to sleep and set an alarm, I'd gotten my wife back. She'd started spending more evening time with me, and had stopped getting up groggy and disoriented.

My gentle, soft-spoken wife was gone—again. Tragedy had stolen her sleep. I hadn't said anything about strong black tea graduating to three cups of coffee, because the alternative was a wife who couldn't get out of bed.

"Thank you, but there's no time. You all will need to change so that we can go downtown. Where's Campbell or Lynell and the kids?"

I did nothing to disguise my yawn. "It's Saturday morning. I have no idea where anyone is." Life getting back to normal meant not everyone being all up under my feet.

"The grand jury's decision is coming this morning," Dinwiddie said, his tone ominous.

Both Myrtle and I stopped in our tracks. Her coffee cup hit the saucer with excessive force. My feet were rooted to the floor.

"It's Saturday. The government is closed on Saturday." I'd woken up this morning rooted in the belief that I had two days off from nail-biting worry about whether we could expect any justice for Troy.

"Mayor Gates and Lori Pope both had their offices call my emergency number. The warmer weather has kept folks outside. They think waiting until Monday is a mistake. Tensions are close to boiling over.

"They should be," I said unapologetically. "Why should we come? I'm sure you can call us to let us know what happened. I'm not sure I need to be there if they don't indict." I didn't think I had it in me to be stoic and accepting in public if this whole thing went the wrong way. The crying blubbering mess that I could turn into, like the day in the alley, wasn't something I wanted to do in public.

"Our grief is not entertainment."

"It might diffuse things." The lawyer had the good grace to wince.

I rested my hands on the piano and brought myself up to full height.

"Let me get this straight. Mayor Gates, who controls the police department whose officer shot my son, and Prosecutor Pope who oversees the county criminal system, that let my innocent son die a painful death, want me to do *them* a favor? You've got to be kidding me. Why would you bring this to me?"

"I…uh…as a lawyer I'm required to relay all information to you." Dinwiddie was backpedaling hard but not hard enough.

"Or are you doing this to get your name out there. The great Dinwiddie who took our case pro bono needs to get out in front of the crowd so that all future paying business comes your way. Or is it because you're cronies with all of these people. Having lunch and dinner or golf with them, while the rest of us do everything we can to stay out of a system that treats us as disposable?"

"Gus. Stop." Myrtle's voice pierced my haze of anger cutting me off before I said something I'd regret. She was right to stop me. I'd worked hard over the years to turn off the part of my brain that saw racism around every corner. It would give me an ulcer and kill me dead before fifty, Myrtle had said. So I'd worked on being one of those jovial guys who acted like I didn't have a care in the world. I hadn't been able to keep the act up over the last month, though.

My wife's words were the only thing that kept me from picking up and tossing the attorney out into the cold.

"Who riots in the winter anyway?" I'd been out to get the paper. It wasn't cold as a witch's tit out there, but I didn't want to pitch a tent either. A predicted high of fifty degrees wasn't exactly rioting weather. Not like July of 1966.

"You saw that story in the paper on Wednesday, right?"

Who hadn't seen it? It was a full two-page feature with pictures of unarmed blacks who'd been shot by police in

Cleveland and Cuyahoga County. It talked about how the timing was right for a department of justice probe into police conduct in the city. The tiny twinge of joy I'd felt at the tables being turned died quickly when a follow-up story detailed how Baldwin had shot another man.

"Saw the Thursday one as well. He shot and killed another man twenty years ago, and they saw fit to put him back on the street. The police chief called it a 'rookie mistake.' That's one hell of a mistake." To think some higher up in the CPD could have pulled the pin on a guy who'd go on to kill again. That my son's needless suffering and death could have been prevented.

"How about a compromise?" Dinwiddie had started to sweat. He took a moment to unwind his gray plaid scarf from his neck.

"What are you suggesting?" Myrtle asked, ever the peacemaker.

"Whether you like it or not, the jury for your case against the city and county is out there. They're watching television and forming judgments as we speak. Money may not be important to you now. Money will not replace your son. I get that. But it can pay for college and get your grandkids off to a good start. Troy would have wanted that for them."

"Don't you presume to know what Troy would have wanted. I bet you if you asked, Troy would have wanted to live to see his kids reach college age more than just the paying for it."

"Sorry. What I'm saying is that you talking to reporters after the decision is handed down, no matter which way it goes, will help keep your son's memory alive. It will keep the issue of police brutality out front and center."

"Fine." I hadn't lost all sense of civic responsibility. "What's your proposal?"

"I'll arrange a press conference at my office. I have a large space on the first floor. We'll set it for twelve-thirty."

"What are we supposed to say?" I swung a finger between myself and Myrtle.

"That we will continue to seek justice through that state and federal courts. That we will not rest until justice is done for Troy Duncan, his family, and other victims of excessive force at the hands of the police."

"You don't think they're going to indict Baldwin, do you?" Myrtle asked. She had always been impervious to hyperbole.

"I did some research. A police officer has never been indicted in Cleveland," he said. "Not for something like this."

I don't know why that took me by surprise, but it did. "Surely it must have happened once?" I blurted.

"Does it matter?" Dinwiddie hung his head and shook. "Some things haven't changed from plantation days."

"Give us half an hour. We'll be ready to go."

The Italian pastries I'd grown to love since I moved to Cleveland sat untouched on the conference room table. I couldn't bring myself to enjoy something as decadent as sugar and sweet cheese when my son could never again have a *sfogliatella.* While we ignored the food and coffee, Dinwiddie's assistant had come into the room with a cart outfitted with a large television. I drummed my fingers on the table as she fiddled with plugs and wires. At ten-fifty sharp, she pressed a few buttons and the screen came to life.

"We're interrupting your regularly scheduled program with a special report. Cuyahoga County prosecuting attorney Lorraine Pope is scheduled to speak at the Justice Center in ten minutes' time."

The screen showed an empty podium in front of the ugly iron sculpture next to the 1970s era courthouse. There were dozens of microphones affixed to the wood. Wind blew across the mics filling my head with white noise.

"A press conference from the prosecutor on a weekend is an unusual move," the anchorwoman said. "The press secretaries for the city and county director of communications have said that they want to announce the grand jury's decision today. They hope to diffuse tension that could build over the weekend."

"Our man on the street, Rick McDaniel is live at the Justice Center," her co-anchor said. "Rick?"

"Thanks. Rick McDaniel, here. I'm standing outside the Cuyahoga County Justice Center in downtown Cleveland. County Prosecutor Lorraine Pope will come to the podium in about five minutes.

"To recap, she's going to announce the decision of the grand jury in the investigation into Troy Duncan's shooting by Cleveland police officer Marc Baldwin. There are two possible ways they could come down in this case. First, the grand jury can move to indict Marc Baldwin. The likely charges include murder, manslaughter, or even assault with a deadly weapon. He would then be arraigned in Common Pleas court where a judge would set bail.

"The grand jury could also issue what they call a no bill. In that case, there would be no charges. That doesn't mean the police officer would be out of hot water. The Attorney General, U.S. Attorney for Ohio's Northern District, and Department of Justice have opened their own investigation into the shooting."

The camera panned to the left of McDaniel while officials lined up behind the podium.

"Mayor Gates and Lori Pope have come to the podium."

"Good Morning. I am Lorraine Pope, the Prosecuting Attorney for Cuyahoga County, Ohio, which includes the city of Cleveland in its jurisdiction."

The prosecutor was reading from a prepared script. She was dressed in a cream-colored wool coat. Her leather gloved hands gripped either side of the podium. I wondered how many hours she'd had the grand jury's decision in her hands.

"When I ran for office," she continued, "I traveled throughout the county and listened to what the honest hardworking citizens of this city and surrounding municipalities had to say. What you want is less crime in your neighborhoods. You want to be able to travel to our downtown destinations without fear. You want the police to work with you to keep your communities safe.

"Our office takes all crimes and shootings seriously. That's why we presented this matter to the grand jury. The decision to indict or not is not up to me or any individual prosecutor. It's up to the grand jury, nine of your fellow citizens who share your values.

"Before I announce the decision, I ask you to remain peaceful. Demonstrations in this city require a permit. Mayor Gates has informed me that no permits have been granted for any protests this weekend. Please stay home if you're there. If you're not working, please return to your homes. The Cleveland Police will enforce a curfew if necessary."

Boos from bystanders drowned out anything else Pope said. It took a good five minutes before the crowd was sufficiently quiet that she could continue.

"The Cuyahoga County grand jury assigned to investigate the shooting of Troy Duncan by Sergeant Marc Baldwin, in the line of duty, has reached a decision."

A man in a dress coat and gloves, handed a single piece of paper to Pope. It flapped in the breeze making it hard for Pope to grasp. When she finally did, she placed the paper on the wood and scanned it as if she didn't already know what it said.

"The grand jury has issued a no bill. Marc Baldwin will not be indicted."

The words "No Bill" flashed across the screen. The diagonal tilt of the words and the bright red color reminded me of a game show.

Even though I had known it was coming. Even though I'd expected nothing from the same county that killed my son, the little bit of hope, I'd had was snuffed out like a candle. Myrtle's soft hand enveloped mine. I looked down at our hands. The brown skin we shared, that we had passed on to Troy, had signed his death warrant.

This time the uproar was longer than the last. News cameras panned past the huddle of reporters to the mostly black and brown crowd spilling from the quadrangle of justice center buildings. Signs were held high. Some had Troy's driver's license photo. Others had a picture I'd never seen before, maybe from one of his cooking jobs. Still more read, "no justice, no peace," and "we have families too."

The moment was truly surreal. It was likely I didn't have enough fingers and toes to count the number of times I'd seen this exact scene play out on television. Never did I think I'd have any relationship to something like this. What no reporter ever told you was how truly horrifying it was to realize your child's life was of little to no consequence when it came down to it.

"At this time, I'm sure you understand, Sergeant Baldwin, his wife, and his children would like to be allowed to recover from this difficult period in peace."

Difficult? I couldn't believe she'd used that word. What could have been difficult for Baldwin? He'd gotten to go to a warm home with his wife and two living children. He would not go to bed fearful of rioters breaking down his doors or police officers shooting his children. From over here, I was thinking Baldwin was as fear-free as one could get.

After Pope left the impromptu stage, Police Chief McCormick and Mayor Gates took to the mics. I didn't listen because it didn't matter what they said. Gates and McCormick would spout platitudes about fairness and justice and process. But it was a system that was only a one-way street for the majority of us.

"It's time to go downstairs." Dinwiddie's assistant escorted us to a big room I'd not seen when we'd come here before. I remembered that he owned the building though. Black men owning commercial real estate was the stuff of legend in Cleveland. It was one of the reasons I'd come to him. I admired a man who reinvested in the community that grew him.

The room was big. Rows of folding chairs looking like they'd been borrowed from the church down the street lined up like soldiers. The assistant sat us on one side of the dais, microphones poised at chin level. As if we would have anything to say, Myrtle and I.

Efficient and experienced, the lawyer's assistant placed small cups of water between us. When I looked up, the room had started to fill. Reporters and producers plugged wires into a console off to the left.

Dinwiddie tapped into the microphone. Ten minutes later, at exactly twelve-thirty on the dot, he rose to speak.

"What we've witnessed today is a travesty of justice. But could we expect any less in light of the current decisions that have come down from the highest court in the land.

"I'm sure Marc Baldwin will tell you that he had a reasonable fear for his safety. But the only basis for that fear was that Troy Duncan was a black man. It wasn't because he was a chef or a father. I was because he was a man who fit a certain profile, plain and simple.

"One hundred thirty years after the end of slavery, fifty years after the end of Jim Crow, here we are no farther than we were those long years ago when the new hope of Reconstruction beckoned. Time and again these hopes have been dashed at the end of a cop's gun. Neither the Duncans nor I will rest until justice is served."

The murmurs of "amen" from the back of the room mingled with whirring camera hand held recorders.

"Mr. Dinwiddie, what's the status of your lawsuit?"

"It was put on hold because of the Grand Jury investigation. We will be pressing forward seeking the justice from the federal court we couldn't get from the county or state."

"Mr. Duncan? Were you surprised by today's decision?"

"Sadly, no. I grew up in Alabama, where white men could kill black men with impunity. I'd hoped when I relocated to Cleveland, my family would be free from that kind of arbitrary justice."

The room was silent for a long second. I wasn't going to be that parent you saw crying on TV or that inarticulate mother you only felt half-sorry for. For better or worse, I was failingly honest and straightforward like I'd taught my boys.

Moment of truth passing, the ruckus of raised hands, shifting sheets, and clicking cameras started up again.

Dinwiddie took a few more questions, but I tuned out both questions and answers. There was no more for me here. This, the rest, was all grandstanding and spectacle.

A shift in the air around me had me turn away from the sea of faces and toward Myrtle. Silent tears streaked down her cheeks. I vowed that minute, this would be the last time we'd be on display. There may be no justice, there may be no peace, but at my house, some things needed to be put to rest.

I stood pulling my wife up with me. I wrapped my arms around her as best I could and walked away from the cameras and microphones. None of this was going to bring back Troy.

27

Marc

February 4, 2006

I slipped into my usual spot in the U-shaped booth. Reluctantly, the guys shifted to give me a little room.

"Have you ordered?"

Silence. I looked at the guys. I'd been eating with more or less the same group, Harry Larson, Roman Ford, and Alden Croft for about a decade. Neither Harry, Roman, nor Alden met my eyes.

"Ah, geez, guys. I know it's been a month, but I had to keep my head down, Captain's orders."

"Do you think you should be here?" Ford asked.

"They got a TV way bigger than the one at my house."

"Why aren't you downtown with your lawyer?" Larson pressed for an answer.

"The way you guys are acting I'm starting to think you don't want me here." I threw up my hands in surrender.

"No, that's not it. It's just—"

"Harry's wife cut off his balls ten years ago," Croft interjected. "What he can't spit out is you seem awful calm for someone with an indictment hanging over your head."

"There ain't *shit* hanging over my head. Watch." To the hostess I yelled, "Turn it up will you?"

Everyone in the diner stopped talking when the TV sound went up. Even the waitress who dropped my breakfast in front of me, barely made a sound.

"This is what I'm talking about," I said to myself. Loved Jan, but she couldn't cook worth a lick. The folks back in the kitchen could do a number on food. I tucked into eggs and biscuits smothered in sausage gravy.

Lori Pope appeared on screen and spit a lot of bullshit before announcing that there would be no charges pressed against me. When the crowd got louder than anyone in front of a microphone, I signaled for the cook to turn it down. It went back to mute. Closed captioned words scrawled across the bottom of the screen.

"You've got motherfucking nerves of steel," Larson said admirably.

I wanted to take the compliment along with some cream in my coffee, but that wouldn't have been fair to the guys.

"My lawyer called me this morning. The prosecutor let her know there was no indictment. They wanted to make sure I steered clear of downtown in case the crowds got ugly."

"But who riots in winter, right?" Larsen asked.

"Gotcha. Cleveland may not have much, but that fucking cold ass wind off Lake Erie kept the bad guys at home for a lot of the winter."

"I heard that," Croft said.

After the waitress cleared our plates, something on the screen caught my eye.

"What in the hell?"

I went over to the kitchen pass through and snagged the remote from the counter. I couldn't fucking believe it. How in the hell had this made the news?

Twenty-year-old footage stared back at me. Then Dinwiddie came back on screen. He was holding some kind of press conference of his own.

"The question is," he said. "Whether this is a pattern of behavior? Maybe it's reasonable for a cop to be scared once. But twice? He's shot and killed two unarmed black men in a city where the black male population is nearly one hundred thousand. I don't know if a full quarter of our city needs to live in fear of a loose cannon like Marc Baldwin."

"To recap, Channel Five has learned that Troy Duncan is the second man Baldwin has killed in the line of duty. The earlier killing of Marcellus Blount was attributed to his then partner. But new information has come forward indicating Baldwin was the trigger man."

"I was fucking cleared of that," I said to anyone who would listen.

No one was looking at me. The face of everyone in the diner was turned to the screen.

The long and sordid history of the Blount killing was rolled out on screen. Only this time, I was the focus.

Giving up on the television, I went back to the booth.

Ford stood, threw a couple of dollars on the table.

"I've gotta be going."

"You're usually the last to leave," I said to the one black cop who'd sat at our table for the last decade or more.

"I gotta be the first today."

"You know I'm not racist, right? We've been buddies for half the time I've been a cop," I said, stuttering over the words.

"I'd just hate to meet you in an alley is all." Ford stood, grabbed his coat, and strode out of the diner toward his car.

"I would never shoot Ford. You guys know that right? He's one of us."

The guys started shuffling their feet. In seconds, I was at the table alone.

Breakfast ruined, I threw down enough to cover a tip and went the hell home.

"Where were you?" Jan practically screamed the question. The kids were huddled together on the couch. There were no lights on in the house.

"At the diner. I go there most mornings before work. You know that. I've done the same thing for twenty years. Why do you have your panties in a bunch?"

"The children and I have been sitting here scared out of our wits. It's been hours, Marc. Five good hours since you walked out the door without a word. The word riot is on every news anchor's lips. For sure, I thought you'd been picked up tarred and feathered."

"It's not the seventeen hundreds, Jan. I'm here now." I turned to the kids, trying to think what could help them snap out of the funk Jan probably put them in with all the worrying and lights out business. "What do you guys want to do this afternoon? Skating maybe?"

"Really, Dad?" they asked in near unison.

"Sure. Go poke around the garage for your skates. Then get suited up in your warmest gear. It'll be fun."

The kids ran in two different directions. I was feeling pretty good as a father.

"I thought you were hurt or worse," Jan whispered her arms wrapped tightly around her body.

"Why, baby? What would happen to me?"

"Did you watch the press conference? See that special report. There were hundreds of people at the justice center. Hundreds more outside that lawyer's office. That's probably thousands of people who wouldn't mind seeing you dead."

"Jan, there's good news. I was cleared of criminal charges. There's no jail coming down the pike. I'll call Captain Todd on Monday. I should be back to work this week."

"There's going to be a riot, Marc. Those people on TV looked really angry. You not being indicted is like throwing a match on an oil slick."

"Calm down. First, I've never heard of a riot in winter. Even if it's a little warm, it's too damned cold. Second, those people always riot in their own neighborhood. Can you remember any riot ever spilling over into Westlake? Third, we're safe. No one knows we live here."

"Captain Todd managed to find us."

"If some reporter manages to do the unethical thing and worm my personal information out of some system, then all they're going to get is that Edgewater address. We all pay that kid to keep his trap shut. I'm safe. You're safe. The kids are safe."

"We're not going to have to move to Cleveland?" Jan said exposing her true worry. It had been her idea to buy a place out here near where she grew up. She'd probably been to the city maybe a few dozen times in her life to see the Browns or the Indians. For her Cleveland might as well not exist.

"Not a chance, Jan. Hey, why don't you come with us? You were one hell of a skater when I met you. I always said you could have gone to the Olympics."

"I was good." A small smile played around her lips. For a long moment, I regretted promising to take the kids out. We could have celebrated in our room, leaving the kids to the Xbox. I shook my head. Later. I still had a few free days coming to me.

"You skate with Donna. She takes after you. I'm gonna work with Mike. I think he wants to try out for hockey next year. But his footing could really use some work. I'd promised him I'd help during winter break. I'm really going to make up for it now." I stepped close tucking my hand under Jan's chin. Her eyes met mine. I could see they were brimming with tears, but not a single one spilled over. She was the rock of our family.

"Promise me you'll stop all this worrying. Everything will be just fine."

"Okay. I promise."

28

Casey

February 13, 2006

"What are they going to ask me that they don't already know?" Baldwin asked.

"Fair question."

Between the department investigation, the grand jury, the department of justice, and every media outlet in Northeast Ohio, everybody and their brother knew what had happened the night of December twenty-eighth. It was like an entire city had a ringside view to the events of that night. And every single one had made their own judgment.

Before I could give Baldwin an honest answer, the intercom buzzed. I left the cop to sit and ponder the mysteries of the Ohio Revised Code books that lined three walls of my shared conference room, while I went outside to greet Dinwiddie.

The small lobby I shared was chock full when I opened the conference room door. Letty gave me the side eye, and I nodded in general greeting while dragging her out into the hall.

"What's going on? Did Dinwiddie suddenly get a merry band of middle age white associates?" I asked as I tried to make sense of the lobby I'd just woven through.

Letty was barely able to cover her laugh. Efficient as always, though, she pulled out a small sticky note.

"It's the assistant city law director, someone from the CPPA, someone from the county prosecutor's office, and a lawyer from the hospital. Also Spencer Milburn's landlord has his own lawyer. Dinwiddie is late."

"I'm being ambushed," I said as it dawned on me that no way in hell was there going to be a deposition today. "Dinwiddie didn't want—"

My comments were cut off by none other than the lawyer-sprite himself coming from around the corner of the elevator bay. His trademark cowboy boots announced his arrival.

"Miss Cort? I believe we met a few years ago. The Grant case?" He extended his hand. Politely, I grasped it and shook. "Met" wouldn't be how I'd have put it. He showed up. The county had destroyed his client's case with a single witness and a DNA test. He'd walked out. I'd be hard pressed to say we'd ever shared a single word.

"I remember," I said. I thumbed toward the plain wood door that held nothing more than a tiny metal plaque with our suite number. "What in the hell is going on in there?"

"Judge Hagemann likes early settlement talks. I figured we could maybe see what we had in common before we put your client through the wringer," he said, like I should thank him.

"We haven't been before the judge yet," I said. We'd had one lightening quick phone conference to postpone this deposition when the grand jury had summoned. Any other communication by one party about a case was ex-parte and prohibited by every state and federal rule I knew.

"Saw him at Big Al's on Sunday. I'd had to tell him that we hadn't done any settlement discussions."

Big Al's. I could have been there. The diner on Larchmere, less than a mile from my apartment was a big leap from the country club, starched linen meal I'd imagined in my head. Of course, if I'd been there, I wouldn't have been able to pick Judge Ralph Hagemann out of a lineup. I wondered if I would always feel like I was barely treading water in the Cleveland legal world.

"Where are your clients?" I asked. They had the right to be here. The right to face down Baldwin. Look him in the eye. Ask him to answer for his actions. It was the part of the day I'd been dreading the most. My own run in with Duncan's wife and son had been difficult enough. But I'd prepped Baldwin anyway. With his steely demeanor, he'd do a fine job of facing them. Honestly, I was more worried about me.

"They're not coming," Dinwiddie answered. Well, then I guess Baldwin wouldn't have to do the cop glare thing. I was probably more relieved that my client. I didn't have his fierce belief that he'd done the absolutely right, moral, legal, and ethical thing. I wish I were a true believer in justice, in the law, in something. Much of my job would be a thousand times easier.

"Okay, then. Let's get this going," I said turning on my heel.

Dinwiddie instructed the court reporter and videographer to cool their collective heels in the closest coffee shop.

I opened the door to the lobby. I raised my voice above the din of gossiping lawyers. Cleveland attorneys were the worst at looking businesslike. I don't know how many times I'd had to reassure clients that everyone took their child custody or criminal matter seriously. Gaggles of laughing and backslapping judges, magistrates, and lawyers did not give that impression.

"Good Morning everyone. I'm Casey Cort. I represent Marc Baldwin. In a moment, we're all going to assemble in my conference room. There's no need to continue to disturb the other lawyers in this office. First, I'll need to consult with my client about the apparent change of plans, then I'll call you in. Please let Letty or the receptionist know if you need any water or coffee."

Proud of my professionalism, I stepped over to the conference room door. The minute I'd opened it, entered, and closed it behind me, Baldwin was out of a chair like a shot.

"I heard a lot of voices out there. What's going on?"

No self-righteous client liked hearing the words settlement or compromise. I took a deep breath and launched into it.

"Judge Hagemann would like us to start settlement discussions—"

"Settlement? The law is on my side. If it weren't, I'd be in jail."

"Mr. Baldwin. Sergeant Baldwin. I understand. I really do. I did *not* call all these folks here today. Dinwiddie did. It's an intimidation tactic, pure and simple."

"So send them home. They can't make me settle."

"Actually, they can." Baldwin's blink told me he wasn't happy with that answer. "Look we're facing two issues at this exact moment. The first is that the Duncans' lawyer ran into the judge this weekend." I used air quotes to emphasize my skepticism of Dinwiddie's story. "Even if they were only at a diner, the Judge... Hagemann emphasized his, hmmm, feelings about settlement discussions."

"What's the second issue?"

"Indemnification."

"You mean the thing about me not being on the hook financially."

"Very much that. If a jury were to find you at fault, and that's a big if, someone has to pay. Any judgment would bankrupt you. Since you were acting in your official capacity, the city's on the hook. If they want to settle, it may be in your best interest to do so."

"You said you'd fight this. If they pay out money, it's going to look like I did something wrong."

"Settlements always include a denial of wrongdoing."

Baldwin looked everywhere but at me.

"Fine. Let in the vultures."

I opened the door and let the predators swoop in. Although everyone appeared to know everyone except me, I insisted on a round of introductions. If I'd known they were coming, I'd have had Letty make place cards. Names weren't my strong suit.

The guy from the prosecutor's office, was chief of the special investigations division. For me Tobias Whelchel was someone in the Brodys' pocket. He'd killed every investigation there'd ever been of that family. I listened to him list his title and tried to swallow bitterness forming a lump in my throat.

The assistant city law director, and likely keeper of the purse strings was Taylor Hollandsworth. Francis Parker was there from the policeman's union. Last but not least, Boyce Scharf was the county attorney representing the hospital. I think Dinwiddie and I were the only people in the room not on a government payroll, even if I was for this case.

Tobias Whelchel spoke first.

"Now that we've done the introduction dance, I want to get down to business. Sergeant Baldwin, we all met yesterday concerning your case—"

"Wait!" I shouted stopping Whelchel mid-sentence. His mouth hung open like a dying fish. I stood and pointed to each of the court men seated round the table. "You had a meeting about my case and my client, and you didn't think to notify either one of us? Did you lose my phone number?"

I reached for the cardholder I'd put on the table, so that the court reporters could spell my name and law firm info. I took a handful and walked around the table. Each and every card was placed carefully face up in front of its intended recipient.

"Ms. Cort. Please let me finish," Whelchel said, his voice full of the condescension I usually only heard from judges.

"Go on. I wasn't stopping you."

"As I was saying. We had a long discussion yesterday and reached a tentative agreement to resolve the Troy Duncan case."

I rested my hands on the back of my chair. I needed to hear this while standing. As the only woman in the room, it was the only advantage I could gain. It was my version of looming over all the self-important men smoothing their ties.

Whelchel, obviously the designated speaker, turned from me.

"Mr. Dinwiddie, we're offering the Duncan family ten million dollars. The payout will be divided equally, half from the county, half from the city. This will settle all claims against the CPD, MetroHealth, Cuyahoga County, and anyone else indemnified by the city and county government."

"Do I get any say?" Baldwin asked. His voice was full of surprise and indignation.

"Mr. Baldwin. I can assure you, there would be no admission of wrongdoing included in any settlement." Whelchel's answer was presumptive.

"But the people out there. The crowd that's permanently assembled on The Mall. They're going to crucify me."

"They already think you're guilty," Hollandsworth interjected. "You've been tried and convicted in the court of public opinion. There's no walking that horse back into the barn."

"Let me call my client," Dinwiddie said and walked from the room.

He was probably about to pocket 3.3 million dollars. There was no reason for him to stick around watching a bunch of lawyers sell Baldwin on settlement.

"I want a judge and jury to hear my case. Once regular law abiding civilians hear my side of the story, they won't find me guilty."

Whelchel and the others gave me a look that said I lacked client management skills. They were likely right on that one. I was not the lawyer you saw at the courthouse beating and berating their client to accept a deal. But I knew a good deal when I saw it. This was a good deal. Now I had to think fast on my feet to get my client to do what was in his best interest even if it was a bitter pill to swallow.

"Marc. Let's have a talk in my office," I said. My tone brooked no argument.

Once we made it across the tiny lobby and were behind closed doors, Baldwin sank deep into one of the chairs his slouch no different from a sulking teen.

"They're not even going to fight for me, are they?" He sounded like a defeated princess forever banished to the castle tower as the knight rode away.

"Give me a minute." I held up my hand and turned to the computer behind me. Google was turning out to be the best thing going. With the Internet, it was like all the knowledge in the world was at your fingertips. The 'Net combined with LexisNexis was going to change the landscape of the law in a few years.

I did two quick searches, one of the Internet in general, and one of the specialized legal database, looking for verdicts. For years, jury verdicts had been cataloged. They were used mostly by plaintiff and defense bar tort lawyers who tried to hedge their bets when picking where to sue.

If a particular county swayed one way, giving plaintiffs everything they asked for, like some in California, plaintiff's attorneys ran there. Where there were others giving plaintiffs nothing, like Rockland county, in New York they were often called judicial hellholes and defendants tried like hell to move a case there. Cleveland and Cuyahoga County were fairer than many.

I took my time clicking and reading.

"What are you looking for?" Baldwin asked. His head bobbed and weaved as he tried to see over my shoulders. I went back to typing and reading.

A few minutes later, I looked away from the screen to find that he'd moved from the chair toward the window. He was staring out at Lake Erie as if the huge body of water possessed answers to life's questions. If he'd asked, I'd have told him that there were no answers to be gleaned from there. I'd tried.

I turned back to the screen.

"Here's what I'm searching for." I pressed print and what looked like a ream of paper furled from the printer one page at a time. The smell of toner filled the room. I rose and collected the collated sheets from the tray. "This lists verdicts and known settlements in cases like yours. It gives me a sense of the value of your case to the plaintiffs and what kinds of dispositions there've been."

"Dispositions?"

"How the case ended. How much was paid out. Whether a jury decided for the plaintiff or defendant. If the case was settled, and if the settlement is public, then for how much."

"Why didn't you look this up before?"

"In most cases the lawyers don't even really start settlement discussions until the discovery, depositions and stuff, are done. Until then no one really knows what they've got. Half the time a plaintiff is full of shit. Sometimes they have the defendant dead to rights."

"Gotcha."

"I was prepared to defend you against Dinwiddie today, not all of the city and county in a room."

"It's a show of force." Baldwin shook his head. "It's a fucking show of force."

"What do you mean?"

"This. What they're doing. We do it all the time. Ten years ago, there were protests for some kind of world trade summit or something. Nearly every officer was called in to suit up in riot gear with tear gas and Tasers on our belts."

"Then what?"

"There were riots in Portland and none here. We held the protestors back. Kept things quiet. Fucking A. I can't believe they're doing this to me. Some kind of fucked up reverse psychology." Baldwin petered off. Stared at the lake some more.

"You know what I'm going to say, right?"

"That I should take the deal."

"Look. If you go to trial, I will make a lot more money. It isn't in my interest to settle your case. But you have a lot moving against you right now. Marcellus Blount, for one."

"Sorry I didn't tell you that. Honestly, I didn't even think about it until that woman in the grand jury asked. It was twenty years ago. My partner and I were cleared in half a minute."

"Which was why you thought this case would go away?" I tapped the radiator cover in emphasis.

"City's changed."

I went over to the window and leaned across the radiator. "Look over there, to the right. What do you see?"

"Nice view. The courthouses, the stadium, the water."

"Look way to the right. Look on the mall." I pointed to a tiny patch of nearly dead grass east of the convention center.

"It's filled with people."

"Those are people who've been camped out nearly every day. Those are people who are as pissed as hell about Troy Duncan. Sometimes a city hits a boiling point, Marc.

Troy Duncan is Cleveland's. The city and county aren't really worried about protecting you, so much as protecting themselves."

"Okay."

"My parents emigrated from Europe. My dad and mom lived through the war. You know what they always said to me? He who has the gold, rules. Those men in there. They have the purse strings. It was never going to be your decision to make despite whatever they said or whatever promises they made."

Baldwin turned away from the lake and the courthouses and the protestors. His eyes scanned the framed diplomas hung over the credenza. Finally, his blue eyes came back down and met mine.

"I'll take it under one condition," he said.

"What's that?"

"They speed up the internal hearing. I'm not going to cool my heels a minute longer. I have a family to support. If they're going to let me go over this, so be it. I can get a job in any of the surrounding towns, but I'm done sitting at home. I have one thing that I do well. One thing. I wasn't the kid who was the hockey star or the football star. I wasn't the kid at the top of his class. But I was the one kid who followed the rules and enlisted in the army, then the police academy and did the right thing. I know how to walk a beat and keep a city safe. It's all I want to do. It's all I ever wanted to do, and now they're keeping me from that one thing. The right to get in there, earn a living for me and my family. I want that hearing. I deserve that hearing. Because if they think that I'm a killer, than they need to tell me that to my face."

"Let's talk to them."

We rose and went back to the conference room. The jovial chatter stopped the minute we stepped through the door. I closed it behind us, relieved Dinwiddie wasn't here.

"Here's the deal folks," I started. "Marc's fine with the settlement. He has a single stipulation."

"We're listening," Whelchel said.

"We get a department decision by this Friday, the seventeenth."

"That's a deal," Whelchel said emphatically and scarily fast. I was grateful no one sat there and pretended they didn't have the power to spur the police process along. I stole a glance around the room. Something told me they'd already made a decision. I was about to ask what exactly it was that they'd decided when Dinwiddie opened the door and stepped in. He tucked his cell phone into his pocket.

"I talked to my clients. I'm going to meet them tonight. I'll have an answer for you in the morning."

"Then I think we're all done here for now." Hollandsworth stood and the rest parroted. They shoved phones and papers into their bags, slipped on their coats and were out the door before I could so much as blink.

Marc Baldwin glanced at me across the empty table.

"What in the hell just happened?"

I didn't have a clue. Instead, I said, "I have a feeling everything will be wrapped all tightly in a bow by Friday. Sit tight. I'll call you."

"There's not going to be a deposition?"

I'd completely forgotten the prep, my morning nerves, and the reason we were here. I hoped that Dinwiddie had remembered to send the court reporters home.

"There will probably never be a deposition. I think your best bet would be to get on over to the CPPA and talk to Francis Parker. The lawyers over there will handle the police hearing. I suggest you meet with him to prep for whatever they're going to throw at you."

"Is there any way you could come with me? You know the case better than Parker or any of the guys over there."

I shook my head.

"The agreement was that I would handle this part. I'm not going to pretend to have any kind of expertise in those kinds of administrative hearings. That's way outside of my wheelhouse. From what you're saying about Blount, though. You've done this dance before. You should be fine."

29

Augustus

February 13, 2006

Myrtle had put the extra leaf into the dining room table. It extended beyond the piano bench. But I didn't think anyone would be up for a rousing rendition of "Build Me Up, Buttercup." My wife had been great at getting a party started back in the old days when the house was full of parents and kids all times of day and night. We'd watched Campbell and Troy circle around each other for years before they got together. I pulled closed a mental shutter on a trip down memory lane. The present needed far too much attention.

I cleared my throat then drank the glass of water in front of me. Myrtle had produced a pitcher and five tall glasses, each on its own coaster. Reminded me of that horrible press conference. Was our life going to be all cold tables and colder water now? I could easily see it. Meetings here, depositions in Dinwiddie's office, courtroom conferences. Water and wood was what happened when you died.

When Dinwiddie knocked, Campbell let him in. I vacated my usual spot at the foot of the table and joined my wife by her side. Campbell sat across from me. Lynell was to her right. The lawyer settled himself in my old chair and snapped open his briefcase. He removed a single pad of paper and pen before clicking it shut and placing it on the floor. Water and wood and leather. I'd forgotten to add leather.

"Gus said they'd already offered a settlement. Is that right? That feels kind of quick." Myrtle and I had spent some sleepless nights over the past weeks preparing ourselves for a months or years long ordeal.

"Have you seen the news today?" Dinwiddie twisted around toward our lone television. It sat silent and blank.

I shook my head. "Not today or any day for the last couple of weeks." Watching had gotten too hard. Troy's picture was flashed across the screen hundreds of times a day. That was followed by howling protests from people who didn't know my son or care about him. People like Reverend Wilkinson who had their own agendas.

"We want to mourn in peace," Myrtle said. She clutched a handkerchief in her hand. She'd unearthed the daintily embroidered clothes from a drawer when we'd run clear out of tissues.

"I understand," Dinwiddie said nodding his head.

I wasn't sure he understood. Lynell, Campbell, and even Myrtle and I had unplugged our phones, stopped answering our doors. What was there to say to ABC, CBS, or CNN? Vulture voyeurs they all were.

"What's the deal?" I asked willing all the other noise from my mind. "You said they'd offered to pay the full ten million dollars we'd asked for."

I watched as Lynell's eyes went wide. I hadn't told her the amount when I'd sent her a text on her cell phone. I didn't want the Powerses running around spending money that wasn't rightfully theirs.

Dinwiddie nodded. "They did. As I've told you before, I'm required by law to discuss all settlement offers with you. Discuss the pros and cons, and help you come to a decision."

"I'm not sure we should take it," I said. Lynell gasped. Poor thing probably couldn't help herself. Even Dinwiddie looked surprised. He had probably already been eyeing more commercial real estate to add to his holdings. Three point five million would be a great payday for the guy.

"Why not? The kids could have everything they've ever dreamed," Lynell said. Or everything she'd ever wanted.

"What have the Cleveland Police learned? I want to teach them a lesson. I want Marc Baldwin to lose his job. I want..." I turned away in disgust at my own emotions. Emotions I'd promised myself to tamp down or I'd kill myself before this was all over.

"What will keep the Marc Baldwins of the world from shooting the next black man he feels threatened by?" Campbell finished asking what I couldn't.

Dinwiddie shook his head.

"Honestly? Nothing. This ten million dollars won't change a thing. This could happen tomorrow or next week or next year. It probably will. This money will not fix the ills of the world. But neither will a trial. At the end of the day, you may feel vindicated. But my experience has been that trials make no one feel better. Trials make no one whole."

"You think we should take it," Myrtle said. "What happens to the cop?"

"Marc Baldwin has been and always will be protected by the police union. Firing cops is almost as hard as firing teachers. That's the system we have. All I can say is that if you take this settlement, the police will probably speed up any disciplinary hearing. There will be no waiting for the outcome of a criminal or civil trial."

"What about the department of Justice?" Campbell asked. "The Plain Dealer said they'd put together a joint task force to look into this kind of thing."

"Those take years. The DOJ pushes one way. A city pushes back. Two or three years from now, they'll all sign a consent decree. The police department will promise reform. Whether that changes anything, who knows?"

"What do you recommend?" I asked. I knew the cold, hard truth of what the lawyer was saying. How many years had I read the papers, watched the news, and seen what he said happen time and again in one city or another. This time it was our son, our city.

"I recommend you take the settlement. More importantly, before I go back to the city and county, you'd need to decide among yourselves *how* you'd split the money."

"What do you mean? Don't his kids get it all? They need food, clothes, maybe even college," Lynell said.

Dinwiddie shifted in his chair, clearly uncomfortable.

"Campbell is Troy's legal wife," he said scribbling on his pad.

"Troy and I were engaged!" Lynell brandished the small diamond on her left hand. Her thumb spun the small gold hoop around as she waived her hand in the air.

The outburst didn't ruffle a single one of the lawyer's feathers. I imagined he'd see it all before. Kissing cousins, fake aunties, common-law marriages. None of them meant anything in the court of law.

"Fiancé's have little legal standing under the law."

"Why can't we let the court decide who was closest to Troy? Huh? Let some judge tell me to my face that money for *my* kids should be paid to someone else." Campbell laid a hand on Lynell's arm.

"You must have seen the coverage of the Anna Nicole Smith case," Campbell insisted. "The lawyers end up with all the money if we go that way."

"The best course of action, in my opinion, is that you all reach a decision, sign an agreement, and present it to the court. They are much more likely to sign a judgment entry put before them where all the parties agree. Judges don't like to make decisions."

"Fine." Lynell actually stomped her foot under the table. "How are we going to do this?" She looked like a kid determined to square off for a playground fight. I wouldn't have been surprised if she'd snatched her earrings from her lobes.

I stood, and stepped away from the table. Without saying a word, I walked over to the fireplace. I could still hear them, but couldn't see them. Carefully, I knelt before the hearth and removed the screen.

I stood the logs like a teepee, then tossed in a couple of rolls of balled up newspaper. Next, I struck a match and watched. The newspaper literally went up in smoke in about a minute. I poked at the smaller logs as they caught flame. We'd all have a roaring fire in twenty minutes or so. I shoved the black metal back in front of the fire then lowered the thermostat.

When I turned around, Myrtle was standing by my side. I'd never heard her come.

"What are you thinking?" she asked in a whisper.

"Do you want to take this money, Myrtle? Do you think we should continue the fight? Hundreds or thousands of people are standing at that mall downtown. People who've stood up for what's right and just. What kind of coward would I be if I backed down?"

"Oh, Gus."

"What? I raised my boys to be strong. To know the difference between right and wrong. To stand up for what they believe in. To stand up for what they know is right. Ten million dollars is nothing to a city like Cleveland. More than that goes out the door in corruption on a monthly basis. It's probably paid by an insurance company which means the city isn't out a penny."

My wife laid a firm hand on my arm.

"Standing up for what's right is one thing. Reverend Wilkinson has made it his life's mission to do that. Maybe even Dinwiddie too. We did not seek out this mission. I'm not even sure it's ours to take on."

"You don't think?" I asked. Relief washed over me. Maybe we didn't have to be the Martin Luther King, Juniors or Malcolm X's of our day.

"No one would think badly of us if we ended the case right now. I've been thinking that we should maybe sell the house. Move to Pittsburgh closer to Malik or even, I don't know, somewhere like New York. I don't want to spend the last chapter of our lives in mourning."

"You sure? You won't be disappointed in me for not doing more to fight for our family, our baby?"

"Never. Gus. Never. Let's go get this over with. Maybe our last act should be to help these girls navigate his money."

We walked around the corner. I sat down to help Dinwiddie walk the minefield between the two women Troy had loved before my dining room turned into the ring for a cat fight.

30

Casey

February 14, 2006

"You didn't go to work today."

That was Miles. Somehow, he'd defeated the boffo security downstairs and was knocking at my door again. Secure building didn't quite mean what I thought anymore. Once my neighbors recognized the polite guy visiting me, they let him in without a thought. I swear if I had a stalker, I'd have to move.

"I'm avoiding downtown for a few days. Crowds of angry protestors are not my friends." I wasn't that worried that anyone would take their anger at Marc Baldwin out on me, but there was no reason to put myself in harm's way. "I'm going to work from home for the rest of the week." Miles nodded, looking thoughtful. "Why don't you come in? It's practically a party in here."

I opened wide to let him step across the threshold.

"Lulu, Jason, Greg. You all remember Miles."

My best friend and my next-door neighbors nodded in greeting, then drank a little more wine. The conversation that had filled my living room a moment ago had come to a grinding halt.

"I'm sorry," I said. "His name isn't really Miles. It's Elephant In The Room. Big gray elephant, meet my friends. Lulu here has known me since law school. Jason and Greg have lived next door since I moved in. And the cat. Simba here isn't afraid of a little elephant, are you?" I said bending down to scratch the cat under the chin.

My lame attempt at humor did nothing to get back the good feeling I'd had moments ago from just shooting the shit with my friends.

"So…well. Happy Valentine's Day?" Miles whipped a huge bunch of red roses from behind his back.

"Is that how the straights do it?" Greg stage whispered.

"I think we should go before we miss our dinner reservations," Jason said. He pulled the glass of wine from Greg's hand and sat both down on my trunk. In a moment, they'd let themselves out.

"Thanks," I said accepting the flowers. I took them to the kitchen so I didn't have to look Miles in the eye. I was embarrassed because he still made me nervous. My heart, breath, and feet were all unsteady when he was around. In the kitchen, I opened and closed all four of my upper cabinets as if a vase would appear by magic on one of the white melamine shelves.

"Can't find a vase?" Lulu said coming up beside me.

"I've never ever gotten flowers before. I don't even know if I like flowers. How am I over thirty and no guy has ever even tried to woo me?"

"Woo? Pitch woo? Is it nineteen fifty up in here?" Lulu looked around like we'd all fallen through a time machine. Except for our clothes it could have been fifty years earlier. Nothing in my apartment had been updated since then.

"Where's Miles?" I whispered.

"He's in your living room. Looks like he's settled in for the night."

"What should I do?"

Lulu mimicked my cabinet search, but came up with a large mason jar where I'd come up empty handed. She took the knife from my hands.

"You're going to massacre these damned flowers. Let me." She pulled the thornless stems from my hands and carefully cut through each one before placing a few in the jar. Sometimes I liked to pretend we were the same, Lulu and I. But the differences showed through. She had that gloss of knowledge and sophistication that I'd never get. I half thought of suggesting she and Miles should give it a go. They had more in common, Jewish parents, money, and class.

"Get me some sugar," she said interrupting my thoughts.

"Sugar?"

"God, you really haven't gotten flowers before. You're serious aren't you?"

"No I take it back. Adrian Kowalczyk brought me a tulip corsage for junior prom."

"Tom never—?"

I shook my head. Sentences starting with "Tom Brody never" could fill a small notebook.

"Why do you need sugar?" I asked looking for the tall glass sugar jar I'd picked up at a second-hand store around the corner.

"Helps keep them alive longer?"

"I may not have gotten flowers before. But I didn't fail high school biology either. They're dead. How can you keep something alive that's already dead?"

"Wow. That's some profound Freudian shit you've got going on there."

I handed her the sugar from the counter. She tipped the glass and white crystals flowed through the hole in the top. She tipped it back up and the tiny metal flap closed back into place saving the rest of the sugar for another day.

"Freudian? You haven't used that psychology major stuff in years."

"I use it every day on clients. It's like a fucking super power."

"That's pretty cool. Like what kind of clients?"

"Oh, snap! You're totally avoiding the living room."

I was so busted.

"There's an elephant in there, remember? Tell me about Freud," I prompted.

"Here's the ten-second analysis. You were comparing these flowers to your relationship. You think it's dead and Miles is trying to bring it back to life."

"Didn't take a degree in psychology to figure that out. Should I add sugar?"

"Don't diss Beloit."

"Go Buccaneers." I raised my fist and arm in mock salute.

"That shit is not funny." Lulu was surprising protective of her small undergraduate college.

"Buccaneers in Wisconsin? That doesn't even make any sense. Worried about pirate attacks from the Great Lakes?"

I asked. I was trying to goad her into a fight rather than deal with the man on my futon.

"Miles is still here."

"Fine," I snapped knowing I couldn't avoid him much longer. "Tell me what to do."

"What do *you* want to do?"

"I want to say yes. I want to give this whole stupid thing another try. Tell me that I'm being stupid. That he's a judgmental ass and this can't work."

"How's the online dating going?"

I rolled my head around my neck. I don't know if the tension was from weeks of Marc Baldwin's case hanging over my head or the fact that I couldn't come to any kind of decision in my personal life.

"That damned eHarmony thing takes forever. Between Miles and Troy Duncan's case I haven't had the time to dedicate to all those questions. Is it that hard to find someone compatible?"

"Go on out there. Talk to that man. He won't wait forever."

"We were supposed to go to dinner together." Lulu gave me a funny look. Fluorescent kitchen light glinted off her rhinestone glasses. Something niggled at the back of my brain. "Wait! Where's the guy you're kind of seeing? How in the hell did I forget about him? Damned Baldwin case. Where is he tonight? Is he with his wife?"

"I told you he's not married."

"Then where is he on Valentine's Day?"

Lulu stuck the final rose in the jar and fluffed them out. They did look really pretty. When in life did people learn things like flower arranging? I was about to ask her when she nearly tripped over herself running out of the kitchen.

"That's my cue. You and Miles can use the reservations."

"You're not answering my questions," I said practically chasing Lulu through my apartment.

"Good bye, love birds," she cooed, then slammed the door behind her.

"What in the hell was all that about?" Miles asked. Carefully, he put down the mint green Ohio Reporter.

"Any good appeals court decisions?"

"I was waiting for you to get up the courage to come out of the kitchen."

Busted, again. This was going to be the day everyone called me on my bullshit. I was thankful my neighbors had left. They were merciless when it came to me facing the music.

"Thanks for the flowers."

"I didn't know if you liked roses."

"They're...nice."

"You don't like roses."

"Miles I don't know what I like. Flowers aren't... They're nice. Thank you."

"Have you thought about what we talked about?"

"I've been up to my ears in Marc Baldwin. I haven't had more than a minute to think about this...us."

"The case can last at least a couple of years, if not more, Casey. If not now, when?"

"The case won't last more than a week, Miles. I'm telling you that as a friend, *not* in your capacity as an assistant U.S. Attorney."

"Settlement?" He zeroed straight in on the reason for the case coming to an end.

"Looks like. Lots of city and county officials aren't thrilled with the idea of this dragging out. They're worried the downtown protests will turn into a riot. Warmer than usual February and all that anger."

I shifted from foot to foot unsure of my next move.

"Do you want to go out to dinner?"

"Lulu and I had reservations," I said trying not to cringe at the last minute invitation.

"Shit. I didn't want her to leave on my account."

"She probably thinks she dodged a bullet. She has a highly unsuitable man that couldn't take her out tonight."

"I'm a highly suitable man who *can* take you out to-night."

"Suitable is really the question, isn't it?"

"I've grown up a lot in the last year, Casey. A lot. Enough to know that I shouldn't have taken what we had for granted."

"We only had reservations at Balaton. If you're up for a lot of Hungarian."

"I'm up for anything." He rose to get his coat. I took the wine and glasses from the living room. Never knew when the cat would have one of its crazy moments and turn the place upside down.

Murmurs came from my bedroom. Damn. The TV. I'd been watching a little Judge Judy. A fake court with low consequences was surprisingly soothing in the afternoon. Judy may have been brash, but she was mostly fair and made swift decisions. Too bad court didn't really work that way.

I slipped on tall leather boots then sat on the edge of my four poster bed to zip them. I glanced at the TV. Looked like another crime show. Maybe it was a rerun of Law & Order. I zipped both boots, marveling at how losing a bit of weight made everything easier. No longer did I have to struggle to get the zipper to stay at the top of my eastern European calf.

I stood and looked for the remote for the small TV. The clock radio pulsed as it moved from 7:44 to 7:45. Forget it. The remote was probably long lost under the pile of duvet and blanket bunched up on the bed.

Rising, I moved to press my finger against the on/off button on the lower right hand corner.

Oh, my God!

It was the scene from the Troy Duncan shooting. It was on TV. Someone else had found Keith Grant and unearthed the video tape. Something scrolled across the bottom of Channel Five's screen. Something about parental discretion. The man who I knew to be Baldwin raised his hand. The flash that was the bullet. Troy Duncan hit the ground. The desk anchors rolled the tape without speaking, without commentary. They let it play out as it happened.

I sat heavily on the trunk at the end of my bed. The law and the police and the prosecutor's office might all have been on Marc Baldwin's side. I didn't think it was going to be enough. He'd been strung up and crucified in the court of public opinion.

I looked up when Miles wandered in. "What?"

"I'm going to have to call and cancel the reservation."

"You changed your mind about us that quickly?"

I shook my head and pointed to the TV screen.

"What? Oh."

"The videotape is out there. I need to do damage control."

I rose and walked to the tiny second bedroom I used as an office as I decided whom I should call first.

31

Marc

February 16, 2006

My first impression of Casey Cort had been less than favorable. Small woman, small office. Nothing impressive or flashy about the lawyer. She hadn't yelled, or jumped up and down, or dismissed me with a flick of her wrist.

Instead, she'd pierced me with her hazel eyes, and had asked hard questions. She'd been a straight shooter all these weeks. No blowing smoke up my ass, no coddling.

Now, Francis Parker, this man was an ass smoke blower if I ever saw one. I didn't think I'd miss the lawyer with her colorless hair and quiet demeanor, but I did. Frank might have been with the police union for years and done dozens of disciplinary hearings. But I didn't get the feeling he gave two shits about me or my case.

"Mr. Baldwin, you understand why you're here today?"

I looked around the hearing room that looked like every other room I'd ever seen in City Hall, all wood paneling, stone floors, and black chairs.

"Yes."

The Deputy Director of Public Safety, Sharda Toby, leaned down and read from one of a stack of papers in front of her.

"We are here to determine whether you violated the following rules of the Manual of Rules for the Department of Public Safety and the rules of the Civil Service Commission of the City of Cleveland.

"Disciplinary action includes, but is not limited to, verbal and written reprimands, and the pressing of divisional charges which can result in suspension, loss of pay, demotion, or termination. I see that you're represented by the experienced and capable police union representative Francis Parker. Has he explained this to you? Do you have any questions?"

"None, Ma'am."

"You've been charged with violating the following rules," she started. I tuned out the ten-page list of things I'd supposedly done wrong, starting with not keeping in contact with dispatch, and ending with the use of deadly force.

"Do you understand the list of possible violations?"

"Yes, Ma'am."

"Sergeant Baldwin, this office is in possession of a videotape that details the actions in question from the night of December 28, 2005. Have you seen this tape?"

I'd never told anyone that Casey had gotten her hands on the tape weeks ago. It was everywhere now, so I said yes without guilt.

"We're going to watch it while I ask you specific questions."

Another city employee moved a television into the area between Toby and Parker and me. We all had to turn in our seat to see the screen.

"Pause here," Toby said to the clerk. We were looking at me frozen in the mouth of the alley. "Where is your partner, Darlene Webb?"

"She was in the car on the corner of Tenth and Front Avenue."

"Did you notify dispatch that you'd split from your partner, give them a description of the suspects, or where your zone car was located?"

"No. There wasn't time to radio in this situation. A silent approach was necessary because we were casing out drug dealers who will run at the least provocation."

Toby had the tape run again. She paused it as Duncan and I approached each other.

"Did you identify yourself?"

"Yes, Ma'am."

"Did you tell the suspect to stop?"

"Yes, Ma'am."

Nineteen seconds elapsed from my approach to the weapons discharge. I watched as Duncan fell to the ground.

"Did you call dispatch after the discharge of your weapon?"

"No, ma'am. I called Webb. I needed to make sure my partner was safe."

"Once you established she was safe, what next?"

"I called dispatch and informed them there'd been a shooting, that a man was down, and that Webb and I were safe."

"Take me through what happened after that."

I led her through the other zone cars and brass showing up, the quick on scene investigation of Duncan's weapon, and the ambulance taking him away.

"You've maintained in your statement and later that you believed Duncan to have a weapon. Can you elaborate?"

"The way his leather pouch was positioned on his body, it looked similar to a short barreled rifle. Additionally, after I told him to stop, after I'd identified myself as a sworn officer, he reached his right hand into his jacket pocket. I thought it was highly probable, after coming upon a drug deal in progress, that he'd have a weapon. Fearing for my life, that of my partner, and the safety of civilians, I fired."

"Thank you."

We spent the next hour and a half detailing my last decade with the department. Parker stood as the hour got close to twelve hundred.

"Deputy Toby. My client and I would like to take a lunch break. We'd be happy to resume this hearing at one or one-thirty."

"Sit down, Mr. Parker. There's no need. I only have a couple more questions of Sergeant Baldwin. Then the two of you are free to enjoy lunch."

"Thanks, Deputy Toby."

"Sergeant Baldwin, please provide your home address."

"Um-"

"I see here in the file, you've listed eleven three oh one Edgewater Drive."

"Yes."

"Do you live at that address?"

"No, ma'am."

"What's your current address?"

"Thirty-nine fifty-one Winterberry Lane."

"What city is that?"

"Westlake. Westlake, Ohio."

"That's outside the city of Cleveland?"

"Yes, ma'am. It is."

"Is there anything else you'd like to tell me? Think of this as a moment to clear your conscience of anything else that you might want to share about your time with the department."

For a moment, my heart beat super quick. Was she signaling that there was something to confess? My mind shot through the last five, ten, fifteen years with the department. But I couldn't think of anything else there was to say. I wouldn't have said my record was spotless, no cop's was, but it was pretty clean. I glanced at Parker, but his face was blank—hard to read.

"Deputy Toby, I have nothing more to add," I finally said.

"I have no other questions, Sergeant Baldwin. I want to thank you for your candor and professionalism as we've gone through this process. We have already held hearings for Patrol Officer Darlene Webb, so there will not be any further delay. We should have a decision before the end of business on Friday."

"Thank you," I said. Parker and I stood once the deputy director shook our hands and left.

"What does all that mean?"

"Don't know. Go have a seat in the hall. I'm going to make a couple of calls."

Half an hour later, Parker approached me on a bench outside the office of Public Safety. I'd seen no less than three or four of CPD's top brass enter and leave. Wonder what business they had down here. Looked like a lot of politics and very little policing to me.

"What the word?"

"Good news." He clapped me on the back like the old buddies we weren't. "The department's going to clear you of all charges related to the shooting. They've determined it to be justified. You can head on over to your supervisor and get back on the schedule for work starting Monday."

I didn't work Mondays, but I didn't say a thing.

Finally.

Finally, it was behind me. Little Donna had been right all along. I'd told the truth, followed the rules, and now I was going back right where I belonged.

32

Casey

February 17, 2006

I'd been in City Hall maybe once before in my life, though I couldn't pinpoint a specific memory. My nerves were jangling as much as the bracelet that Lulu had convinced me was a necessary accessory.

It was one of those chunky statement jewelry pieces that was supposed to bring gravitas to my professional demeanor. I'd put on my best dove gray silk suit and white blouse. Even I had to admit I looked like I could have walked off the set of a network legal drama.

Too bad I didn't feel like that on the inside. When Tommie Gordon had called last night, for a long second I'd assumed he had the wrong number. But he hadn't. He'd expressly asked me to come down to City Hall and bring my client. I had no idea what to expect. That's exactly what I'd said to Marc Baldwin when I'd pulled him away from dinner with his family.

We had only spoken hours before when he'd let me know the department had exonerated him. That he wasn't on the hook for the shooting. I'd mostly talked about putting his case on hold. If something came down the pike from the department of justice, we'd open the file back up. But was mostly me wishing him and his family well, and him probably glad as hell to get back to it.

Baldwin was in full dress uniform again, his peaked cap under his arm when he approached.

"Good Morning," I said. I stood and shook his hand. The weight of the multicolor linked bracelet pressed against my wrist.

"Have they told you anything?" Baldwin asked. He looked as perplexed as I felt.

"Not a word. Have a seat. Let me tell them that you're here," I said. Lifting my messenger bag by the small handle, I took myself into the door.

A clerk nodded, told me to go to room 418.

Baldwin stood again when I exited.

"Let's go," I said. "Do you know what's on the fourth floor?"

"No idea."

We walked the stone stairs to the top floor, while I tried to hold myself steady. Heels were all well and good, but they were like wearing socks on glass when it came to these old buildings. Worn smooth marble and granite was hell on me.

I turned the knob and let us in to the small conference room.

"Make yourself at home," I offered.

Baldwin chose to stand at the end of the small wood table. I laid my bag down and mimicked his stance at the other end of the overheated room. The city and county buildings had one temperature in the winter: hot. It wasn't much different from my apartment. But with the unseasonably warm outside temperatures, the rooms were often unbearable. This was no exception.

The radiator hissed at the same moment the door opened. Tommie Gordon, whom I recognized from some bar luncheon, stepped in first. I extended my hand, ready to introduce myself, but I was quickly cut off when more people filed into the room. I recognized Tobias Whelchel, dear friend of the Brody's from Prosecutor's office. He was followed by an older woman and a couple of other people I didn't know.

"Please have a seat," Gordon said.

I pulled out a chair at the far end of the table and sat. Baldwin and the government suits all did the same.

"Ms. Cort. Sergeant Baldwin. Thank you for coming on short notice. We're going to give a press conference at noon, but wanted to speak with you first."

There weren't going to be any introductions, niceties, or offers of water. This was as serious as cancer. I leaned forward then glanced around the table. No one would meet my eye. All the ways I could have possibly fucked this up went through my head. But I couldn't figure out where I'd put a foot wrong.

"Thanks for your candor, Mr. Gordon," I said because I was doing the thing nervous women always did, fill the empty space with conversation.

"We all met last night regarding issues that have come to our attention in the ranks of the Cleveland Police Department," Whelchel started. That man loved to run a meeting.

"During our investigation of the Troy Duncan shooting, we were informed that nearly two dozen officers were in violation of Rule twelve point three, subsection 'a.' Twenty of you were using the address that Sergeant Baldwin has admitted to. Four officers were using friends' and relatives' homes."

"What does this have to do with Sergeant Baldwin?" I asked, although it was starting to dawn on me exactly what it might have to do.

"As I said. We're going to have a press conference in ninety minutes. We're going to announce the termination of Sergeant Baldwin and the twenty-three other officers in violation of the city employee residency requirements."

"You're firing me? For not meeting some stupid residency requirement half the city violates?"

"Sergeant Baldwin. You were aware of the rule at the time you accepted the job. It's been in place since nineteen eighty-two." Whelchel pulled a single piece of paper from a thin folder on the table before him.

"Here's the agreement you signed at the time you accepted employment." He slipped it across the table. Baldwin only glanced down at the sheet, but didn't touch it.

"The rank and file can't afford Old Brooklyn, West Park, or Shaker Square. Everyone knows the Cleveland schools are shit. Who wants to live in a city of thugs and drug dealers? I dare one of you to put your money where your mouth is. To ride on over to the east side at night. You'll be wishing we were all there to protect you."

"Thank you, Sergeant Baldwin. We wish you luck with your future endeavors. Captain Todd will walk you over to the department and help you complete your separation papers."

"That's it? Twenty plus years of service and that's it. You're picking the criminals over loyalty." Noisily, Baldwin shoved his chair across the floor. It landed backside down, with a noisy thud. I stood.

"Thank you gentlemen and...lady." I'd hastily added the last as I remembered there was another woman in the room besides myself. "Let's go, Sergeant Baldwin," I said and pulled him from the door.

"Did you have a fucking clue?" He rounded on me, but the anger pulsing from his neck wasn't aimed at me.

"Another ambush. I swear no one in Cleveland uses a phone."

"I can't believe this. I can't believe this. Do you think this was a backdoor way of pushing me out?"

"I honestly don't know," I said. That wasn't entirely true. I thought there might be some validity to his argument. "Firing twenty-three others to get rid of you seems excessive."

"Cover your ass month continues."

Captain Todd exited the room, pulling the thick wood door closed behind him. "Sergeant Baldwin. Let's get this over with."

"Thanks for nothing," he spat at Todd.

"We went to bat for you over this Troy Duncan. We went to bat for you over Marcellus Blount. How did you repay the department? You defied a rule and tried to get over. There's no way to walk that horse back into the barn. No way. There are dozens of small city departments. The pay is better. You'll bounce back fine."

"Those cities are a snooze."

"Maybe quieter is your speed now."

Todd tipped his head toward me and lifted his hand in a half salute. "You did great work for us. The department won't forget your loyalty."

"Thank you." I nodded at the men. Then they turned all their shiny brass and stripes and walked toward the stairs. In a few minutes, I followed the path to the stairs. I had no idea if I'd won or lost.

33

Augustus

February 18, 2006

“Gus! Come down here!”

I set the picture album aside. There’d been a lot of days lately when I flipped through these old cracked plastic pages.

“Lunchtime?” I asked as I stepped carefully down the stairs. The hip had been acting up and the fear of falling in my own house had come back full force.

My wife was standing in the living room, cordless phone in hand.

“Dinwiddie called.”

“What now? I thought we were all done with the settlement.” Four million was to go into trust for the kids. Campbell and Myrtle and I had split the rest after fees and costs. Campbell was going to donate hers to some kind of nonprofit that helped free the wrongfully convicted. Myrtle and I were going to buy a house somewhere far from here. That and put aside money for Malik's kids. We hadn't told my other son and his wife yet, but it was our plan.

"There's another press conference." Myrtle lifted the remote from the top of the piano.

"What now? The settlement's been announced. Baldwin kept his job. He's not facing criminal charges. Is it the feds? Did they decide to step up?"

"I don't know, Gus." She pressed the button, turning on the TV.

"Our correspondent Rick McDaniel is inside City Hall. What are we waiting for, Rick?"

"Thanks. I'm here in the pressroom at City Hall. All that we've heard so far is that Mayor Foster Gates, Police Chief Kelley McCormick, and the deputy director of Public Safety, Toby Sharda, are going to come to the podium in a moment. Here they are." The camera shifted from McDaniel to another block of brown wood, this one inside city hall.

"Good Morning. I'm Foster Gates, Mayor of the City of Cleveland. In the last few weeks, during the investigation of the Troy Duncan shooting, we've learned that several of our officers have flouted the city's residency rules. In nineteen eighty-two, we as a city decided that those who work to make it better, should live here as well. Building a strong community requires members of the community have a stake in what happens. Twenty-four officers decided not to invest in our community."

He stepped away, his back sweeping against the three large flags.

"I'm Toby Sharda, Deputy Director for the Cleveland Department of Public Safety. We are serious about our residency requirements, as the mayor touched on. After careful consideration, it's our decision to terminate those officers who violated the rules. We're handing out a list of those officers who've been terminated effective immediately."

Chief McCormick had barely been at the podium a second when the questions started.

"Chief McCormick, Sergeant Marc Baldwin is at the top of the list of those being terminated. Is this all to cover up your termination of Troy Duncan's shooter?"

"No, this isn't a smoke screen. We have completed our internal investigation of the Duncan shooting. Per our department rules, the shooting was justified. The standard we use is the standard the Supreme Court uses. That is, if an officer reasonably fears for his life, his actions to protect not only his life, but the lives of others around, other officers, and civilian bystanders, then protection of life trumps any one person's rights. It's what we have to do to maintain a civilized society, one in which the police aren't the only ones armed."

When the clamor of questions took over, I turned to Myrtle.

"They fired Baldwin. Dinwiddie didn't call you because of the address violation. He called you because this is the way they found to get rid of a bad cop."

She nodded. Tears streamed down the same face I'd known for more years that I could comfortably count. "Praise God."

"They found a way to do what was right," I whispered. I couldn't believe it. Nothing would bring back our son, but at least we weren't going to be the only ones who suffered. Maybe the city would see peace. There had been justice.

ABOUT THE AUTHOR

Aime Austin is the author of smart women's fiction. Her compelling stories are boldly told, designed to keep readers turning the pages. Whether you're reading romantic women's fiction written as Sylvie Fox or The Casey Cort Series of legal thrillers, she wants you to enjoy the heroine's journey.

Before turning to writing full time, Aime practiced law for nearly a decade.

She splits her time between Los Angeles and Budapest, where she enjoys yoga, knitting, farm-to-table cooking, and life with her husband and son. When she's not writing, her nose is stuck in a book.

Also Available from Aime Austin

The Common Pleas Lawyer, A Casey Cort Prequel Novella

Casey crosses a powerful family...

It's spring in Cleveland, Ohio, but Casey Cort isn't going to let rain and gray skies get her down. The last year of law school is a magical time. At any moment her long-time boyfriend, Tom Brody, is going to pop the question. She's ready to finish a successful year as a senior editor on the law review, and her dream job at Morrell Gates is right around the corner. The bar exam is her last hurdle, and she's more than ready to jump it.

Or so she thinks.

When Casey reports an honor code violation to the dean of the law school, her perfect future comes crashing down around her as friends and fellow students fail to come to her rescue.

In this prequel novella of the Casey Cort series, Aime Austin—a former trial lawyer in Cleveland—weaves a tale that blends the best of today's top legal thrillers with the heart and soul of women's fiction, in a story ripped from real-world headlines.

Qualified Immunity, Casey Cort Book One

Sheila Harrison Grant is the first African American woman ever nominated to the federal bench in Cleveland. But when her thirteen-year-old daughter Olivia shares a family secret with a well-meaning guidance counselor, she sets the wheels in motion to feed a partisan senate's opposition, threatening her mother's position...and both of their lives.

Once an ambitious young law student with promise, Casey Cort made the mistake of

crossing a classmate from a prominent and influential family. Now she works as an unfulfilled, faceless cog in a broken legal system.

When fate gives Casey a second chance, she has to set aside her lack of faith in justice and find the strength to fight for those with nowhere else to turn.

In this first novel of the Casey Cort series, Aime Austin—a former trial lawyer in Cleveland—weaves a tale that blends the best of today's top legal thrillers with the heart and soul of women's fiction, in a story ripped from real-world headlines.

Under Color of Law, Casey Cort Book Two

Losing the most high profile case of her career ironically made Casey Cort a winner. Well-heeled clients now knock on her door, and Tom Brody, her rich ex-boyfriend, wants her back. But entry into the upper echelon comes at a price.

The newest assistant United States attorney, Miles Siegel, has set his sights on nailing a public figure he believes to be corrupt: Cuyahoga County Juvenile Court Judge Eamon Brody. But Brody's brothers, one the presiding judge of the county, the other the state attorney general, aren't about to let that happen.

When Casey gets retained by single mom Claire Henshaw, to wrest custody from her son's irresponsible father, Casey handles her first case before the controversial judge . . . and learns something that will force her to make the hardest decision of her life.

In this continuation of the Casey Cort series, Aime Austin—a former trial lawyer in Cleveland—weaves a tale that blends the best of today's top legal thrillers with the heart and soul of women's fiction, in a story ripped from real-world headlines.

In Plain Sight, Casey Cort Book Three

Struggling to pull together the pieces of her life after another falling out with Ohio's most powerful political dynasty, Casey Cort turns her attention toward her budding relationship with rising assistant U.S. Attorney Miles Siegel. Things come to an abrupt halt when circumstances catapult them onto the scene of a horrific crime.

Miles investigates the identity of an unlikely criminal mastermind, known on the street as Sledge Hammer. Meanwhile Casey discovers she may hold the key to solve the crime—and to the freedom of innocent women and children in the sex trafficking ring. Can Miles and Casey put the clues together to solve the mystery before the trail runs cold?

In this continuation of the Casey Cort series, Aime Austin—a former trial lawyer in Cleveland—weaves a tale that blends the best of today's top legal thrillers with the heart and soul of women's fiction, in a story ripped from real-world headlines.

Romantic Women's Fiction written as Sylvie Fox

The Good Enough Husband

What would you do if you met your soul mate, but you were already married?

In *The Good Enough Husband*, Sylvie Fox delivers a riveting story about a woman who refuses to let her past define her future.

For years, Hannah Morrison Keesling's marriage to Michael was good enough. Then she wakes up one morning and it isn't. Taking her puppy Cody along, Hannah drives north to put distance between herself and her past. Planning to go as far as her SUV will take her, she has to stop on the Lost Coast when her dog gets sick. There she meets small town veterinarian Ben Cooper.

Ben is the man Hannah wishes she had met first. He's perfect for her, but gun shy because he's been lied to before and vows not to be betrayed again. Hannah leaves Michael and moves to Ben's rural town to pursue a future with the man she knows is her soul mate. But Michael won't let go so easily. Forced to make a decision between the man she chose and the man she loves, Hannah soon realizes that her choices will define everyone else's consequences.

Don't Judge Me

Fill a lonely city with one dash of playboy comedian.
Add a splash of adult webmistress.
Do not shake.
Stir.

One-night gigs, one-night stands, even one-night in jail…comedian Raphael Augustine is not about the repeat performance. Now he's closing in on a TV deal that might be his route to stardom, he can't let anything unexpected shakeup his careful plans. Or so he tells himself.

During Raphael's striptease act at a gay bar, a young woman catches his eye—and his shirt. Daisy is gorgeous, but she's also from world more prim and proper than anything Raphael knows. Falling for her may be the biggest joke the world's played on him yet.

Despite her Ivy League education, Daisy's wound up doing the one job she never imagined: working as an adult webmaster. Her degree's collects dust on the wall while she clings to a failing business and spends her days in virtual chat rooms. It's enough to make her want to give up on men entirely—after all, they only seem to want one thing. But when Daisy meets a rakish comic, she begins to doubt her cynical view of love. Could he be the one?

The Secret Widow

Whoever said that time heals all wounds . . . lied.

A decade after the death of her husband, Nari Yoon still mourns. On the ten-year anniversary of the worst day of her life, co-worker Lucas Tucker tries to save her from self destruction in a tropical paradise. But Nari doesn't want salvation, she wants to keep her past buried.

Nari wants to forget, but Lucas wants to remember . . .

Tall and blond, Lucas always stood out in the short, brunette adoptive family. Driven by his search for truth, he flies two thousand miles to the Hawaiian island where he was born, determined to find his birth parents.

The truth may be more than he is ready for . . . .

When Lucas forces Nari to confront her past, she tries to forgive herself. But once Lucas discovers the truth about Nari, can he move past judgment to love?

Unlikely—L.A. Nights Book One

Divorced and done with her dry spell, Holly Prentice is ready to get back in the game. At six years her junior, Nick Andreis is a perfect stand in for Mr. Right as Mr. Right Now. Will Holly's unexpected pregnancy change the rules of the game? Or can they both decide to play for keeps?

Impasse—L.A. Nights Book Two

There are only two things Sophie Reid doesn't do: lawyers and sex. When sexy lawyer Ryan Becker waltzes into her life, he persuades her to pursue their attraction. But a Hollywood union strikes, and Ryan and Sophie find themselves on opposite sides of the bargaining table. Can their sparks in the bedroom overcome their standoff in the boardroom?

Shaken—L.A. Nights Book Three

After he married Jessie Morales, Cameron Becker made a solemn vow: Once mine, always mine. Years later, Cameron still holds fast to this belief, even though he and Jessie are legally separated. When a natural disaster brings them together, Cam is poised to get his wife back. But will Jessie choose family and career over love a second time?

Stirred—L.A. Nights Book Four

Globetrotting cartoonist Zoe Andreis comes to Los Angeles to help her father recover from a serious medical scare. When she meets bus driver Max Kiss she is forced rethink the meaning of home.

Made in the USA
San Bernardino, CA
24 August 2018